How to Sell Your Way through Life

How to Sell Your Way through Life

Napoleon Hill

PRABHAT
PAPERBACKS

Published by
PRABHAT PAPERBACKS
4/19 Asaf Ali Road,
New Delhi-110 002 (INDIA)
e-mail: prabhatbooks@gmail.com

ISBN 978-93-5266-440-5
HOW TO SELL YOUR WAY THROUGH LIFE
by Napoleon Hill

Edition
2018

Price
₹ 275.00 (Rupees Two Hundred Seventy Five only)

Printed at
R-Tech Offset Printers, Delhi

Dedicated to
ALL WHO HAVE TRIED AND FAILED
BUT STILL FIGHT ON
WITH
DETERMINATION
TO MAKE LIFE PAY

CONTENTS

FOREWORD

LIKE millions of others, I am a big fan of Napoleon Hill's timeless classic, *Think and Grow Rich*. First published in 1937, it has the distinction of being the best read self-help book of the twentieth century.

Not so well known is how Napoleon Hill earned his livelihood before he wrote *Think and Grow Rich*. In *How to Sell Your Way Through Life*, Hill explains how he spent many years perfecting his skills as a master salesman and sales trainer. *How to Sell Your Way Through Life* was written in the depths of the Great Depression. To write it, Hill drew upon contacts, interviews, and the cooperation of the most successful men in the country, including Andrew Carnegie, Henry Ford, Thomas Edison, and others.

The information in *How to Sell Your Way Through Life* is as relevant in today's economy as it was in a time very similar to ours. Hill could have been writing about today when he said, "Business depressions do not destroy the market for imagination; they merely increase the need and extend the demand for imagination. The world stands in need of men who will use their imagination."

From the psychology of negotiation and selling to an analysis of proven methods, positive thinking, and the all-important Golden Rule, *How to Sell Your Way Through Life* is an outstanding course in salesmanship. Invest some time in reading these pages and you'll understand why Napoleon Hill stands as one of the most masterful business philosophers of our time.

—Ken Blanchard,
co-author of *The One Minute Manager*®
and *The One Minute Entrepreneur*

THE AUTHOR SOLD HIS WAY INTO THIS FAMOUS "CASTLE ON THE HILL."
A glimpse of the magnitude and magnificence of Napoleon Hill's "Model American Home" overlooking beautiful Lake Dora, Florida.

One of the Fine Things about This Book Is That "It Works"

TO write a book of theories on "how the other fellow should succeed" is quite common. But for an author to definitely demonstrate that his ideas *will work*, and that he personally can *make them work*, is quite rare.

Hence, it is not for the purpose of boasting—but to give you confidence that what you are about to read is practical, workable, proven philosophy—when we mention the following. As you read this book, you will feel as though the author was present in the pages. The lessons were not just written; they were first *lived*, and then put into print.

The author has sold his way through life so successfully using the philosophy and methods taught in this book, that he lives in a castle in Florida, which is one of the famous showplaces of the entire South. From it he commands not only a rare view of beautiful Lake Dora, but also of the entire town of fashionable Mount Dora, in the "Golden Triangle."

He is the first to occupy this castle, upon which it is reported the builder spent about $100,000. It is to be developed into a "model American home." It is here that 15 children are to be adopted who will be schooled in these principles, so that they, too, may sell their way through life successfully

This visible evidence of opulence demonstrates in a definite way that the author can not only prescribe the "medicine of success, but that *he can make it work for himself*. In a personal letter to his publishers (not intended for publication), he wrote:

"There is one thing of which you can be sure. Mrs. Hill and I have whipped life and actually made it pay in terms of complete and continuous happiness. We have found 'that something' which brings peace of mind and genuine joy in just living. I am astonished at not having discovered our vast riches before this.

"If I were only able to paint word pictures that truly represent the fortune Mrs. Hill and I have captured, *by applying the philosophy I am trying to teach the American public,* I believe you would not be able to produce books fast enough to meet the demand."

And so, in this spirit, we pass on to you *How to Sell Your Way Through Life.*

—The Publishers

> The great Edison failed 10,000 times before he made the incandescent electric light work. Do not become discouraged and quit if you fail once or twice before making your plans work.

THE CHALLENGE TO LIFE

The Spirit in which the Author of This Book Has Related Himself to Life

Life, you can't subdue me, because I refuse to take your discipline seriously.

When you try to hurt me, I laugh, and laughter knows no pain.

I appropriate your joys wherever I find them. Your sorrows neither discourage nor frighten me, for there is laughter in my soul.

When I get the thing I want, I am glad, but temporary defeat does not make me sad. I simply set music to the words of defeat and turn it into a song about laughter.

Your tears are not for me. I like laughter much better, and because I like it, I use it as a substitute for grief and sorrow and pain and disappointment.

Life, you are a fickle trickster, don't deny it!

You slipped the emotion of love into my heart so you might use it as a thorn with which to prick my soul, but I have learned to dodge your trap—with laughter.

You try to lure me with the desire for gold, but I have outwitted you by following the trail that leads to knowledge, instead.

You induce me to build beautiful friendships, then convert my friends into enemies so you may harden my heart, but I sidestep your fickleness by laughing off your attempt and selecting new friends in my own way.

You cause men to cheat me in trade, so I will become hard and irritable, but I win again because I possess only one precious asset, and this is something no man can steal—IT IS THE POWER TO THINK MY OWN THOUGHTS AND BE MYSELF, plus the capacity to laugh at you for your pains.

You threaten me with death, but to me death is nothing worse than a long, peaceful sleep, and sleep is the sweetest of human experiences—except laughter.

You build the fire of hope in my breast, then sprinkle water on the flames, but I go you one better by rekindling the fire on my own account—and laugh at you once more.

You plant vicious enemies in my path who try to assault my reputation and destroy my self-reliance, but you fail again because I turn their efforts into publicity that brings me to the attention of new friends whom I would never know without this perfidy.

For a quarter of a century, you hurdle-jumped me over every conceivable form of failure, but I coined the knowledge gained from these failures into a philosophy of success that now renders useful service and brings countless thousands of others the joy of laughter; and these newly made friends willingly pay me compound interest for every second of failure you have imposed upon me.

You bore me into this world in poverty, but this has proved to be a blessing in disguise because poverty has taught me patience and industry and imagination and temperance and humility and a hundred other useful traits that the idle will never know.

Life, you are licked as far as I am concerned, because you have nothing with which to lure me away from laughter and you are powerless to scare me.

This book was not written for the purpose of expressing heroism or brilliancy. Its sole purpose is to convey practical information on the psychology of negotiation; information that is known to be sound because it was obtained from the life experiences of hundreds of successful people who began at scratch and made for themselves enviable positions in the world. For this reason the book should be the handbook of every person who has just finished school and is ready to sell himself through life successfully. If I could place a copy of the book in the hands of the members of every family having children of the high school age, and every person graduating from business college, I would feel I had made a definite contribution to the successful lives of hundreds of thousands of young people who are today groping in the dark for the path that leads to self-determination.

—The Author

> All anyone really requires, as a capital on which to start a successful career, is a sound mind, a healthy body, and a genuine desire to be of as much service as possible to as many people as possible.

Preface

THIRTY-FIVE years ago a young man dropped from a moving freight train in East Orange, N. J., and hurriedly made his way to the laboratory of Thomas A. Edison. When asked to state his business before being permitted to see Mr. Edison, the young man boldly replied, "I am going to become his partner!"

His boldness got him past the secretary. An hour later he was at work, scrubbing floors in the Edison plant. Five years later he was a partner of the great Edison. The man's name is Edwin C. Barnes, known throughout the United States as the distributor of the Ediphone dictating machine. His home is in Florida, not very far from my own home. I have known him for a quarter of a century; have known him through the relationship of close personal friendship that gives me the privilege of saying that he sold himself to Edison through the psychology of selling described in Part 1 of this book.

Edwin Barnes has accumulated a fortune far greater than he needs, and he owes every cent of it to the hour he spent in private conversation with Edison. During that hour he sold himself so thoroughly that it gave him his opportunity to go into partnership with one of the greatest men this country ever produced. Roughly speaking, that hour of selling was worth in actual cash the millions of dollars Edwin Barnes afterward accumulated.

My first job was that of secretary to General Rufus A. Ayers, for whom I went to work while I was still in my teens. Long before I was 20, I became the general manager of one of General Ayers's coal mines. The jump from secretary to general manager was made in less than one hour, during which I sold myself into the better position by voluntarily rendering confidential service for which I neither expected nor asked pay. That sale changed the entire trend of my life and led directly to my alliance with Andrew Carnegie, with its far-flung effects on myself and thousands of others.

If you asked me to tell you why this book may be of benefit to you and demanded I give you proof that I am an authority on How to Sell Your Way through Life, I would be compelled to pull aside the curtains that hide from view my private life and give you the information in these frank but truthful words:

Thirty years ago I began, at the request of, and in collaboration with, Andrew Carnegie, to organize all the causes of success and failure into a philosophy of individual achievement. During those 30 years of research it became necessary for me to contact, interview, and gain the cooperation of the most successful men of the country, including Henry Ford, Thomas A. Edison, John Wanamaker, Luther Burbank, Woodrow Wilson, and others of their type from whose rich experiences I organized the first practical philosophy of individual achievement, under the title of *The Law of Success.*

The best evidence the philosophy is sound and practical may be found in the use I have made of it in selling my way through life. The blessings this philosophy has given me are many, the greatest of them being the fact that I can truthfully say I have sold my way through life so successfully that I have everything I need or can use for the attainment of happiness, including, of course, absolute freedom from all manner of worry over money.

I am married to the woman of my choice, with whom I have found harmony and understanding sufficient to give me continuous peace of mind and inspiration to hitch my wagon to higher stars than any I had aspired to reach before I found her.

Having converted my philosophy into the privilege of living my own life, in my own chosen way, in any part of the world I desire, Mrs. Hill and I have established a permanent home in Lake Dora, Florida, where we have an abundance of sunshine, in a castle surrounded by trees and fresh air, far enough removed from the rest of the world to give us privacy, close enough to keep us attuned to the hearts and minds of our neighbors.

From 1 to 3 hours, out of every 24, we devote to our private Master Mind conference, at which we analyze our plans and prepare some form of service for the benefit of others who have been less successful than us in selling their way through life.

We have no fears of any nature whatsoever. We have no worries. We have no feeling of suspense over the past, the present, or the future. We have perfect health and enough years ahead of us, we hope, to enable us to write a score of books after this one. We have open minds toward all things and all people, and we make it our business to learn something of interest or value from every person we contact.

Mrs. Hill's major hobby is children. Having none of her own she has begun the adoption of a family that will not be complete until we are feeding, clothing, sheltering, and educating 15 homeless children, ranging in ages from 6 to 10 years, for whom we shall become responsible until we turn them back to the world fully capable of selling their way through life successfully.

My major hobby is Mrs. Hill!

I spent 15 years searching for my wife before I found her. I sold myself to her through the principles of salesmanship described in this book. This is, I believe, the best evidence of the soundness of the rules of selling I have described.

If you read this book, you will have your mind temporarily connected with that of a man who is thoroughly happy, who can truthfully say, "Life has nothing to offer that I do not already have." During these days of turmoil, when half of the world is arming itself to the teeth and threatening civilization with its spirit of greed and lust for power, it seems almost a miracle to find even one person who has made life pay on his own terms without damage to others.

The philosophy with which Mrs. Hill and I have sold our way into happiness is fully and frankly described in this book. The spirit of our philosophy may be found in the challenge to life that I wrote nearly 10 years ago, the day after the Depression had shut off my income and destroyed my entire fortune. (See the first pages of this book.)

The rhythm of our Florida home is both positive and contagious because it has been established by a blending of the minds of two people who are doing exactly what they wish to do and through their work have found supreme happiness. This environmental rhythm is so definite it affects everyone who contacts it, including all the members of our household, our secretariat, our adopted children, and all who visit us. It is so noticeable that it is the first thing our visitors observe when they enter our home, and always they speak of the inspiring effect it has upon them.

This same rhythm of opulence and peace of mind has been written into the lines of this book, every word of which was carefully examined, weighed, and evaluated by both Mrs. Hill and myself before the manuscript was given to the publisher. We would be greatly surprised if any reader of the book failed to pick up the influence of this rhythm as he reads.

The book consists of four parts. Part 1 describes the psychology of negotiation through which successful men and women sell their way through life with a minimum amount of friction in their relationships with people. Part 2 is devoted entirely to the psychology of selling personal services of every nature, with particular emphasis on facts of great value to young men and young women just beginning their careers. Part 3 is a comprehensive analysis of the methods by which America's number one citizen, Henry Ford, sold himself from poverty to fame and fortune.

The facts described in the four parts of this book were not merely written; they were lived by men and women who have made America the greatest industrial nation on earth. I got the facts directly from the distinguished people who lived them which, of itself, was a job of selling that continued for 30 years and gave me access to the rich store of experience of such men as Frank A. Vanderlip, John D. Rockefeller, Dr. David Starr Jordan, Harvey S. Firestone, William Wrigley, Jr., F. W. Woolworth, James J. Hill, Charles M. Schwab, and scores of others who sold themselves into fabulous riches with the aid of the principles of selling I have described.

I cannot overemphasize the importance of studying carefully the story of Henry Ford's rise from poverty to riches, as described in Part 3, for here you have an authentic outline of the principles that everyone who sells himself through life successfully must use. It may be helpful if you measure yourself point by point on the 17 principles of achievement described in the Ford analysis, taking care to observe wherein you differ from Ford in applying each of these principles.

Part 4 has been devoted to analysis of a principle that has been responsible for all that is good in our present civilization: The principle that must be understood and applied by every person who attains and holds any worthwhile station in life. Unless you make this principle a part of the foundation of your salesmanship, you may sell your way into a high station but you will not be able to hold your gains. Perhaps some may complain that Part Four sounds like a preachment on ethics. Very well, what if it is? I can think of nothing right now that you and I and most of the others now living need more than to improve the manner in which we relate ourselves to one another in business and social dealings.

Part Four should be interesting to every American who has the right to vote, because it accurately describes the principle through which Franklin D. Roosevelt did one of the finest jobs of selling in the history of the United States during his first term in office, when he stopped the stampede of fear and resold the people on the merits of their country. It will be interesting to observe if, by a neglect to apply this principle during his second term in office, the president loses the confidence of the people, which he at first had in so great a measure.

Part 4 also describes what I believe is going to happen because of the relations between the president and John L. Lewis. The business recession cost thousands of people their jobs. Any principle of human conduct capable of such far-flung results as these is worthy of careful analysis by all who are trying to sell their way through life.

The principle analyzed in Part 4 reveals the path by which the world may sell itself out of the spiritual bankruptcy into which it has been drifting since the World War. It is the only principle that will prevent another World War. It is the only solution for all this controversy between the president of the United States and the business and industrial leaders who supply the economic lifeblood that keeps the nation alive. It is the only solution of the widespread labor racket that is costing working men both their peace of mind and millions of dollars of their wages. It is the only solution available to those who are suffering religious and racial persecution throughout the world.

This great universal principle has been the very foundation on which Mrs. Hill and I have made life pay us off in coin of our own mintage, and we sincerely believe it is the only principle through which any person can find and retain peace of mind, prosperity, and happiness. For these reasons, Part 4 could not well be omitted from a book whose chief purpose is to inform people on how to sell their way through life successfully.

I

The Principles of Practical Psychology Used in Successful Negotiation

ABILITY to influence people without irritating them is the most profitable art known to man. The entire first section of this book has been devoted to an analysis of the accepted principles of psychology, through which anyone may negotiate with others without friction. These are the only known principles by which one may win friends and influence people without unnecessarily flattering them. The principles were organized from the life experiences of some of the most successful leaders in business, industry, finance, and education known to the American people during the past 50 years. In this section of the book, one may find modern salesmanship in its most fitting, streamlined clothes.

EMPLOYERS are always on the lookout for a man who does a better job of any sort than is customary, whether it be wrapping a package, writing a letter, or closing a sale.

1

Introduction

Definition of Salesmanship

A Master Salesman is an artist who can paint word-pictures in the hearts of men as skillfully as Rembrandt could blend colors on a canvas. He is an artist who can play a symphony on the human emotions as effectively as Paderewski can manipulate the keys of a piano.

A Master Salesman *is* a strategist at mind manipulation. He can marshal the *thoughts* of men as ably as Foch directed the allied armies during the World War.

A Master Salesman is a philosopher who can interpret *causes* by their *effects* and *effects* by their *causes.*

A Master Salesman is a character analyst. He knows men as Einstein knows higher mathematics.

A Master Salesman is a mind reader. He knows what thoughts are in men's minds by the expressions on their faces, by the words they utter, by their silence, and by the feeling that he experiences from within while in their presence.

The Master Salesman is a fortune teller. He can predict the future by observing what has happened in the past.

The Master Salesman *is master of others BECAUSE HE IS MASTER OF HIMSELF!*

The attributes of mastery in selling will be described in this book as well as the means by which these qualities may be acquired. The purpose of the book is to enable the reader to transform mediocrity into mastery in *the art of persuasion.*

Life is a series of ever-changing and shifting circumstances and experiences. No two experiences are alike. No two people are alike. Day after day we experience life's kaleidoscopic changes. This makes it necessary for us to adapt ourselves to people who think and act in ways different from our own. Our success depends, very largely, upon how well we negotiate our way through these daily contacts with other people *without friction* or opposition.

This sort of negotiation calls for an understanding of the art of salesmanship. We are all salesmen regardless of our calling. But not all of us are *Master Salesmen*!

The politician must sell his way into office. If he remains in office, he must keep himself sold to his constituency.

The salaried person must sell himself into a job. Salesmanship must be used to keep the position after it has been obtained.

If a man seeks a loan at a bank, he must sell the banker on making the loan.

The clergyman must sell his sermons, and himself as well, to his followers. If he is a poor salesman, he soon finds himself looking for another "call."

The lawyer must sell the merits of his client's case to the judge and jury even if he knows his case has but little merit.

If a man chooses to marry, he must sell himself to the woman of his choice, although the woman may, and often does, remove many of the obstacles in the path of the sale.

Everybody will agree with this statement.

The day laborer must sell himself to his employer, although the form of salesmanship required is not as difficult as that which must be employed by the man who sells himself into a job at $50,000 a year.

These are examples of salesmanship through which people sell intangibles. Any form of effort through which one person persuades another to cooperate is salesmanship. Most efforts at salesmanship are weak; and for this reason most people are poor salesmen.

If a man attains a high station in life, it is because he has acquired or was blessed with native ability as a salesman. Schooling, college degrees, intellect, brilliancy, are of no avail to the man who lacks the ability to attract the cooperative efforts of others, *thus to create opportunities for himself.* These qualities help a man to make the most of *opportunity* once he gets it. But he must first contact or create the opportunity to be worked on. Perhaps, by the law of averages, opportunity is thrust upon one out of every hundred thousand people. The others must create *opportunity.* Moreover, salesmanship is often as necessary in the development of opportunity as in its creation.

"Salesmanship" in this book applies not merely to marketing commodities and services. *You can sell your personality. You must do it!* As a matter of fact, the major objective in writing this book was to teach men and women how to sell their way through life successfully using the selling strategy and the psychology used by the Master Salesman in selling goods and services.

Herbert Hoover was handicapped during his youth by the loss of his parents. Millions of other orphans have lived and died without having had the *opportunity* to make themselves known outside of the local communities in which they *existed.* What distinguishing features did Mr. Hoover possess to enable him to set his sails in the direction of the White House and ride with the winds of fortune to that high goal? *He discovered how to sell his way through life successfully.* This book is to teach others to do the same.

Jean Beltrand has given five definitions of salesmanship, as follows:

FIRST: Selling is the ability to make known your *faith, goods,* or *propositions* to a person or persons, to a point of creating a desire for a privilege, an opportunity, possession, or an interest.

SECOND: Selling is the ability of professional and public men to *render services, assistance,* and *cooperation,* to a point of creating a desire on the part of the people to remunerate, recognize, and honor.

THIRD: Selling is the ability to *perform work, duties,* and *services* as an employee, to a point of creating a desire on the part of an employer to remunerate, promote, and praise.

FOURTH: Selling is the ability to *be polite, kind, agreeable,* and *considerate,* to a point of creating a desire upon the part of those you meet to respect, love, and honor you.

FIFTH: Selling is the ability to write, design, paint, invent, create, compose, or accomplish anything, to a point of creating a desire upon the part of the people to acclaim its possessors as heroes, celebrities, and great men.

These definitions are very broad. They might easily cover a great variety of all human activity. The whole of any life is one long, unbroken chain of sales endeavor.

The newly born babe is a salesman! When it wants food, it *yells* for it and *gets it*! When it is in pain, it *yells* for attention and gets that, too.

Women are the greatest salespeople on earth. They are superior to men because they are more subtle, more dramatic, and use greater finesse. Men often believe they are selling themselves to women in proposals of marriage. Generally, however, it is the woman who does the selling. *She does it by making herself charming, attractive, and alluring.*

While Mr. Beltrand's definitions are comprehensive, I would add to his list one more, viz:

"Selling is the art of planting in the mind of another a *motive* which will induce favorable *action.*"

The importance of this definition will be apparent throughout the book.

The Master Salesman becomes a master because of his or her ability to induce other people to *act* upon *motives* without resistance or friction.

There is but little competition with Master Salesmen because there are so few of them!

Master Salesmen know what they want. They know how to *plan* the acquiring of what they want. Moreover, they have the *initiative* to put into *action* such a *plan.*

There are two forms of sales endeavor. One: when the salesman is negotiating with but one person. Two: when the salesman is negotiating with a group of people. The latter is commonly known as group selling or public speaking.

The Master Salesman's education is not complete unless he has the ability to persuade groups of people as well as influence individuals. The ability to speak to groups with that force which carries conviction is a priceless asset. It has given more than one man his *big opportunity.* This ability must be self-acquired. It is an art that can be acquired only through study, effort, and experience.

Here are some specific instances:

William Jennings Bryan lifted himself from obscurity to a position of national prominence through his famous "Cross of Gold" speech, during a Democratic National Convention.

Patrick Henry immortalized himself through his famous "Give me liberty or give me death" speech in the days of the American Revolution. But for that speech, his name might never have known its heritage.

Robert Ingersoll changed the trend of theology by his eloquent art in forceful group salesmanship.

The Master Salesman has the ability to influence people through the printed page as well as by the spoken word.

Elbert Hubbard accumulated a modest fortune and indelibly impressed his name upon the minds of men through the selling power of his pen.

Perhaps Thomas Paine, through the power of his pen, did more than any other one person to inspire the American Revolution.

Benjamin Franklin immortalized himself and left his imprint for good upon civilization by the forceful simplicity and quaintness of his written salesmanship.

Abraham Lincoln immortalized himself through a single speech, his Gettysburg Address—simple in theme, pure in composition, moving in thought.

The spirit of Jesus Christ goes marching on, influencing hundreds of millions of people 2,000 years after his death because he was a Master Salesman. He built his sales presentation around a *motive* universally acceptable.

Caesar, Alexander, Napoleon, the ex-kaiser Wilhelm of Germany, and hundreds of others of their type were also Master Salesmen. But *they built their sales presentations around motives that were destructive of the best impulses in civilization.* They sold and delivered wars—wars for which the people paid in blood and tears and suffering.

Enduring success in selling is always predicated upon *sound motive*! Remember this, you who aspire to mastery in selling. Sell neither stones nor serpents nor swords!

The world now faces the greatest opportunity for Master Salesmanship in history. The Business Depression left wounds in millions of hearts that must be healed. Only *master salesmanship* can do it. New leaders and a new brand of leadership are needed throughout the world in almost every line of human endeavor. This is a great reconstruction period. It is rich with opportunity for Master Salesmen who have the *imagination* to build their sales efforts around motives that are beneficial to the general public, and who release their full *energies* through their work.

Class privileges are passing! Mass privileges are in the ascendancy. Remember this, too, when selecting a motive as the guiding spirit of your sales efforts: The *people* must be served.

The whole of America stands at the crossroads of progress waiting for able leadership. Millions of people have been slowed down by *fear* and *indecision.* Here is an unparalleled opportunity for men and women who are prepared to adapt themselves to the new brand of leadership, fortified by *courage,* dedicated to *service.*

High-pressure salesmanship, of which we heard so much during the last 20 years, is now a thing of the past. The "go-getter" will have to make room for the "go-giver" in every walk of life, selling included.

The successful leader of the future, whether in the field of selling or in other walks of life, must make the Golden Rule the basis of his leadership.

In the future, the question of paramount importance will be: "How much can I give in the way of service to others?" not, "How much can I get away with and keep out of jail?"

A great economic renaissance is sweeping the entire world!

The man who cannot see this is mentally and morally blind. The old order of things in business and industry has already been swept away, and a new order is rapidly taking its place. Wise beyond description is the person who sees this change and adapts himself to it harmoniously—without force!

We are approaching an era during which we shall see the reincarnation of the spirit of Thomas Jefferson and Benjamin Franklin and George Washington and Abraham Lincoln in politics and the reincarnation of the spirit of Marshall Field and John Wanamaker in the fields of industry, business, and finance.

The people have become rebellious against the oppression forced upon them by the avaricious and the greedy. This spirit of resentment is not transient. It will remain until it rights a wrong. It will gain organized momentum. America will not soon again see the sad spectacle of millions of people starving to death in the midst of an overabundance of both the necessities and the luxuries of life.

We are on the grand concourse that leads out of the wilderness of human exploitation, and we are not going to be driven or coerced into giving up our rights to remain on this highway.

These statements of fact and of prophecy may be helpful to those who aspire to leadership in the field of selling or in some other walk of life. Men who have imagination will not wait for time to prove their soundness. They will anticipate the changes that are to take place and will adapt themselves to the new conditions.

The great changes occasioned by the economic upheaval that has thrown millions out of adjustment in all fields of human activity accentuates the need for discovering those fundamental principles by which one may come back into the path of ordered progress. Since all people must use some form of salesmanship to right themselves and to adjust themselves into satisfactory relations, both social and commercial, it behooves one to lend an ear to a presentation of those fundamental principles with suggestions of their practical application. This book attempts to teach such principles.

The person who masters these fundamental principles of persuasion can sell his way through life successfully, surmounting obstacles, overcoming opposition, harnessing and redirecting adverse forces. No matter who you are or how much you know, you will not succeed unless you are a salesman! You must sell your services. You must sell your knowledge. You must sell yourself. You must sell your personality.

As you approach the study of fundamentals, keep ever before you the fact that your only limitations are creatures of your own mind. Remember, too, you can remove any limitation that you can create.

This book was written for men and women who will not permit themselves to be bound down by blind circumstance nor hedged in by psychological limitations.

2

You Need Intelligent Promotion to Succeed

IT may be true that the world will make a beaten path to your door if you make a better mousetrap than your neighbor, even though your house may be far back in the woods, but you may as well know that the big rush toward your place of business will not begin until you have given the location and have been properly promoted.

Jack Dempsey was an unknown prize fighter, and a good one at that perhaps, but he stepped up front and won the World Championship with its million dollar income only after Jack Kearns had promoted him into that highly desirable position. Jack Dempsey's fists and arms did the punching, but Jack Kearns' brains did the guiding of the blows so they found their way into big bank balances. The promoting job that Kearns did for Dempsey was so effective that even now, long after the championship was lost, Dempsey is able to collect big dividends for the mere use of his name.

Thomas A. Edison, with less than three months of schooling, became the world's greatest inventor because he possessed that rare quality of being able to promote himself. Where he succeeded, no fewer than 10,000 other inventors, many of them as capable as he, never have been heard of and never will be.

Arthur Brisbane was a run-of-the-mill newspaperman, no better and no worse than a thousand others in his profession, until William Randolph Hearst spread his name on the front page of all his newspapers; then he became America's leading columnist. I can name a hundred men who can write better stuff than anything Brisbane ever wrote, but you would not recognize one of them because they have not been properly promoted.

During the World War my attention was called to a man by the name of Arthur Nash, a Cincinnati merchant tailor, who had taken his employees into business with him and had given them a part of the profits because his business was on the rocks and he saw no other way of saving it from bankruptcy. I went to Cincinnati, interviewed Nash, and wrote the first story about him. In my story I called him "Golden Rule" Nash. The story was taken up by the newspapers and magazines of the country and he received free publicity for more than five years. When he died a dozen years later, he was a wealthy man and his business was among the more successful of its type.

Kate Smith, as all who know her will testify, is "a dear sweet girl" who sings on the radio. Kate does not have anything but a fine character and a pleasing voice, but *she does have* Ted Collins, therefore she draws a weekly salary of a staggering figure, to say nothing of side incomes from moving pictures and other endeavors.

Edgar Bergen and Charley McCarthy trooped up and down Broadway, eating now and then when the now famous pair could get an engagement, until one night when they appeared on the Rudy Vallee Program. The promotion they received on that occasion gave them a start toward radio stardom that has made the pair among the best features of the air. Bergen was as good five years ago as he is today, but he was not then properly promoted, so he often found himself "temporarily at leisure."

Ely Culbertson was a competent bridge player, but nothing to brag about until his wife took him in hand and began to promote him, and now he receives free publicity in newspapers throughout the nation. Moreover, he has made himself wealthy as a bridge expert. He is probably no more an expert now than he was when his better seven-eighths began to promote him, *but he is better paid!*

Ziegfeld picked up Will Rogers when he was an unknown gum-chewing, rope-throwing vaudeville specialist (when he could get an engagement). By proper promotion, Ziegfeld catapulted Rogers into stardom almost overnight, to say nothing of paving the way for moving picture and other money-making opportunities from which Rogers made millions of dollars. Before Ziegfeld's promotions caught up with him,

Rogers was glad to do his stunts before clubs and on other occasions for his lunch, in cities where he was playing on the vaudeville stage. This same "promoter" took over the banjo-eyed Eddie Cantor and started him on a career that is said to now pay him $10,000 a week for merely reading lines that someone else writes! Not bad, eh? Ziegfeld also promoted the tall, slender Fanny Brice into the big money. Not one of these favorites would have piled up the huge fortunes the public has paid them to do their parlor tricks if it had not been for clever promotion.

When I was organizing The Law of Success philosophy, Andrew Carnegie sent me to call on Henry Ford. "You want to watch this man Ford," said Carnegie, "for one day he is going to dominate the motor industry of America." I went to Detroit and met Ford for the first time. That was in 1908. When I first looked him over, I wondered how as shrewd a judge of men as Andrew Carnegie could have been so definitely mistaken in his estimation of Ford, but that was 30 years ago. Year by year I have watched Ford climb to the top in his field, and back of his stupendous achievement I have observed highly organized, systematic, and effective promotion. Perhaps no man who was ever connected with the Ford promotion was of greater service to him than the late Senator Couzens, unless it is W. J. Cameron, the present chief Ford promoter, who sees to it that the Ford interests are never neglected in the eyes of the public. Since Ford began business, I have seen no less than a hundred other makers of automobiles rise and fall like mushrooms because they had not the foresight to surround themselves with promotion experts.

By "promotion experts," I do not mean advertising men. Promotion is one thing, advertising is something entirely different. Promotion, the sort to which I have reference, is the art of keeping an individual favorably sold to the public all the time.

The late Ivy Lee was one of the greatest promotion men of his time. It was he who removed the odium from the name of the elder Rockefeller and kept that name before the public in a favorable light almost continuously. Ivy Lee seldom worked through paid publicity. He preferred free space and other forms of more efficient promotion for keeping his clients properly sold to the public. While I was publishing the *Golden Rule Magazine*, I wrote a brief editorial praising the work of John D. Rockefeller, Jr., in connection with his fine humanitarian work in going to Colorado to settle the famous coal strike in 1919. Almost before the print had dried on my article, I received a wire from Ivy Lee, inviting me to visit him in New York. When I met him, he got down to business without ceremonies, offering me $10,000 a year to join his staff and write similar editorials about other clients of his. Promotion experts earn and receive big money because they have the ability to recognize and the good sense to appropriate the forces needed to further the interests of their clients. I declined the Ivy Lee offer, but I have often regretted the mistake, for I now know that a few years of schooling under that genius would have been worth many times the sum he offered me.

During my negotiations with Ivy Lee, I was astounded to learn that the world-famous Billy Sunday revivals were a well organized, Ivy Lee-guided promotion! Sunday fought the Devil up one side of the country and down the other, to the tune of millions of dollars. The Devil has Ivy Lee to thank for whatever damage Billy did him, which probably was not very much. My personal opinion is that Billy Sunday set Christianity back a thousand years. One thing is certain, religious revivals of the Sunday type—emotional orgies as they are called by many who think—have gone forever. They died about the time Ivy Lee passed on.

Rudolph Valentino (the late silent movie star, in case you have forgotten him) danced up and down Broadway, at a few dollars per dance, until a moving picture director discovered him and placed back of him a clever promoter. Then Valentino became the screen's great lover. The women of America, in the slang of the street, "ate it up!" When the talkies came, all the stars of the silents had to be replaced overnight because most of them had no real ability in talking parts. The great lovers of the silents were great only because they had been cleverly promoted as such. The talkies proved that!

When the late Theodore Roosevelt came back from Africa, just after he left the White House in 1909, he made his first public appearance at Madison Square Garden. Before he would agree to make the appearance, he carefully arranged for nearly one thousand *paid applauders* to be scattered throughout the audience to applaud his entrance on the platform. For more than 15 minutes, these paid hand-clappers made the place ring with their enthusiasm. The other sheep took up the suggestion and joined in for another quarter hour. The newspaper men present were literally swept off their feet by the tremendous ovation given the American hero, and his name was emblazoned across the headlines of the newspapers in letters two inches high. Splendid! Teddy understood and made intelligent use of personal promotion. That was the major reason why he was a great statesman!

One does not have to be an expert on propaganda or personal promotion tactics to observe how effectively these forces are used by Mussolini, Hitler, and Stalin, to maintain their standing in the eyes of the world. They keep themselves constantly promoted in all sorts of favorable lights because they know the necessity of appeasing home folks and impressing foreigners.

For a great number of years, I served as my own business and promotion manager, yet I saw other men in my field going by me in an ever-increasing line of procession. I now know that the habit of serving as one's own promotion manager is something like the equally foolish habit of cutting one's own hair. A man can cut his own hair, but it does not improve his appearance. A man can also serve as his own lawyer, but he who does so usually follows his own counsel into difficulty. There is no wisdom in following such a course.

Even a street can be made to take on a different reputation and yield greater rents under the right sort of promotion direction. Fifth Avenue in New York is known the world over as the bonton street of Manhattan. The reputation enables the owners of the ground to ask for and receive fabulous rentals for their property. Fifth Avenue's reputation is a promotion, maintained by the Fifth Avenue Association, through a carefully managed promotion plan that keeps out the riff-raff that has reduced Broadway and Forty-Second Street to nothing short of a hunting ground for mendicants and street peddlers. Stores on Broadway bring but a fraction of the rentals received on Fifth Avenue.

Alvin York was merely another illiterate Tennessee mountaineer who objected to conscription during the World War. He put up such a howl about his "conscientious objection" that he attracted much attention and plenty of newspaper space. After his return from war he was still illiterate, but a clever little promoter took him over and now he dominates a large school for mountain folks that was promoted in his name; the State of Tennessee has dedicated one of its main highways to him; and he has received financial and other forms of aid from influential people from all over the country. Verily, it pays to be properly *promoted.*

Thousands of Catholic priests throughout America have never been heard of outside of their own parishes. Father Coughlin, self-promoter extraordinaire, made himself and his influence felt all over the country, and to some extent all over the world. He shone for a little while, then his candle flickered out. Father Coughlin could not, or did not, take counsel from promotion experts. He talked himself into the limelight and out again. Under promotion management such as that of the late Ivy Lee, Father Coughlin would have become one of the political and economic factors that this country would have been compelled to heed, whether for weal or for woe to the rest of us.

I wonder how many readers of these lines know or ever heard of America's greatest thinker? I venture the guess that not half a dozen people could name him. He lives in Dallas, Texas, practices law, and his name is Stuart Austin Wier. He is, in my opinion, the most suitable man in the United States as the successor to Franklin D. Roosevelt. I doubt that there is living in the world today any person who has the depth and balance of thought that Mr. Wier possesses, and I doubt seriously that any philosopher, from Socrates to Elbert Hubbard, ever possessed the flexibility of thought, the variety of knowledge, the balance of judgment possessed by Wier. But Wier is practically unknown because he does not choose to avail himself of professional promotion service. Remember the name. You may hear of it again. If you do, it will be for the reason that someone who has a penchant for uncovering and publicizing men with brains has voluntarily smoked Wier out into the open where the world can take a look at him.

Mrs. Franklin D. Roosevelt is not known as "the President's wife." She is known as herself. Professional promotion experts see to this! Whether or not this exploitation of Mrs. Roosevelt as an individual separate and distinct and independent from the President is good taste, it is not my business to say, but I do know that she is neither idle nor without income from her independent sources of service. One might think that a person as prominent as the wife of the president of the United States would not need professional promotion, but Mrs. Roosevelt is keen enough to know that no one is so big or important that he cannot be raised higher through well-organized promotion.

Now, how do these ideas apply in your case?

One of the major duties of life is that of selling one's way to some definite goal. Not all of us are efficient salesmen, therefore most of us need the services of experienced promotion experts who will assume the responsibility of keeping us steadily and favorably before the public.

Over 30 years ago an enterprising young lawyer in Chicago, by the name of Paul Harris, conceived the brilliant idea of circumventing the rule against a lawyer advertising. He gathered around him 30 or so of his business friends and organized the first Rotary Club, the idea being, of course, to promote himself into a variety of contacts that might conceivably be converted into clients as the result of his personal relationship with them once a week. Today the Rotary Club movement has spread all over the world and has become an international power for good. The movement did its founder no harm!

Doctors, dentists, lawyers, architects, and other professional men, whose professional ethics make direct advertising of themselves inadvisable, might well profit by Paul Harris's example. Ethics is one thing; building up a professional practice is another! The two can be made to harmonize. That is the business of expert promotion men. And that goes for the rest of us as well. If we wish to get ahead in the world, we must find ways and means of bringing ourselves to the attention of people who need whatever we have to offer the world. Building a better mousetrap than one's neighbor will avail one nothing unless sound, intense, and continuous sales promotion is placed back of the trap.

Ham actors walk hungrily up and down Broadway, *trying to sell themselves.* Once in a blue moon a Ziegfeld discovers a Cantor, or a Will Rogers, or a Fanny Brice, and promotes him or her to the top, but blue moons do not rise often. The better plan is not to wait for "discovery," no matter who you are or what you have to offer the world. The better plan is to search until you find the one person best equipped to market the sort of services you have to offer, then give that person a good block of stock in yourself and tell him to go ahead and promote you!

While I was writing this story, my doorbell rang. My visitor was a young man who has been acknowledged in America and abroad as one of the coming musical composers and pianists. He spent two hours trying to convince me there is virtue in the old habit of an artist starving in an attic rather than commercialize his art. He tried conscientiously enough to convince me that the philosophy of opulence, as outlined in my book, *Think and Grow Rich,* was an insult to great artists whose major business, from his viewpoint, should be a willingness to starve for their art. I liked the young fellow. He had a pleasing personality, a brilliant mind, and a truly great passion for classical music. But I also felt very sorry for him—sorry because I knew his warped view of life would cost him his much coveted goal: the desire to be recognized as a truly great musician. He is already a great artist, but the world does not know him. Unless he allies himself with a set of brains skilled in marketing his services, he may go through life an unknown genius. There is no greater tragedy.

The irony of this story is that the genius of whom I write came to my apartment to pick up a cast-off suit and an overcoat I had promised him! Great heavens, this genius accepting alms merely because be does not believe in professional promotion.

A little while ago, I was in the office of one of the editors of a syndicated service with my manager, negotiating for the sale of some of my works. He told me that every well-known man in the literary field reached the top through clever promotion. He mentioned, in particular, the late Dr. Frank Crane who wrote, in a light vein, a daily column for the newspapers.

"When Dr. Crane first came to us," said this distinguished editor, "he was peddling his stuff here and there, wherever he could get a country weekly newspaper to buy it, not earning enough to keep him and his family." I happen to know that when Dr. Crane died he was paying an income tax on upwards of $75,000 annually, all of it made from the sale of that same light vein column, marketed by an expert promotion man.

Elbert Hubbard made a sizable fortune by writing and marketing his own works, but the world seldom knows more than one Elbert Hubbard at a time. He was one of those very rare persons who have the ability to create and to market the products of their creation. Most of us are lucky if we have the ability to *create,* much less sell our products.

I spent a quarter of a century organizing the philosophy of individual achievement. I wrote into that philosophy all that had been retrieved from the experiences of such men as Andrew Carnegie, Henry Ford, Thomas A. Edison, John Wanamaker, and others of their type, yet I found myself outmoded by men who wrote books that they had thrown together overnight, as far as financial income was concerned. I finally awakened to myself, placed myself under the management of my wife, and duty impels me to admit that I accomplished more in the way of recognition during the first year of her management than I had accomplished during all my previous years, while serving as my own manager.

It is each person's duty and responsibility to provide himself with whatever form of promotion is needed to help him attain success in his chosen calling. R.L. Sharpe expressed the thought beautifully in these lines:

Isn't it strange that Princes and Kings,
And clowns that caper in sawdust rings,
And common **folks like you** and me
Are builders for eternity?
To each is given a bag of tools,
A shapeless mass and a book of rules
And each must make 'ere life has flown,
A stumbling-block or a stepping-stone.

Self advancement cannot be built on bluff, fear, or flattery!

Life demands of the successful man sterner stuff than these. Mere words and fine platitudes will never take the place of a practical plan doggedly put into action. And this, despite the fact that a book recently published was purchased by nearly a million people in which the central theme admonished the reader to flatter those whom he wished to sway and attract.

A book on flattery may be helpful to those willing to stoop to flattery, but what of the "flatterees"—those unfortunates on whom the million purchasers of the book will work their magic? Are they to be deprived of protection against these seductive flatterers?

Personally, I resent all attempts of people to flatter me. If I used flattery in my work, I would be instantly pegged as a charlatan, and rightfully so. I get better results by frankness in my dealings with people, for I find that direct, straight dealing not only wins friends, but it also *holds* them!

The greatest asset I have, or shall ever have, is a friend I won, not by flattery, but through the most scrutinizing analysis. That friend is my wife. I won her not by telling her she was pretty, or smart, or witty. On the contrary, I called her attention to all her weaknesses and suggested how she might correct them—*by marrying me!*

Morons and nitwits like to be flattered, there is no denying that fact. People who think or make any real pretense of thinking, resent all forms of flattery. It is an insult to their intelligence.

When anyone starts to flatter you, it is a sure indication that person wants something you possess or some favor from you. Flattery is a form of dope that sidetracks the reasoning faculty of the one flattered, and while it may, and often does, permit the flatterer to gain temporary advantages, the time comes when the effect wears off and the victim comes out from under the spell with resentment in his heart.

The most that can be said of flattery is that it is sometimes a cheap psychological trick with which charlatans and dishonest people lull others into a state of carelessness while they pick their pockets. Flattery is the chief tool of all confidence men. Through its use, crooked stock salesmen take millions of dollars away from men and women annually. Through its use, vicious spies wriggle their way into the confidence of military men and wheedle information out of them.

Gold diggers and women of questionable morals use flattery as a weapon with which to break down the resistance of men who will not respond to mere sex appeal. It is said that one highly publicized show girl, who has been married many times, managed to pick a millionaire every time she married because she is adept at the art of flattery. *But the marriages did not last!* Nothing built on flattery can last, for flattery is a weapon for ensnaring people designed and executed by the Devil.

The person who permits himself to be influenced by flattery is whipped before the battle begins. Samuel Insull's downfall really began when he started to pay more attention to the flattery of Grand Opera and opera stars than he gave to his business.

Some executives demand an affiliate of yes-men around them. They would be safer if they employed a staff of "no men!" The human ego is a tricky piece of mental equipment. It needs constant protection against all forms of flattery, the one element to which the ego responds most readily.

One of the commonest mistakes is that of seeking the counsel of friends, even though they have been properly "influenced and won." The reason is that most so-called friends would rather flatter than be frank. They do not wish to offend, therefore their opinions are usually worth much less than the cost, because these opinions are generally misleading.

Moving picture stars and other quick-money victims shine for a time and then flicker out, mainly because they blow up and burst by feeding too freely on public flattery.

It is said that John W. Davis is paid an enormous sum annually by the J. P. Morgan banking firm, not for what he tells the members of the firm they can do, but for what he tells them they cannot do. He is the official "no-man" of the firm. He does no flattering to win and influence the Morgan partners. Astute businessmen that they are, they prefer cold facts to flattery. Perhaps this is why the Morgan firm is tops in the financial world.

Al Smith climbed from the fish market to within a stone's throw of the White House. His greatest help was Mrs. Bell Moscovics, his official "no-woman." It is no mere coincidence that the Brown Derby began to decline when Mrs. Moscovics died. Men who love to be flattered need immunity against this form of malady, and the ones who really think see that they get it.

Truly great business leaders do not depend upon flattery to get results. They have a better formula. Andrew Carnegie did not flatter Charles M. Schwab. He got more dependable results by paying Mr. Schwab as much as a million dollars a year for his brains and his personality, *demanding loyalty and getting it!*

The train dispatcher does not flatter the conductor. He gives the conductor definite orders that he does not question. Once in a while the orders may be neglected, then a wreck costs the conductor his job—or his life.

There are times when one should say "yes" and times when one should say "no." The author of a recent bestseller who advised her readers, as one of "The Twelve Disciplines," to say yes to all questions asked them for one whole day, could have been deeply embarrassed had she literally followed her own counsel. Life is made up of situations and circumstances calling for yeses and nos. The person who negotiates his way through life successfully learns to use each in its proper place.

Lincoln kept bitter enemies as members of his Cabinet because he needed their frank analysis and criticism. Woodrow Wilson ousted Cabinet Members who did not agree with him. The difference in the records of the two presidents is very great, and it will become greater with time.

How far would a military man get in warfare if soldiers were managed by flattery?

Flattery would not help one very much with most policemen and taxicab drivers.

The person, who makes himself indispensable to others by rendering more service and better service than he is paid to render, will accomplish more permanent results of a desirable nature than he could accomplish with all the flattery in the world.

If you would sell your way through life successfully, look around you, see what useful service you can render to as many people as possible, make yourself of value to others, and you will not need to learn the art of flattery in order to win people and use personal influence. Moreover, those whom you do win will stay won!

To be well-liked gives one great advantages, but flattery is not the tool with which this desirable end may be attained and held. A Pleasing Personality is worth a king's ransom to those who possess it, but such a personality is not developed through speaking honeyed words of flattery that mean nothing. A Pleasing Personality consists of 21 different characteristics that can be developed. You will find the complete description of these 21 assets in a subsequent chapter. Master them and make them your own property; then you will be able to *attract* and *hold friends.*

There are practical and tried rules for *attracting and holding friends.* You will find them all in the subsequent chapters of this book. These are not the rules used to gain temporary advantages over others. They are the rules gleaned from the lifework of Abraham Lincoln, Benjamin Franklin, Thomas Paine, Thomas Jefferson, Samuel Adams, Richard Henry Lee, George Washington, and half a hundred other truly great men who laid the very foundation of this country. They are the rules used also by the most successful business and industrial leaders the country has produced, such men as Andrew Carnegie, Thomas A. Edison, Henry Ford, Owen D. Young, Cyrus H. K. Curtis, Frank A. Vanderlip, and John Wanamaker.

If any of these men had advocated flattery as a means of getting ahead in the world, I would have been impressed by their recommendation, but not one of them used or recommended so low and vulgar a method as a means of self advancement.

When flattery and direct frankness are placed side by side, the latter will win over the former 999 times out of every 1,000. Every truly great trial lawyer knows that attempts to flatter a jury are always fraught with definite hazards to his case. The most successful lawyers are those who deal with *facts* instead of relying upon flattery. The same is true of successful business executives. How far, for example, do you believe one would get by trying to influence Henry Ford through flattery?

If I appear to be overemphasizing the importance of guarding against the dangers of relying upon flattery as a means of selling one's way through life, it is because of the possible effects upon the large number of people who have been taught to use flattery as the hub of the wheel of personal advancement. I believe that philosophy is dangerous to all who embrace it, and especially is it hazardous to the young person just starting out, with little or no experience in the business world.

There are sound and commendable ways of winning friends and influencing people through appeal based upon some combination of the Nine Basic Motives described in another chapter. If you wish to climb to the top of the ladder of success and remain there, it will be much safer to use these nine motives as the rungs of your ladder instead of depending upon flattery.

Every move, every act, and every thought of every human being of sound body and mind, who has reached the age of reason, is influenced by one or more of the Nine Basic Motives. When you come to the description of these motives, study it carefully and learn how to influence people by genuine appeal to natural motives. Then you will experience no resentment from those whom you influence.

Success in any calling is largely a matter of one's being able to negotiate his way through life with a minimum amount of friction in connection with his relationship with other people. By mastering, understanding, and applying the Nine Basic Motives, you may reduce misunderstandings, opposition from others, and friction to a minimum. Do this and you will be a great salesman, no matter what may be your calling.

Lest all this counsel impress you as a mere preachment, I am taking the liberty of citing at least one illustration of a circumstance in connection with which practical application was made of the principles of salesmanship recommended in this philosophy of personal negotiation.

Let me mention my own use of this idea.

At the end of the first year of the world depression, I found myself divested of my money and most of my worldly property. People were not interested in books, they were interested in eating. I closed my New York office and moved to Washington, D. C., where I planned to remain until the economic storm had passed.

Months stretched out into years, and instead of the Depression passing it became worse. Finally, I reached a decision not to wait for the end of the business stagnation, but to go on the lecture platform and work my way back into useful service to others who also had been wounded.

I decided to make my start in Washington. For this purpose, I needed newspaper space for advertising. The amount of space I required would cost over $2,000 and I did not have this amount, neither could I get it from the usual banking sources. Here I was face-to-face with a situation similar to that which you and every other person on earth must sometime experience. *I was in need of something 1had to procure with mere words.*

Here, then, is a brief description of exactly what I did and said in order to surmount my problem:

I went to Colonel Leroy Heron, advertising director of the *Washington Star*, and made known to him my needs. In approaching him, I had two courses available to me. I could flatter him; I could tell him what a great paper he represented, what a fine record he made in the World War, what a great advertising man I believed him to be, and all that sort of piffle, or I could lay all my cards on the table and tell him what I wanted, why I wanted it, and why I believed I should get it. I chose the latter method of approach.

Then, I was forced to decide whether I would disclose to Colonel Heron *all* the facts, including my financial weakness, or skip over these embarrassing subjects without clearly discussing them.

Again, I chose to rely upon frankness and directness. There come times in one's life, when no other plan will secure the desired results.

As well as I can remember, here is a word for word statement of what I said:

"Colonel Heron, I wish to use the *Washington Star* in an advertising campaign to announce a series of public lectures on the philosophy of individual achievement. The space I require will amount to approximately $2,500. My problem is in the unpleasant fact that I do not have that amount of money available. I had that amount and more a short time ago, but the Depression consumed it.

"My request for this credit is not based upon the usual commercial credit rating. On that basis, I would not be entitled to the credit. My appeal is based upon the fact (plenty of evidence of which I am prepared to present to you here and now) that I have devoted a quarter of a century to the study of the principles of individual achievement. During this time, I have had the active cooperation of such men as Andrew Carnegie, Thomas A. Edison, Frank A. Vanderlip, John Wanamaker, and Cyrus H. K. Curtis. These men thought enough of me to give freely of their time and experience over a long period of years while I was organizing the philosophy of success. The time each gave to me was worth many times the amount of credit I am asking of you. Through their cooperation, I am now prepared to take to the world a philosophy of self-help that all the people of the world badly need. If you do not wish to extend to me the credit as a sound business risk, then extend it in the same spirit of helpfulness that these men of affairs gave to me of their time and experience."

The credit was extended to me by Colonel Heron on my brief statement of my case with this significant remark:

"I do not know what your chances are of paying for the space you want, but I believe I know enough of human nature to understand that you intend to pay for the space. I also believe that any philosophy organized from the life work of such men as Edison and Carnegie is sound and needed at this time. Moreover, I believe anyone to whom these men would devote their priceless time is worthy of much more credit than you seek with the *Star*. Bring in your copy and I will run it. We will talk to the credit manager afterward."

After the transaction had been completed and the advertising had been paid for, I called on Colonel Heron again and had a very intimate personal talk with him. I asked him to tell me frankly why he extended the credit in face of the fact I had told him all about my financial weakness and nothing whatsoever of my ability to pay the account.

His reply was illuminating. "I gave you the credit," he exclaimed, "because you made no attempt to cover up your financial weakness. You resorted to no subterfuge and did not set your best foot forward first."

How far do you suppose I would have gotten had I appealed to Colonel Heron on anything but frankness?

The old-time salesman carried with him a supply of cigars, good liquor, and burlesque stories with which to entertain his prospective buyers. All these have been supplanted by moving picture films and highly colored graphs and charts with which the salesman can paint in the mind of his prospective buyer a perfect picture of the merchandise he sells.

There are nine windows and doors through which the human mind can be entered and influenced. Not one of these is labeled "flattery." The nine doors are the Nine Basic Motives by which all people are influenced.

Remember, as you read and digest the contents of this book, that it is not a book on flattery. It is not a book of pleasantries and platitudes. It is not a book on psychological tricks and legerdemain. But, it is a book based on the recorded *facts and realities of life as they have been organized from experiences of the most able leaders the country has ever produced.*

> Seek the counsel of men who will tell you the truth about yourself, even if it hurts you to hear it. Mere commendation will not bring the improvement you need.

3

The Strategy of Master Salesmanship

MOTIVE is the seed from which a sale may be germinated. All seed must contain the life germ or it will not germinate, regardless of the kind of soil in which it is planted, *Motive,* too, must contain the life germ or it will not germinate into a *sale.* The man who understands how to inject the germ of life into *motive is a* Master Salesman—a *master because he captures the prospective buyer's own imagination and makes it work for him!*

When an appropriate *motive* has been painted in the mind of the prospective buyer by a *real artist,* it begins to work from within, as yeast works in a loaf of bread. Let us illustrate this point, viz:

The late Dr. Harper, while serving as president of the University of Chicago, *desired* to construct a new building on the campus, the estimated cost of which was $1,000,000. His available funds were not sufficient for his needs, nor did he see any chance of securing the necessary funds from the university's annual budget. After analysis of the situation, it became apparent to Dr. Harper that he would have to seek the million dollars from an outside source.

Here begins the description of the modus operandi of a Master Salesman.

Dr. Harper *did not* start buttonholing wealthy men for donations. He did not put on a drive for donations. He made up his mind to get the entire sum through a single sale; moreover, he assumed personally the responsibility for making the sale.

His first move was to *lay out a plan of action!* (Here it is that all except Master Salesmen usually fall down for lack of a plan that is both *definite* and *sound.)* His plan when completed involved only two prospective donors. From one or the other he intended to secure the needed funds. His plan was conceived with ingenuity and rounded out with strategy—keen, penetrating strategy that was alive and filled with *lure!* It was also loaded with dynamite. What did he do?

He chose, as his two prospective donors, two Chicago millionaires whom he knew to be *bitter* enemies. Yes, yes, I know. You are beginning to see the point before it has been explained. But follow on and get the technique of a Master Sales Artist.

One of these men was the head of the Chicago Street Railway system. The other was a politician who had accumulated a great fortune by gouging the street car company and by other methods.

Dr. Harper's selection of prospective buyers of his plan was perfect. (Here again is a point at which all but Master Artists at Selling are usually weak. They do not use sound judgment in the selection of prospective buyers.)

After turning his plan over in his mind for a few days, and carefully rehearsing his sales presentation, Dr. Harper swung into action!

Choosing the noon hour as the most favorable for his call, he presented himself at the office of the street car magnate. Observe with profit his *reason* for choosing this particular hour. He deduced that the executive's secretary would be at lunch at that hour and that his prospect would be alone in his office. His deduction proved to be sound. Finding the outer office empty, he walked on into the private office. The magnate looked up at the intruder in surprise and asked, "What can I do for you, sir?"

"I beg your pardon for the intrusion," Dr. Harper replied, "I am Dr. Harper, president of the University of Chicago. I found no one in the outer office, so I took the liberty of walking in."

"Why, yes, of course," the other exclaimed, "have a seat, Dr. Harper, I am glad to have the honor of a visit."

"Thank you," the doctor replied, "I am in a great hurry and will stand, if you don't mind. I just dropped in to tell you of an idea that has been running in my mind for some time. (Here comes the *motive.* Watch how deftly it is planted in fertile soil.) First of all, I want to tell you how greatly I admire the wonderful system of street railway transportation you have given the people of Chicago (neutralizing his prospect's mind). I believe it to be the greatest system in the country. It has occurred to me, however, that while you have built a great monument to your name, it is of such a nature that the world will forget who built it the moment you die. (Watch the master go back now to *motive.*)

"I would like to see you build a monument that will endure forever. I have thought of a plan by which you might build such a monument, but I have met with some difficulties which, I am sorry to say, may stand in the way. (Pulling the *lure away* from the prospect to make the idea more desirable.) I had thought of securing for you the *privilege* of constructing a beautiful granite building on the university campus, but some of the members of our Board want this privilege to go to Mr. X (mentioning the name of the political enemy). I am holding out in your favor and just came by to ask if you can think of any plan that may help me to secure this rare privilege for you."

"That is most interesting!" the magnate exclaimed. "Please sit down and let us talk about the matter."

"I am exceedingly sorry," Dr. Harper replied, "but we are having a board meeting in an hour and I must hurry along. If you think of an argument I might use on your behalf, please telephone me as promptly as possible and I will go to bat for you before the Board. Good day, sir."

Dr. Harper turned and walked out. When he reached his office, he found that the street car magnate had already telephoned him three times requesting that Dr. Harper call him as soon as he came in.

The doctor was obliging. He telephoned the magnate, who requested that he be permitted to come out and present his case to the Board in person. Dr. Harper replied that this would be inadvisable; that in view of the opposition some of the Board members had expressed toward him, Dr. Harper might present the matter more "diplomatically" (*intensifying* the *lure*).

"If you will telephone me tomorrow morning," Dr. Harper suggested, "I will let you know what luck I have had."

The next morning upon arriving at his office, he found the street car magnate already there. They were closeted together for half an hour. What happened probably will never be known to the public. The interesting thing, however, is that *the street car magnate assumed the role of salesman, while Dr. Harper became the "buyer" and was "persuaded" to accept a check for a million dollars and to promise that he would try to get it accepted by the Board!*

The check was accepted!

What arguments Dr. Harper used with his board no one knows, but the million dollar building now stands on the campus of the university, silent but impressive evidence that mastery in selling is never accidental. The building bears the name of the donor.

Hearing of this incident, I called on Dr. Harper and asked him to tell me why some of the members of his board should prefer to honor a racketeering politician. In reply, he merely shrugged his shoulders and smiled at me, a queer little twinkle in his eyes. His *answer was sufficient.* I got the idea. The opposition existed mainly in Dr. Harper's imagination. To place the transaction in the category of "justified strategy," Dr. Harper probably developed the idea of friendly opposition in the minds of some of the members of his board.

Let us analyze this transaction to make sure that the fine points are not overlooked. First of all, observe that no *high-pressure methods* were used by Dr. Harper. He depended entirely upon *motive* to turn the trick for him. No doubt he spent days planning his approach. Incidentally, the *motive* that he chose is one of the most alluring of all the motives. In fact, he made his appeal through two motives, namely:

1. The motive of desire for fame and power.
2. The motive of revenge.

The street car magnate saw instantly that he could perpetuate his name in the role of public benefactor in such a way that it would go marching on long after his remains had gone back to dust, and his street railway system had, perhaps, been supplanted by some other mode of travel. He saw also (thanks to Dr. Harper's sound strategy) an opportunity to get *revenge* on his bitterest enemy by depriving him of the privilege of a great honor.

No great amount of imagination is required to enable one to see what would have happened if Dr. Harper had made his approach in the usual manner, by writing a letter to the street car magnate asking for an appointment, thus giving him an opportunity to anticipate the *motive* behind the request. Any but a Master Salesman would have made the approach either in this way or by presenting himself at the man's office and requesting him to "help the university out of a hole" by *giving* it a million dollars.

Suppose, for illustration, that Dr. Harper had not understood the psychology of *motive* and had not been a Master Salesman. He would have visited the magnate, and this is about the conversation that would have taken place:

"Good morning, sir. I am Dr. Harper, president of the University of Chicago. I have come to ask for a few minutes of your time. (Asking for favors to begin with *instead of offering favors!* Failure to neutralize the prospective buyer's mind.) We need an extra million dollars for a new building that we intend to erect on the campus of the university, and I thought you might be interested in donating the amount. You have been successful. You have a great street railway system from which you earn big profits, profits which really have been made possible through the patronage of the public. Now, it is only fair that you should show your appreciation of the success that the public has made possible for you by doing something for the public good."

Observe in your mind's eye this scene. The street car magnate is fidgeting in his chair and nervously fussing with some papers on his desk, groping for an alibi with which to refuse. As soon as the doctor hesitates for a moment in his sales presentation, the magnate takes up the conversation.

"I am exceedingly sorry, Dr. Harper, but our budget for philanthropic purposes has been entirely exhausted. You know we make a liberal annual donation to the Community Chest fund. There is nothing more we can do this year. Besides, a million dollars is a large sum of money. I am sure our board could not be persuaded to donate so much money to *charity.*" (He beats the doctor to that "board" gag.)

That word *"Charity!"*

You see, of course, that a poor presentation would have placed Dr. Harper in the unhappy position of one who begs for charity. Giving to charity, as such, is not listed as one of the nine basic motives that move men to action. But lift the word "charity" out of its humble setting and give it the color of *privilege, fame,* and *honor,* and it takes on an entirely different meaning. *Only a Master Salesman can do this.*

One way is clever; the other is crude.

The act of selling, if scientifically conducted, may be compared to an artist at his easel. Stroke by stroke, as the artist develops form and harmony and blends the colors on a canvas, the Master Salesman paints a *word picture* of the thing he is offering for sale. The canvas on which he paints is the *imagination* of the prospective buyer. He first roughly outlines the picture he wants to paint, later filling in the details, using *ideas* for paint. In the center of the picture, at the focal point, he draws a clearly defined outline of *motive!* As a painting on a canvas must be based upon a *motive* or theme, so must a successful sale.

The picture that the Master Sales Artist paints in the mind of his prospective buyer must be more than a mere skeleton outline. Details must be perfected so the prospect not only sees the picture in perspective as a finished whole, but the picture must be pleasing to him! *Motive* is the thing that determines how pleasing the picture can be made.

Amateurs and little children may draw a rough picture of a horse that can be recognized to be the picture of a horse. But when the Master Artist draws a picture of a horse, those who see it not only recognize it as a horse but exclaim, "How wonderful! How like a living thing!" The artist paints action, reality, and life into his picture!

There is the same difference between men who call themselves salesmen and a Master Salesman, as there is between the dabbler and the master painter. The inefficient salesman hurriedly sketches a crude outline of the thing he wishes to sell, leaving *motive* out of the picture. He says, "See? There it is, as plain as the nose on your face! Now will you buy?" But the prospective buyer *does not see* that which the salesman has kept hidden within his own mind. Or he may see but does not *feel*. He is not moved to *action* by any rough sketch or unfinished, lifeless picture. No seed of *desire* has been planted in his mind; no appeal to *motive*.

That's why he doesn't get desired results.

The Master Salesman paints another picture. He omits no detail. He mixes his word-colorings so that they blend with harmony and symmetry that capture his prospective buyer's imagination. He builds the picture around a motive that dominates the entire scene, putting the prospective buyer's own mind to work on his behalf. That is Master Salesmanship!

A little while ago, a great sales artist came to sell me life insurance. As everyone knows, life insurance is abstract, intangible, and one of the hardest things in the world to sell. One cannot see it; one cannot smell it, or taste it, or feel it, or sense it through any of the five senses. In addition to these handicaps, one must in a sense, and under certain conditions, *die in order to profit by it.* Even then, the profit goes to someone else.

No amateur is a successful life insurance salesman!

But this artist was no amateur. Through study and preparation, he had gained the status of a Master. He had familiarized himself with the *motives* that most quickly and effectively appeal to the prospective purchaser of life insurance. He had prepared himself to analyze his prospective buyers accurately in order that he might readily catalog them as to the *motive* best suited to each case.

He placed before my eyes an invisible canvas and on this canvas, with only words for brushes and paints, he drew a picture of me 20 years hence, with shoulders drooping and fast-graying hair. Around me, he grouped my family. In this picture, he transformed my wife from a woman of youth and vigor, beauty, and independence, into an aging, *dependent* person! He played upon my heartstrings through that word *dependent,* as a master violinist would play upon the strings of a Stradivarius. Nor was the picture yet complete. He added another scene in which I saw myself lying cold in death! I felt the shivers running down my spine as the artist played upon that word *death!* (Reaching me through the motive of *fear,* one of the strongest of the nine basic motives.) By my coffin was my wife, a helpless, dependent, old woman; the woman whom he knew I loved and whose future he knew I would want to make secure. (Reaching me through the motive of *love,* another of the nine basic motives.)

Only an artist can paint such a picture. It was so realistic that it still haunts me!

I took that picture to bed with me that night. It was a nightmare that caused me to groan and turn from side to side, seeking to escape its horror. In sleep, my subconscious mind seized upon it and tortured me with terrible dreams. (By planting in it the motive of fear, the salesman had made a friendly ally of my mind.)

Only an artist can paint such a picture, yet artists are *made,* not born! They may be born with the inherent potentialities for artistic creation, but they become finished artists only by mastering the technique of harmony, form, and color. Sales artists, too, *are made* and not born. They become masters by studying technique and motive; they develop expert methods of analyzing buyers and the things they buy!

Dr. Harper was not a born salesman. He was small in physique and unprepossessing in appearance. He became a great salesman by studying men and the *motives* that cause men to act. That is exactly what all who would attain to mastery in selling must do. The old bromide about salesmen being "born and not made" is as weak as it is old. The 30,000 salesmen whom I have trained have taught me that salesmen can be made.

I have had the privilege of knowing intimately perhaps as many as 100 Master Salesmen during my days as an educator of salesmen; most of the others in the sales field whom I have known, numbering well into the thousands, have been just plain order takers.

The difference in earning capacity between a Master Salesman and an order taker is very great. It runs all the way from several thousand dollars to as much as a million dollars a year. The late John W. Gates earned $1 million a year with much less effort than most salesmen earned $3,000. He was an artist. The late "Diamond" Jim Brady had no difficulty in converting his talents into a like amount of money. He, too, was a master. These two men (and all others in their class) used showmanship and technique and method where most salesmen depend upon shoe leather instead of technique and method.

Master Salesmanship consists of a series of picture impressions that are deftly painted in the mind of the prospective buyer through one or more of the five senses. If these word-pictures are not clear and distinct, beautifully harmonized, and properly fertilized with *motive*, they will not move the prospective buyer to action.

Master Salesmen paint their pictures in the minds of their prospective buyers through as many motives and through as many of the senses as possible. They often supplement mere word-pictures with samples or actual pictures of their wares, knowing that sales are more easily made when the presentation reaches the mind of the prospective buyer through more than one of the five senses and also when more than one motive for buying has been planted in the buyer's mind.

Master salesmanship begins and ends with proper motive! As long as the right motive has been injected into the selling argument, it makes very little difference what happens between the opening and closing of a sale.

All selling is like this, in a way. Men are moved to buy or not to buy because of motive! Base your sales presentation upon the right motive and your sale is made before you start.

Remember, however, that motive usually must be established in the mind of the prospective buyer; most people have neither the imagination nor the inclination to build their own motives for *your* wares. Only a weak-willed person will permit himself to be *sold*, unless a sufficiently impelling motive has been tactfully but forcefully planted in his mind by the salesman.

Showmanship is not only one of the important factors in Master Salesmanship, it is important in practically every other calling.

An efficient showman is one who can dramatize the commonplace events of life and give them the interesting appearance of uniqueness. Efficient showmanship calls for sufficient imagination to be able to recognize things, people, and circumstances that are capable of being dramatized.

Through the aid of efficient showmanship, Roger Babson has made a fortune out of dry statistics and monotonous columns of figures. Through the use of graphic charts and appropriate illustrations, he has literally made figures talk. His success is due almost, if not entirely, to his showmanship ability.

Theodore Roosevelt was one of the most colorful presidents who ever occupied the White House, although many doubt that he was one of the most brilliant or capable executives. He was popular because he was a master showman and understood publicity and dramatic values and made use of both effectively.

Perhaps Calvin Coolidge had the least colorful personality of any man who ever occupied the White House. He appeared frigid and reserved. Theodore Roosevelt was vital and enthusiastic. Moreover, he understood how to display his magnetism. Roosevelt will be remembered and talked about long after the "Mayor of Northampton" has been forgotten, because he knew how to dramatize the commonplace and prosaic events of life so they would stand out and attract attention. Great personalities are remembered.

People buy personalities and ideas much more quickly than they buy merchandise. For this very reason, the salesman who is an efficient showman makes sales where other salesmen cannot. The life insurance salesman who knows nothing about showmanship and does not possess a magnetic personality, usually tail ends the list of producers. The life insurance salesman who is an efficient showman and possesses a magnetic personality, sells everything except statistics and seldom mentions the word "policy." He does not have to. He deals in ideas and uses them to paint alluring pictures that interest and please his prospective buyers.

An efficient showman makes effective use of enthusiasm. The poor showman knows nothing of enthusiasm. He trusts his case to his own colorless statements of fact, which he intends as an appeal to the prospective buyer's reason. Most people are not influenced largely by reason; they are swayed by *emotion* or feeling. The man who is not capable of arousing his own emotions very deeply is not apt to be able to appeal to others through their emotional nature.

During the heyday of his career, Billy Sunday was the greatest showman who ever went gunning for the Devil. He could sell tickets into heaven and make the crowds stand in line and like it. The public paid him millions of dollars while other preachers, who lacked a sense of the dramatic, starved to death. Had Sunday been selling patent medicine, instead of tickets through the Pearly Gates, he would have been arrested for profanity.

Be an able salesman and you can be almost anything else you wish to be.

Jimmie Walker is an efficient showman, however poor a mayor he may have been. Ex-Mayor James F. Hylan was, perhaps, one of the best mayors New York City ever had and the least capable in showmanship. The difference in their popularity was the difference between showmanship and the lack of it!

Will Rogers made himself popular through his comments on the highlights of world news because he had a sufficient sense of the dramatic to make his remarks fit people's moods. That is not only showmanship; it is salesmanship of the highest order.

Arthur Brisbane was the highest paid newspaper columnist in America. His yearly income was well above half a million dollars. He made a fortune through his "Today" column because of his ability to dramatize what people think about or what they want to think about, and to color the news of the day.

The Sales manager who is not an efficient showman is defeated before he begins. He must bring out showmanship qualities in his salesmen.

A sales presentation, delivered by an able showman, is a show all by itself and as interesting as a play. Moreover, it carries the prospective buyer through exactly the same mental processes that a good play does. A salesman who is an able showman can change the prospective buyer's mind from negative to positive at will. He can accomplish this change of mental attitude, not by accident or luck, but by a carefully prearranged plan. An able showman can neutralize the mind of his prospective buyer regardless of the state of mind he may be in when approached, and what is more important, the able showman knows enough not to try to reach a climax or close his sale until this change has been successfully effected.

The farmer cannot raise wheat in paying quantities without preparation of the soil *before the seed is sown.* No more can a salesman plant the seed of desire in the prospective buyer's mind while that mind is negative. The salesman who understands showmanship prepares the mind of the prospective buyer as carefully and scientifically as the farmer prepares his ground. If he does not, he is not a salesman.

A little while ago, a salesman walked into a man's office while the man was engaged in a heated argument with his wife over the telephone. When the conversation was finished, the man turned to the salesman and barked, "What the hell do you want?" Undismayed by the unfortunate moment of his call, the salesman replied in a soft drawl and with a kindly grin, "I am organizing a defense club for husbands," going on to explain that he also had "that kind of wife." The two men talked about women for 10 minutes, after which the salesman tactfully switched the talk to his own wares and went away with a $10,000 sale. That was showmanship plus salesmanship. The salesman who knew nothing about showmanship would have failed in this case. This salesman, knowing the value of the dramatic, turned an unfortunate situation into an advantage for himself.

William Burnette converted a plan of sales strategy into $5,000,000 in five years by teaching salesmen how to sell *ideas* about kitchen utensils made of aluminum. His entire plan can be described in one sentence, viz: He taught his salesmen how to organize clubs of housewives, for the purpose of selling them aluminum ware.

More specifically, Burnette's plan was to invite the housewives of a community to luncheon at one of their homes, all expenses to be paid for, and the meal to be cooked by one of his salesmen with the aluminum ware he was selling. After the luncheon, the salesman would take orders for the aluminum ware running all the way from $25 to three times that amount.

It was the sales strategy of the plan that turned the trick for Burnette. Because he was a Master Salesman, William Burnette lifted himself from the lowly work of house-to-house canvassing, in which he had previously been engaged, to make himself a multimillionaire in five years.

Bear in mind the fact that his salesmen were selling a complete kitchen set of aluminum ware, not merely a few pots and pans. Also, no individual selling was done. The work consisted of group sales that took place after the luncheon had been served. The woman at whose home the luncheon was given usually signed the first order, the others quickly falling in line.

As the reader may observe, page after page of this book is devoted to emphasizing the importance of sales strategy or a plan that has been carefully built around the proper motive. One of the major differences between a Master Salesman and a sales agent is the fact that the Master Salesman is familiar with the nine basic motives and uses at least one of them as a foundation of his selling plan, while the sales agent uses neither motive nor plan. He tries to sell by "main strength and awkwardness" through the hit-or-miss method, which sometimes works but usually misses.

We shall soon describe the attributes of a Master Salesman, as well as the fundamental rules and principles of salesmanship. The preceding portion of this book has been intended to prepare the reader's mind to assimilate more quickly these rules and principles and to illustrate how they have been applied by men who have attained mastery in selling.

In the next chapter, we will describe the qualities that a Master Salesman must possess. In subsequent chapters, we will describe how these qualities may be developed and applied most effectively.

4

Qualities the Master Salesman Must Develop

THERE are many factors that enter into the equipment of the successful salesman. Most of these factors are personal in nature and have more to do with the salesman than with the goods or services he sells or the institution or organization he represents.

We will investigate these factors in detail.

In cultivating or inducing the principles here discussed, there are necessarily involved, first, a self-searching analysis to determine the presence or absence of these desirable qualities and, second, deliberate effort in cultivating them.

As most so-called mental traits have a physical basis, many of these desired qualities can be attained by doing or attempting to do those things that lead to the desired end. Science has abundantly proved that even a state of mind reflects a physical condition and that chemical and physical factors within the body itself bring about the moods and feelings and thoughts that academic psychology has in the past been wont to classify as purely mental.

Even thought has been proved by scientists, including the great John B. Watson, to be intimately bound up with speech. Watson declares that thought is, in effect, but inarticulate speech; and that thinking is but a highly organized physical activity.

Therefore, talk to yourself about the things you want to take root and grow in your mind and character. This is the very first step.

And it is a very profitable step, too.

The second is like unto the first in that it is a physical activity also. This second consists in doing the thing that you would like to do. We learn by experience. After all, it is the greatest of all teachers. Habits can be cultivated as well in the mind as in the body because both mind and body function on a physical plane.

Now, then, what are some of the absolutely necessary things for the Master Salesman to have in his mental equipment?

There follows a list of very desirable qualities that almost any normal and reasonable person can come to possess and exercise. The list is long and perfection may be only slowly attained. Therefore, before entering into a detailed consideration of the things you would like to have your mind and body capable of doing, let's at once enumerate those that are absolutely necessary.

1. *Physical fitness* is of tremendous importance for the simple reason that neither mind nor body can function well without it. Therefore, give attention to your habits of life, proper diet, healthful exercise, and fresh air.
2. *Courage* must be the part of every man or woman who succeeds in any undertaking, especially that of selling in these trying times of intense competition after a devastating period of depression and discouragement.
3. *Imagination* is an absolute requisite of a successful salesman. He must anticipate situations and even objections on the part of his prospective customer. He must have such a lively imagination as to enable its operation to place him in sympathetic understanding with the position, needs, and objectives of his customer. He must almost literally stand in the other man's shoes. This takes real imagination.
4. *Speech.* The tone of voice must be pleasing. A high-pitched squeaky voice is irritating. Words half swallowed are hard to understand. Speak distinctly and enunciate clearly. A meek voice indicates a weak person. A firm, clean-cut, clear voice that moves with assurance and

color, indicates an aggressive person with enthusiasm and aggressiveness.

5. *Hard work* is the only thing that will turn sales training and ability into money. No amount of good health, courage, or imagination is worth a dime unless it is put to work; and the amount of pay a salesman gets is usually fixed by the amount of very hard, intelligent work that he actually puts out. Many people sidestep this factor of success.

The above principles are simple. There is nothing unusual or impossible or even striking in them separately or collectively, unless perhaps it is the fact that most salesmen fail to possess one or more of these five primary requisites.

Some salesmen may work hard and even intelligently, using their imaginations well until they meet a succession of rebuffs and turndowns. It is here that the salesman with sand in his soul, stamina in his backbone, and courage in his heart comes right back and whips the salesman who hasn't these qualities, so courage is essential.

Then again, many salesmen have been known to possess courage, imagination, and hard work, yet by dissipation and bodily excesses handicap themselves so as to be physically unfit half the time to carry on their work.

Other qualifications considered by experienced sales managers as necessary in the equipment of successful salesmen may be listed as follows:

6. *Knowledge of the merchandise he sells.* The supersalesman analyzes carefully the merchandise or service that he sells and understands thoroughly every advantage that it embraces, because he knows that no salesman can sell successfully that which he, himself, does not understand and believe in.
7. *Belief in the merchandise or service.* The supersalesman never tries to sell anything in which he does not have implicit confidence because he knows that his mind will broadcast his lack of confidence to the mind of the prospective buyer, regardless of what he may say about his wares.
8. *Appropriateness of merchandise.* The supersalesman analyzes both his prospective buyer and his needs and offers him only that which is appropriate to both. He never tries to sell a Rolls Royce to a man who ought to purchase a Ford, even if the prospective buyer is financially able to buy the more expensive car. *He knows a bad bargain for the buyer is a worse bargain for the seller!*

9. *Value given.* The supersalesman never tries to get more for his wares than they are actually worth, realizing that the sustained *confidence* and *goodwill* of his prospective buyer is worth more than a long profit on a single sale.
10. *Knowledge of the prospective buyer.* The supersalesman is a character analyst. He has the ability to ascertain, from his prospective buyer, which of the nine basic motives he will respond to most freely, and he builds his sales presentation around those motives. Moreover, if his prospective buyer has no outstanding motive for buying, the supersalesman creates one for him, knowing that a motive is essential in closing a sale.
11. *Qualifying the prospective buyer.* The supersalesman never tries to make a sale until he has properly qualified the prospective buyer, thereby informing himself, in advance of his efforts to close a sale, on the following points:
    a. The prospective buyer's *financial* capacity to purchase.
    b. His *need* for that which is being offered for sale.
    c. His *motive* in making the purchase.

    Endeavoring to make sales without first qualifying the prospective buyer is a mistake that stands at the head of the list of causes of "no sale."
12. *Ability to neutralize the mind of the buyer.* The supersalesman knows that no sale can be made until the mind of the prospective buyer has been neutralized or made receptive. Because he knows this, he will not endeavor to close a sale until he has opened the mind of the buyer and prepared it as a background or base upon which he may put together the word-mosaic of his story. This is the point where many salesmen fail.
13. *Ability to close a sale.* The supersalesman is an artist at reaching and successfully passing the closing point in selling. He trains himself to sense the psychological moment when terminal facilities may be reached successfully. He rarely, if ever, asks the prospective buyer if he is ready to purchase. Instead, he goes on the assumption that the buyer is ready and conducts himself in conversation and general demeanor accordingly. *Here he uses the power of suggestion most effectively.* The supersalesman avoids trying to close a sale until he knows in his own mind that he can close successfully. He so conducts his sales presentation that his prospective buyer believes he has done the buying.

Other principles to be acquired have more to do with the personal makeup and self-organization of the salesman than with his goods. Some of these follow:

14. *A pleasing personality.* The supersalesman has acquired the art of making himself agreeable to other people because he knows that the prospective buyer must buy the salesman as well as the merchandise he sells or no sale can be made. (See the 21 factors of a pleasing personality, Chapter 14.)
15. *Showmanship.* The supersalesman is also a super-showman! He has the ability to reach the mind of his prospective buyer by dramatizing his presentation and by giving it color sufficient to arouse intense interest through an appeal to the prospective buyer's imagination.
16. *Self-control.* The supersalesman has *and exercises* complete control over his head and his heart, at all times, knowing that if he does not control himself, he cannot control his prospective buyer.
17. *Initiative.* The supersalesman understands the value, and uses the principle, of initiative. He never has to be told what to do or how to do it. Having a keen imagination, he uses it and creates plans that he translates into action through his initiative. He needs but little supervision and, generally speaking, is given none.
18. *Tolerance.* The supersalesman is open-minded and tolerant on all subjects, knowing as he does that open-mindedness is essential for growth.
19. *Accurate thinking.* The supersalesman thinks! Moreover, he takes the time and goes to the trouble to gather facts as the basis of his thinking. He does no guessing when *facts* are available. He has no set or immovable opinions that are not based upon what he knows to be facts.
20. *Persistence.* The supersalesman is never influenced by the word "no" and he does not recognize the word "impossible." To him *all things are possible of achievement.* The word "no" to the supersalesman is nothing more than a signal to begin his sales presentation in earnest. He knows that all buyers take the line of least resistance by resorting to the "no" alibi. Because he has this knowledge, he is not susceptible to negative influence by sales resistance.
21. *Faith.* The supersalesman has the capacity for "super-faith" in:

    a. The thing he is selling
    b. Himself
    c. His prospective buyer
    d. Closing the sale

Moreover, he never tries to make a sale without the aid of this faith because he knows that faith is contagious; his faith is picked up through the "receiving station" of the prospective buyer's mind and acted upon as if it were the prospective buyer's own state of mind. Without the quality of faith, there can be no supersalesmanship! Faith is a state of mind that may be described as an intensified form of self-reliance. It is said that faith moves mountains, but it also makes sales.

22. *Habit of observation.* The supersalesman is a close observer of small details. Every word uttered by the prospective buyer, every change of facial expression, every movement is observed and its significance weighed accurately. The supersalesman not only observes and analyzes accurately all that his prospective buyer does and says, but he also makes deductions from that which he *does not* do or say. Nothing escape the supersalesman's attention!
23. *The habit of rendering more service than is expected of him.* The supersalesman follows the habit of rendering service that is greater in quantity and finer in quality than he is expected to render, thereby profiting by the law of increasing returns as well as by the law of contrast.
24. *Profiting by failures and mistakes.* The supersalesman experiences no such contingent as lost effort. He profits by all of his mistakes and, through observation, by the mistakes of others. He knows that in every failure and mistake may be found (if analyzed) the seed of an equivalent success!
25. *The master mind.* The supersalesman understands and applies the "master mind" principle, through which he greatly multiplies his power to achieve. (The master mind principle refers to "the coordination of two or more individual minds, working in perfect harmony for a definite purpose.")
26. *A definite major aim.* The supersalesman works always with a *definite* sales quota, or goal, in mind. He never goes at his work merely with the aim of selling all he can. He not only works with a definite goal in mind, but he has a definite time in which to attain the object of that goal. The psychological effect of a definite chief aim will be described in Chapter 5 on autosuggestion.
27. *The Golden Rule applied.* The supersalesman uses the Golden Rule as the foundation of all his business transactions, putting himself in the other man's shoes and seeing the situation from his viewpoint. This quality will be a greater necessity in the future than it has been in the past because of the changes in business ethics that have taken place as the result of the Business Depression.

Of all the qualities that a salesman must possess none is more necessary, none more valuable than the next one, which is:

28. *Enthusiasm.* The supersalesman has an abundance of enthusiasm that he can use at will. Moreover, he knows that the vibrations of thought that he releases through his enthusiasm will be picked up by the prospective buyer and acted upon as if it were his own creation.

Enthusiasm is a difficult thing to explain, but its presence is always easily recognized. Everybody likes the enthusiastic person. He is high of spirit and radiates an atmosphere of good fellowship, high faith, and lofty purpose. Perhaps, enthusiasm is born as much of his own deep faith in himself, the mission of work he carries on, and the good he does in his work, as anything. Enthusiasm in people and the lack of it may be compared to the light that surrounds a flashing diamond on a jeweler's tray with its spontaneity and iridescence, which compel admiration and give value to it, and the dull leaden atmosphere surrounding a piece of glass the same size. The glass can be bought for a song with none willing to sing it, while the diamond is eagerly sought by all, great and small, rich and poor.

Therefore, to every salesman this advice is given as though from Sinai: *With all thy getting, get enthusiasm.*

Mastery in connection with these major factors in selling entitles those who sell to rate as supersalesmen! Study the list carefully and make sure you are not weak in connection with any of these qualities if you aspire to mastery in selling.

You will observe that every quality may be acquired!

This does not harmonize with the false notion held by some people that "*Salesmen are born and not made.*" Salesmanship is an art and a science and may be acquired by those with the will to acquire it! Some people are blessed with personalities that are favorable to quick mastery of the factors of supersalesmanship, while others must develop such a personality, but it can be developed.

The Nine Basic Motives to which People Respond Most Freely

Science has catalogued the responses of which normal people are capable and has set forth for us the types of appeal that will induce desired responses.

Response may be of a low grade, such as scientists would call purely physical or which are prompted by physio-chemical stimuli. You may cause a man to get out of the office by kicking him out—that is purely physical—or he may be induced to act by reason of those chemical reactions incident to a peculiar condition of the physical body. Temperature, atmosphere, and physical comforts or discomforts, as well as foods and drink, bring about such chemical conditions as to prompt certain reactions.

But forgetting these more elementary and purely physical responses, we may classify the appeals that induce appropriate responses under three heads. These appeals are the only ones to which we need address ourselves in this study. They are:

1. Appeals to instinct
2. Appeals to emotion
3. Appeals to reason

The appeals that cause most people to buy food, clothing, and shelter fall primarily into the first group, though in lesser degree they may find a field of expression in the other two.

All beautiful things in the world that are desirable because of their beauty may be sold because of suitable appeals made under the second heading: emotion.

Love, marriage, and religion deal largely in appeals that are emotional. Many goods and services are sold on emotional appeal. Education, books, the theater, music and art, life insurance, advertising, cosmetics, luxuries, toys, and a long list of things are all sold on emotional appeal.

Investments, savings, mechanical appliances, business machines, and scientific works often change hands on appeals to reason.

There are nine basic motives to which people respond and by one or more of which they are influenced in practically every thought and deed. When the supersalesman qualifies his prospective buyers, he looks first for the most logical motive with which he may influence their minds. The nine basic motives are:

1. The motive of self-preservation
2. The motive of financial gain
3. The motive of love
4. The motive of sexual urge
5. The motive of desire for power and fame
6. The motive of fear
7. The motive of revenge
8. The motive of freedom (of body and mind)
9. The motive of desire to build and to create in thought and in material

These motives are listed in the approximate order of their importance and greatest usefulness.

The supersalesman checks his sales presentation against these nine basic motives to make sure that it embraces an appeal through as many of them as possible. He knows that a sales presentation is more effective when based upon more than one motive.

No salesman has any right to try to sell anything to anyone unless he can present through his sales argument a logical motive for the purchaser to buy, and no supersalesman will try to do so. Supersalesmanship contemplates the rendering of useful service to the buyer. High-pressure methods do not come within the category of supersalesmanship, mainly for the reason that such methods presuppose the lack of a logical motive for buying. The very fact that high-pressure methods are employed is evidence that the person doing the selling has no logical motive to offer the prospective purchaser as to why he or she should buy.

High-pressure salesmen usually depend upon superlatives to take the place of motives for buying. This is a form of hijacking to which Master Salesmen never resort.

If your sales presentation plan does not emphasize one or more of the nine basic motives, it is weak and should be revised. Careful analysis of over 30,000 salespeople disclosed the fact that the outstanding weaknesses of approximately 98 percent of them were to be found among the following:

Weaknesses in Technique

1. Failure to present a motive for buying
2. Lack of persistence in sales presentation and in closing
3. Failure to qualify prospective buyers
4. Failure to neutralize the minds of prospective buyers
5. Lack of imagination
6. Absence of enthusiasm

These deficiencies are common among the majority of salespeople in all fields of selling. Any one of these weaknesses is sufficient to destroy the chances of a sale.

You will observe that "failure to present a motive for buying" heads the list of the six most common weaknesses of salespeople. Nothing but indifference or lack of knowledge of scientific selling could explain this weakness.

The Major Weaknesses in Personality and Habits of Salesmen

Success in selling is the result of positive qualities that one must possess and use. Failure in selling is the result of negative qualities that should be eliminated. Among the more outstanding negative qualities are the following:

1. *The habit of procrastination.* There is no substitute for prompt and persistent action.
2. *One or more of the six basic fears.* The man whose mind is filled with any form of fear cannot sell successfully. The six basic fears are:
   a. The fear of poverty
   b. The fear of criticism
   c. The fear of ill health
   d. The fear of loss of love of someone
   e. The fear of old age
   f. The fear of death

To this list of basic fears should, perhaps, be added fear that the prospective buyer will bite the salesman.

3. *Spending too much time making calls instead of sales.* A call is not an interview. An interview is not a sale. Some who call themselves salesmen have not learned this truth.
4. *Shifting responsibility to the sales manager.* The sales manager is not supposed to go with the salesman to make calls. He has not enough hours or legs to do this. His business is to tell the salesman what to do, not to do it for him!
5. *Perfection in creating alibis.* Explanations do not explain. Orders do! Nothing else does! Don't forget that!
6. *Spending too much time in hotel lobbies.* A hotel lobby is a fine place to "park" but the salesman who parks there too long is bound to get walking papers sooner or later.
7. *Buying hard-luck stories instead of selling merchandise.* The Business Recession is a common topic of discussion, but don't let the purchasing agent use it to switch your mind from your own story.
8. *Imbibing too freely the night before.* Parties are exciting, but they do not add to the following day's business.
9. *Depending on the sales manager for prospects.* Order takers expect prospective buyers to be hog-tied and held down until they arrive.

Master Salesmen catch their own prospects on the wing. This is one of the chief reasons why they are Master Salesmen.

10. *Waiting for business conditions to pick up.* Business is always good with the robins, but they do not wait for someone to dig the worms out of the ground. Be at least as clever as a robin! Orders are not being slipped under the salesman's door this year.
11. *Hearing the word "no."* This word, to a real salesman, is only a signal to begin fighting. If every buyer said "yes," salesmen would have no jobs, for they would not be needed.
12. *Fearing competition.* Henry Ford has plenty of competition, but he apparently does not fear it because he had the courage and ability to turn out an eight-cylinder car at an amazingly low price during a period in which many motor manufacturers were retrenching.
13. *Devoting too much time to the "poultry" business.* The only sort of chickens that lay eggs are the feathered variety, and they roost on farms, *not on Broadway or Main Street!*
14. *Reading the stock market reports.* Let the suckers bite at this bait. You may be smart enough to dodge the hook, but think how the sales manager would feel if you won a fortune on the stock market and quit the house, as 1 out of every 10,000 who play the market do—*sometimes!*
15. *Plain pessimism.* The habit of expecting that the prospective buyer will give you the gate is likely to result in your getting it. Life has a queer way of trying to please. It usually gives that which is expected!

This is not a complete list of salesmen don'ts, but it is a fair sample. Perhaps some may interpret the list to be a little too personal and flippant. Others may see in it a touch of sarcasm. Remember, as you read, that it was intended only for those who have corns on their toes. Others will not be offended. If you have any doubt as to whether or not you are suffering from any of these "don'ts," pick up courage and check the list over with your sales manager, first assuring him with hands crossed on your heart that you want him to be perfectly frank with you!

This list of don'ts is not original with me. It was compiled from observation of more than 30,000 salesmen whom I have had the privilege of training, some of whom I have directed.

Need I suggest that not one of these don'ts is an attribute of a pleasing personality?

5

Autosuggestion, the First Step in Salesmanship

EVERY supersalesman knows that every sale is first made to the salesman, himself, and that the extent to which the salesman convinces himself in making this sale measures perfectly the degree of conviction that can be induced in the buyer's mind.

Because of the importance of self-selling, the subject of autosuggestion assumes an important role in the teaching of salesmanship. This is the principle through which the salesman saturates his own mind with belief in the commodity or service offered for sale, as well as in his own *ability* to sell.

Autosuggestion is self-suggestion. It is the principle through which one imparts to one's subconscious mind any idea, plan, concept, or belief. The subconscious mind is the broadcasting station that voluntarily telegraphs one's thoughts and beliefs (or disbeliefs) to others. The supersalesman knows he must educate his subconscious mind to broadcast belief in that which he offers for sale.

Repetition of a suggestion to one's subconscious mind is the most effective way of educating it to broadcast only such thoughts as will be beneficial. The subconscious mind will not be influenced by any suggestions made to it except those that are mixed with feeling or emotion. The head, or cold reasoning faculty, has no influence whatsoever on the subconscious mind. It responds only to the impulses of thought that have been well mixed with feeling. The subconscious mind is influenced by the negatives as readily as by the positives. Supersalesmen never overlook this fact! This is one reason they are supersalesmen!

The Seven Major Positive Emotions

1. The emotion of sex (placed at the head of the list because it is the most powerful emotion)
2. The emotion of love
3. The emotion of hope
4. The emotion of faith
5. The emotion of enthusiasm
6. The emotion of optimism
7. The emotion of loyalty

The world is controlled by the emotional faculty!

Most of our activities, from birth until death, are induced by our feelings. The salesman who appeals to his buyers through their emotions or feelings will make 10 sales to 1 made by the salesman who appeals to his buyers through their reason alone. Buyers generally make purchases because of some motive that is closely associated with the emotions, as one may readily discern by studying the table of motives that prompt people to buy.

In the foregoing list of seven major positive emotions, the supersalesman will find nature's elixir, which he must mix with the suggestions he plants in his subconscious mind if he expects to broadcast to his prospective customers thought impulses that will influence them in his favor.

The Seven Major Negative Emotions

1. The emotion of anger (quick and transitory)
2. The emotion of fear (prominent and easily discernible)
3. The emotion of greed (subtle and persistent)
4. The emotion of jealousy (impulsive and spasmodic)
5. The emotion of revenge (subtle and quiet)
6. The emotion of hatred (subtle and persistent)
7. The emotion of superstition (subtle and slow)

The presence of any one of these emotional impulses in the conscious mind is sufficient to discourage the presence of all of the positive emotions. In extreme cases, the presence of a combination of these emotions in the conscious mind may lead to insanity.

Obviously, any suggestion planted in the subconscious mind while any one or more of these negative emotions is present, will carry with it a coloring of a negative nature; and when the subconscious mind broadcasts any such suggestion, it will register a negative result in the minds of those who pick up the vibration.

Understand this principle and you will know why a supersalesman must first sell himself before trying to sell others. You will also know why the negative-minded salesman hears "no" so often. Feelings, beliefs, and thoughts released by the salesman, through his subconscious mind, speak more loudly than words. Remember that people are motivated to buy, or not to buy, through their feelings. Remember also that much of what they believe to be their own feelings consist, in reality, of thought impulses that they have unconsciously picked up from the vibrations of thought released by the salesman.

The supersalesman neither permits his subconscious mind to broadcast negative thoughts nor gives expression to them through words, for the reason that he understands that like attracts like and negative suggestions attract negative action and negative decisions from prospective purchasers.

The salesman who knocks anything or anyone thereby destroys the advantage he might obtain through positive suggestion. The presence in the mind of even one of the negative emotions has a tendency to attract to it a flock of its relatives. Knowing this, the supersalesman takes care not to plant negative thoughts in the minds of his prospective purchasers.

Politics and politicians, as is well known to every reader, are in ill repute all over the country today. Analyze the brand of salesmanship used by politicians, and you may readily understand why they have lost the confidence of their "buyers." It is customary for those who seek office to do so by attacking their competitors for office instead of selling themselves to the voters on their own merit. No well-managed business would permit salesmen to seek patronage by knocking competitors. Sales managers have enough common sense to know that sales made by belittling competitors or competitive merchandise are not really sales and that business obtained in this way is a liability in the long run.

Any political speech is, as a rule, a fine example of just this sort of salesmanship.

A wise philosopher once said, "Whom the gods would destroy, they first make mad." Anger is a negative emotion. It makes a very poor salve when mixed with salesmanship, whether or not there be just cause for anger. Silence is far more effective than words inspired by and mixed with the emotion of anger.

Satire, sarcasm, and negative thoughts expressed by innuendo may give a salesman a reputation as a wisecracker, but they will not aid him in selling his wares. Out and out statements of a negative nature are the equivalent of suicide in selling.

The taxicab companies of New York City engaged in a price war some time ago. The public resented their tactics and registered its resentment through a loss to the business of over $750,000 in one year!

It used to be a popular pastime for automobile salesmen to endeavor to make sales by knocking competitive cars. More than a hundred automobile manufacturers were forced to the wall before they awoke to the fact that anything that hurts one man's business hurts all business in that line.

Life insurance men used to follow the practice of "twisting" (inducing the owner of a policy in a competitive company to give up that policy and purchase one in his company). Intelligent life insurance officials stopped the practice except in isolated cases. Twisting, with most life insurance companies, is considered the equivalent of a discharge. The agent who does it will not be tolerated any longer than is required to find him out.

Negative statements in selling not only set up resentment in the minds of the prospective buyer, they magnetize the salesman's own subconscious mind so that it throws off negative vibrations that are picked up by other people and acted upon to the detriment of the salesman.

> Never, in the history of the world, has there been such abundant opportunity as there is now for the person who is willing to serve before trying to collect.

6

The Master Mind

IN selling, as in every walk of life, noteworthy achievement is predicated upon power.

Power is acquired through organized and intelligently directed knowledge. The Master Mind principle makes available unlimited sources of knowledge, because one may, through its application, avail one's self of the knowledge possessed by others, as well as all knowledge that has been accumulated and recorded in books.

The term "Master Mind" means the coordination of two or more minds, working in perfect harmony, for a definite purpose.

There are two separate and distinct phases of this principle. One is economic in nature, the other psychic. Through the aid of the economic phase, it is obvious that one may, through friendly alliance with others, avail one's self of their knowledge, experience, and cooperative efforts. The psychic (spiritual) phase leads in an entirely different direction from the economic phase. This portion of the Master Mind principle may be used to connect one's conscious, thinking mind with the higher forces of Infinite Intelligence. I regret that limited space makes it impracticable to describe here in detail the psychic phase of the Master Mind. (This principle has been fully covered in *The Law of Success* by this same author.)

The economic phase. Let us keep in mind the fact that power is essential for successful achievement in every walk of life. Also, let us remember, power is organized and intelligently directed knowledge. These facts indicate clearly that power in great quantities can be accumulated only through coordinated efforts of a plurality of minds. No one individual, functioning independently, can ever possess great power, no matter how intelligent or well informed he may be, for the reason that power must be transmitted before it is effective; one individual is limited as to the amount of power he can transmit or apply.

The reader should gain a clear understanding of the two phases of the Master Mind principle at the outset of this chapter, even at the risk of dealing with principles that seem more abstract than concrete. The Master Mind principle is the basis of all great, enduring power. It must, therefore, be understood and applied by all who aspire to mastery in any calling, in selling as well as in other vocations.

Henry Ford has organized one of the most efficient Master Mind groups known in the entire field of distribution. This group consists of his thousands of trained dealers who operate in practically every part of the world. Through the cooperative efforts of his dealer alliance, Mr. Ford can estimate, well in advance of the actual building of his cars, how many can be distributed. He knows where his market exists and the extent of that market, even before the raw materials for his cars have been assembled. His greatest asset is his Master Mind sales alliance. This is an indisputable fact. Mr. Ford owes his stupendous success to his understanding and application of the Master Mind principle.

Andrew Carnegie first brought to my attention the Master Mind principle. He attributed his huge fortune to his use of it. His Master Mind group consisted of about 20 men, his executive staff, whose combined technical knowledge and experience enabled him to make and market steel successfully. Mr. Carnegie informed me that he could have made his fortune in the grocery business or banking business or railroad business or in any business that rendered useful service to a large number of people, just as easily as he made it in the steel business, by merely surrounding himself with men whose knowledge and temperament were suited to the pursuit of the business in which he might be engaged.

The Master Mind principle is the basis of every great fortune; even inherited fortunes were originally accumulated through the Master Mind principle.

Successful achievement is the result of power!

Power in great quantities can be accumulated only through application of the Master Mind principle. I have repeated this statement many times for the sake of emphasis because it contains the very warp and woof of mastery and achievement.

7

Concentration

ONLY through the principle of *concentration* can the psychic phase of the Master Mind principle be reached and used. Concentration is the focusing of the attention, interest, and desire upon the attainment of a *definite* end. In view of these facts, it will be readily observed that concentration is essential for the effective use of the Master Mind principle, the two being inseparable when practical results are to be obtained through their use by two or more people.

Autosuggestion (self-suggestion) is the principle through which the subconscious mind may be reached and influenced; concentration is the principle through which autosuggestion must be applied, a fact that has been clearly illustrated in the chapter on that subject. We have termed it "the first step in salesmanship."

Let us state these important facts in another way, viz:

The Master Mind principle, the principle of concentration and the principle of autosuggestion, constitute a triumvirate that must be used in reaching and influencing the subconscious mind.

The subconscious mind will not recognize nor be influenced by any suggestion given it, unless that suggestion is mixed with one or more of the emotions mentioned in the chapter on autosuggestion.

Thus, it will be seen that these three chapters on the Master Mind, autosuggestion, and concentration constitute the very heart of Master Salesmanship. If you miss complete understanding and assimilation of these three chapters, the book will have lost for you much of its value.

In this chapter is described the method by which the principle of concentration may be applied effectively. Don't fail to make the most of it, for it is of supreme importance to you.

Concentration is defined as "the habit of planting in the mind a definite aim, object, or purpose, and visualizing the same until ways and means for its realization have been created."

The principle of concentration, as it applies to and constitutes a part of mastery in selling embraces planting in one's conscious mind a definite chief aim, idea, plan, or purpose, and the continuous focusing upon it of the conscious mind.

The principle of concentration is the medium by which procrastination is overcome. The same principle is the foundation upon which both self-confidence and self-control are predicated.

The principle of habit. The principle of habit and the principle of concentration go hand in glove. Habit may grow out of concentration and concentration may grow out of habit.

The object of concentrating upon a definite aim is to train the mind until it forms the habit of focusing upon the object of that aim. By focusing upon one's definite aim through concentrated effort and attention, this habit comes to influence the subconscious mind, so that it picks up the mental concept of that aim and translates it into its physical counterpart through the most practical and direct methods available.

Every human being makes use of the principle of concentration whether he realizes it or not. The person who permits his conscious mind to dwell upon the negative thoughts of fear, poverty, ill health, and intolerance, thereby applies the law of concentration and sooner or later the subconscious mind will pick up these suggestions and act upon them and translate them into their physical counterpart.

Instructions for Applying Concentration

1. Master and apply the principles described in the chapter on *auto-suggestion* by following the habit of giving orders to your subconscious mind, mixing your thoughts with one or more of the positive emotions, and repeating your orders over and over. Keep up this procedure until you get satisfactory results, remembering that eternal vigilance is the price of mastery in this effort.
2. Empty your conscious mind of all other thoughts. After a little practice, you will be able to focus your mind entirely upon any subject that you please. The act of focusing upon one subject and keeping your mind upon that one subject is concentration.

3. Hold your thoughts to the object of your concentration with a *burning desire* for the attainment of whatever object you have in mind. When concentrating upon your Definite Chief Aim, do so in perfect faith that you will realize the object of that aim.
4. When you find your conscious mind wandering, drive it back and focus it upon that subject again and again until you have developed such perfect self-control that you can keep out of your mind all other thoughts. Mix *emotions or feelings with your thoughts when concentrating; otherwise they will not be recognized by your subconscious mind.*
5. The principle of concentration may be best applied when one is in an environment of silence where there are no counter attractions or noises of any disturbing nature. The best time for concentrating is after one has retired at night, for then the number of distractions is minimized.
6. Your subconscious mind can best be reached and influenced when you concentrate in your conscious mind upon an idea, plan, or purpose in a spirit of *intense enthusiasm*, for the reason that enthusiasm arouses your faculty of creative imagination and puts it into action.

Any idea, plan, purpose, or definite aim that you persistently submit to your subconscious mind through the medium of concentration here described, brings to your aid the force of Infinite Intelligence until eventually practical plans of procedure will flash into your mind during your period of concentration.

When you first start your practice of concentration, you may not experience the feeling that you are in communication with a superior intelligence, but in time if you develop the habit of regular concentration, you will be thoroughly cognizant of the fact that a superior intelligence is influencing you.

It is a well-known fact that the jack-of-all-trades never achieves success. Life is so very complicated, and there are so many ways of dissipating energy unprofitably, that the habit of concentrated effort must be formed and adhered to by all who succeed.

Power is predicated upon organized energy. Energy can only be organized through the principle of concentration. It is a fact worthy of serious consideration that all men of outstanding success in all walks of life are men who concentrate the major portion of their thoughts and efforts upon some one definite purpose or chief aim.

By analyzing the principle of the Master Mind, you will observe that when two or more people ally themselves in a spirit of harmony for the purpose of achieving some definite objective, that alliance functions through the principle of concentrated effort.

From my analysis of more than 25,000 men and women who were rated as failures, I observed that not one of them followed the habit of focusing his or her mind upon a definite chief aim through the principle of concentration. The 30 major causes of failure may be either controlled or eliminated entirely through the principle of concentration, indicating the importance of this principle as a part of the working equipment of the successful salesman.

Nearly everyone has a definite chief aim at one time or another. Ninety-five percent of the people who have such aims, however, make no attempt to realize them, for the reason that they have not learned the art of concentrating on their definite aims for sufficient length of time to fix in the subconscious mind the object of their aims. The majority of the people who adopt a definite aim do so more in the nature of a wish than in the form of a definite, determined, well-defined intention.

Merely permitting a definite aim to come into one's mind is in no way beneficial. Such an aim, to be of permanent value, must be fixed in the mind through the principle of concentration.

Concentration develops the power of persistence and enables one to master all forms of temporary defeat. The majority of people never learn the real difference between temporary defeat and permanent failure, for the reason that they are lacking in the persistence necessary to stage a comeback after they have experienced temporary defeat. Persistence is merely concentrated effort well mixed with determination and faith.

From these facts you will readily understand that the principle of a definite chief aim and the principle of concentration are complementary. One can be applied successfully only with the aid of the other.

Every human being is ruled by the law of habit. Because this is true, the person who learns to build his habits to order practically controls the major cause of successful achievement. Concentration is the principle through which one may build one's habits to order. It has been correctly said that "we first make our habits and our habits then make us."

We have habits of mind and habits of body. Both are subject to control and the medium of that control is concentration. The mind is just as susceptible to the influence of habit as is the physical body. Through concentration, we may force the mind to dwell upon any subject we desire until the mind falls into the habit of dwelling on that subject. It then follows the habit automatically.

There is no point of compromise between a man and his habits. Either he controls his habits or his habits control him. The successful man, understanding this truth, forces himself to build the sort of habits by which he is willing to be controlled.

Habits are formed step-by-step through our every thought and deed.

Center your thoughts upon a definite aim, through concentration, and very soon your subconscious mind will pick up a clear picture of that aim and aid you in translating it into its physical counterpart.

All thought has a tendency to externalize itself. This is a truth well-known to every psychologist, as it was known to him who wrote, "Whatever a man soweth, that shall he also reap."

Your financial condition is not the result of chance or accident. It reflects perfectly the nature of your dominating thoughts, desires, and aims. In analyses of men who have accumulated huge fortunes, I particularly studied the source of those fortunes and in every case discovered that they represented the consummation of the state of mind of those who had accumulated them.

The man who understands the possibilities of concentration need rarely know the word "impossible."

Throughout the book, I have repeatedly made reference to the power of Infinite Intelligence. If such a power can be influenced to inject itself into man's affairs and made to help man achieve the object of his aims and purposes, I feel certain that this stupendous result can be attained only through the principle of concentration.

I owe eternal allegiance to Infinite Intelligence. No church nor creed would quarrel with such an attitude. This statement is made for the sole purpose of enabling every reader to become more familiar with a great universal law that is capable of being harnessed and induced to separate man from all of his causes of doubt, worry, and fear.

I am a firm believer in the power of prayer. Let me explain, however, what I mean by the term "prayer." To me, a prayer is any fixed or *definite aim* that is founded upon faith in the realization of that purpose or aim. Concentration without faith appears to bring no results. Concentration with faith appears to achieve results that border on the miraculous.

The process of mixing faith with a definite chief aim is one that is indeed difficult to describe and more difficult still to apply. Faith can only be induced through concentration upon the object of one's hopes, aims, and purposes.

A little while before his death, I had the privilege of visiting with F. W. Woolworth. In these words did he describe the method through which he built what was at that time the tallest building in the world:

"I had an architect draw up a set of plans. Every day for more than six months, I went into my private office, shut the door, and looked over these plans for more than half an hour. Each time that I looked at them, the actual physical building seemed nearer a reality. Finally, the day came when the exact method by which I financed the Woolworth Building flashed into my mind, and I knew instantly that the building was a reality. From that point on, I had no difficulty whatsoever."

The Woolworth Building became a reality because F. W. Woolworth concentrated upon that building *until concentrated thought externalized itself in physical reality.*

Writing in *The Christian Science Monitor*, Mr. Willis J. Abbot recently said:

"Not long ago, I was in the original Menlo Park laboratory of Edison, which Henry Ford, with pious reverence for the great inventor, has erected at Dearborn, Michigan. All the earlier tools of Edison's craft are there—the first electric incandescent light—it had a life of eight hours; the first phonograph, in which a needle played over a tin foil, recorded and emitted a squeaky imitation of the human voice. Thousands of bottles of chemicals lined the walls. 'Mr. Edison had to have every known chemical where he could put his hand on it,' said the custodian, who had worked with him half a century ago.

"But to me, more interesting than the material relics was a picture the custodian drew for me, little thinking how impressive it was. 'Often Mr. Ford comes in here,' said he. 'He pulls up that chair and just sits and thinks. Sometimes he'll sit almost an hour and then go out without a word to anyone.'

"What are the thoughts of the giant of industrial organization as he sits thus surrounded by the relics of the earlier triumphs of Edison's wizardry. 'Thinking,' he once said, 'is the hardest work that any man can do.' Perhaps he found it easier to think out his problems in an environment which had witnessed the solution of so many. At any rate, the spectacle of Henry Ford thus plunged in meditation amidst the evidences of Edison's struggles and victories is one to challenge thought."

It is difficult for anyone to say which of the principles described in this book is the most important, but I always feel when I approach the subject of concentration that I am dealing with the keystone to the arch of the whole subject.

> Your employer does not control the sort of service you render. You control that, and it is the thing that makes or breaks you.

8

Initiative and Leadership

INITIATIVE means the doing of things without being told to do them. It means the selection of a Definite Aim and the building of plans for the achievement of that aim.

Its most profitable application is in the selection of a Master Mind group. If you use judgment in the selection of this group, your Master Mind alliance will give you the power of real leadership.

The Major Attributes of Initiative and Leadership

In applying initiative and leadership, certain definite steps are essential. The following are the most important of these steps:

1. Know *definitely* what you want.
2. Build a practical plan or plans for the achievement of that which you want, making use of the counsel and advice of your Master Mind group.
3. Surround yourself with an organization made up of men who have the knowledge and experience essential for carrying out your Definite Aim.

4. Have sufficient faith in yourself and in your plans to see your aim a finished reality even before you begin to carry out your plans.
5. Do not become discouraged no matter with what obstacles you may meet. If one plan fails to work, substitute other plans until you have found the one that will work.
6. Do no guessing but get the facts as the basis for all of your plans.
7. Do not be influenced by others to abandon your plans or your aim.
8. Have no set hours of labor. The leader must devote to his task whatever hours are necessary for success.
9. Concentrate upon one thing at a time as you cannot dissipate thought and energy and still be efficient.
10. Whenever possible, relegate to others the responsibility of details, but have a system for checking your subordinates to see that these details are accurately attended to. Hold yourself accountable at all times for carrying out all of your plans, bearing in mind that if subordinates fail, it is you yourself who have failed.

Persistence is the keynote to success for all great leaders. If you are going to become discouraged at the first signs of opposition or adversity, you will never become a great leader. Leadership means the capacity to assume great responsibility. If you lack the quality of persistence, you must have associated with you in your Master Mind group some person or persons who have this quality. An efficient leader never permits himself to be loaded down with small details. One of the outstanding qualities of a leader is the ability to so organize his plans that he is free at all times to place the weight of his personal effort wherever it is most needed. I have met and interviewed, many times, many of the most able industrial leaders of America. Not one of these ever seemed to be rushed with work, for the reason that in every case the responsibility of details had been relegated to others.

The man who boasts of the habit of inspecting personally all the details of his business is either not an able leader or he is at the head of a very small business. The sentence, "I haven't had time" is said to be the most dangerous sentence in the English language. Any man who makes such an admission confesses his lack of ability as a leader. The real leader has time for everything necessary to his successful leadership. The stock alibi of more than 90 percent of the world's failures, to justify them in not having selected a Definite Chief Aim in life, is "I just haven't had time to get around to it." An efficient leader is not necessarily the person who appears to be the busiest, but he is the person who can so organize his plans that he can efficiently direct and keep large numbers of other people busy. The man who can get things done is much more profitable to a business house than the man who actually does the work.

The efficient leader is also an efficient salesman. He gets people to do things because they wish to do them *for him*. The efficient leader has a pleasing personality. He is optimistic and enthusiastic and he knows how to transmit his enthusiasm and his optimism to his followers. An efficient leader is courageous. No man wishes to follow a leader who is lacking in courage, and in fact, will not do so. The efficient leader has a keen sense of justice and deals with his followers fairly and justly. An efficient leader assumes full responsibility for the acts of his subordinates. If they make mistakes, he assumes that it is he that has really made the mistake because it was he who chose the subordinates. The efficient leader understands the rules of pedagogy and is in reality an able *teacher. An efficient leader reaches decisions quickly and changes them slowly.*

There are circumstances, of course, which call for slow deliberation and the examination of facts before an intelligent decision can be reached. However, after all the available facts have been gathered and organized, there is no excuse for delaying decision, and the person who practices the habit of delay cannot become an effective leader unless he masters this shortcoming. For more than a hundred years, there had been talk about the building of the Panama Canal, but the actual work of building the canal never got much beyond the talk stage until the late Theodore Roosevelt became the president of the United States. With the firmness of decision that was the very warp and woof of his achievements and the real basis of his reputation as a leader, Roosevelt took the initiative, had a bill framed for Congress to pass, providing for the appropriation, organized his Master Mind group of engineers, went to work with a spirit of self-confidence, and lo, the much talked of Panama Canal became a splendid reality.

We have had more learned men than Theodore Roosevelt in the White House, but we have had few, if any, greater leaders than he. Leaders are men of action!

General Grant said, "We will fight it out on this line if it takes all summer," and despite his many other deficiencies, he stood by that decision and won.

When asked by one of his sailors what he would do if they saw no signs of land by the following day, Columbus replied, "If we see no land tomorrow, we will sail on and on." He, too, had a Definite Chief Aim and a plan for its attainment, and he, too, had reached a decision not to quit or to turn back until success had crowned his efforts. Columbus was a man with great ability as a leader.

Napoleon, when surprised by the enemy, having discovered that there was a deep camouflaged ditch just ahead of the line of march, gave orders for his cavalry to charge the ditch. He waited until the dead bodies of men and horses filled the ditch, then marched his troops across and whipped the enemy. That required courage and quick decision; moreover, it required instantaneous decision. One minute of faltering or hesitation and he would have been flanked by the enemy and captured. He did the unexpected or impossible. His capacity to act quickly *without waiting to be told by others what to do* was the quality that marked him as a great leader.

The first step essential to the development of initiative and leadership is that of forming the habit of prompt and *firm* decision. The great leader must have a tremendous amount of the capacity for quick and prompt decision. The man who hesitates between vague notions of what he wants to do or should do, generally ends by doing nothing.

This is an age when initiative and leadership are in demand in practically every calling. Never in the history of the world have these qualities meant as much as they do today for the reason that millions of people throughout the world are in an unsettled, undecided state of mind. In America, the doors are wide open to men who have the qualities of initiative and leadership in statesmanship, religion, industry, finance, transportation, merchandising, education, and in a score of other lines of endeavor. At the present time, there are few outstanding men in any of these great fields.

There is a mistaken notion in the world to the effect that a man is paid for what he knows. This is only partly true, and like all other half-truths, it does more damage than an out-and-out falsehood. The truth is: A man is paid not merely for that which he knows, but more particularly *for what he does with what he knows, or that which he can get others to do.*

Not long ago, the author received a letter from a man who said, "I have a splendid education and I could be a great success if someone would only show me what to do and how to do it."

Successful men never wait for others to show them what to do or how to do it. They take the initiative themselves, appoint themselves to leadership, enlist the necessary assistance and capital, and forge ahead despite all opposition. Self-confidence is one of the essentials for success in leadership. One of the natural tendencies of human nature is that of willingness to follow the man with great self-confidence. No one wishes to follow a man who does not seem to be sure of himself. It was said of Napoleon that his soldiers would willingly follow him to their death because of his example of courage and self-confidence.

A real leader is always persistent and never accepts temporary defeat as failure. The leader who changes his mind often soon loses the confidence of his followers. When a leader changes his mind often, he thereby puts his followers on notice that he is not sure of himself, and if he isn't sure of himself, how may he expect his followers to be sure of him.

The real leader shows no partiality among his followers. If he has friends or relatives in his organization, he treats them exactly as he does the rest of the staff.

A real leader not only has self-reliance and courage himself, but he imparts these qualities to his subordinates. When Mr. Cyrus H. K. Curtis placed a man in charge of one of his publications, he said to that man, "I am turning this property over to you to be managed and run just exactly as if you had the legal title to it. Make your own decisions, select your own help, create your own policy, lay out your own plans, and then accept the entire responsibility for its success. All I wish to see is a satisfactory balance sheet at the end of the year."

Mr. Curtis was one of the most successful publishers in the world. He was successful because he himself was a great leader and his leadership was based primarily upon his understanding of the principle of relegating responsibility to others. He would not permit his subordinates to shift any responsibility back to him. In this way, he created efficient leaders.

The president of the United States would get nowhere if he undertook to instruct all of his associates how to plan and conduct their campaigns. He places on their shoulders the responsibility of planning and carrying out the plans. The able business leader must do this. A man always does his best work when he feels that he is acting upon his own initiative and knows he must assume full responsibility for his actions.

There can be no real leadership in any calling without assumption of responsibility. We all want to be leaders in one way or another. Most of us would like to have the authority and the pay that belongs to the man who tells other people what to do, but few of us wish to accept the responsibility that goes with that authority. A real leader has no set hours of labor for the reason that it is his business to carry out his plans no matter how many hours he may be called upon to devote to the task.

The real leader makes due allowance for the ordinary weaknesses of his subordinates and lays his plans so he will be protected against these weaknesses. The real leader does not merely surround himself with a number of subordinates selected at random. He selects with care the right man for the special job, later shifting and changing men from one job to another whenever and wherever he finds he has made a mistake. The real leader has a keen imagination and he induces action on the part of his followers by an appeal to their imaginations. He does not rely upon his authority or power over his men, nor does he try to instill fear in their hearts. The real leader relies mainly upon his ability to sell his followers on doing what is most advantageous to him, through presenting the advantages to them. He uses *persuasion*, not power. There are two types of leaders in the world. One resorts to power and controls his followers through fear; the other resorts to persuasion and controls his followers through able salesmanship. Men of the latter type are Master Salesmen, regardless of their calling.

In warfare, leadership based upon power and authority and fear may be essential, but in business that form of leadership is despicable. The successful leader in business and industry is a man who induces people to do things because it is to their advantage to do them and not merely because he happens to be in power.

The Master Salesman is essentially a leader. He induces people to cooperate with him in a spirit of harmony by planting in their minds adequate motives. He uses persuasion instead of coercion, therefore, his leadership endures. The Master Salesman reaches his followers and influences them favorably through their emotions as well as their reason.

All great leaders are Master Salesmen!

And all Master Salesmen are great leaders. They understand the art of persuasion; they understand how to set up in the minds of their followers, motives that will induce favorable, willing cooperation.

Master Salesmen can sell anything they choose to sell because they have sufficient initiative to create markets. Moreover, they can sell one commodity, idea, plan, form of service, or motive just as easily as any other.

Great leaders and Master Salesmen use the same philosophy. They sell their followers or patrons whatever they choose to sell by establishing a relationship of confidence.

> One of the greatest leaders who ever lived stated the secret of his leadership in six words as follows: "Kindness is more powerful than compulsion."

9

Qualifying the Prospective Buyer

IN the actual process of selling, the first step is to qualify the prospective buyer. That is, the salesman should ascertain tactfully from the prospective buyer, and from other sources if possible, the following information that he will need in presenting his sales plan to the best advantage:

1. How much money is the prospective purchaser prepared to spend and how much should he be asked to spend?
2. Are conditions, including the prospective buyer's state of mind, favorable for closing the sale? If not, when are they likely to be?
3. Will the prospective buyer act for himself or must some lawyer, banker, wife, husband, relative, counselor, or other person be consulted before a decision can be reached? If so, who is the person to be consulted and for what specific purpose?
4. If the prospective buyer must consult another person before making a decision, will he permit the salesman to be present at the consultation? *This is highly important.* No salesman can afford for a third person to sit in judgment upon him and his wares without being present to present his own case.

5. Does the prospective buyer like to do most of the talking? If so, be sure to give him the opportunity. Every word a prospective buyer speaks will serve as a cue to what is in his mind. If the prospective buyer is not inclined to talk freely, induce him to do so by asking leading questions that will bring out the desired information.

While qualifying the prospective buyer, the salesman will find it easy to ascertain just what alibi and what objections are likely to be offered when the closing point has been reached. The following are some of the most commonly used alibis, to which practically all prospective buyers resort:

- The prospective buyer will claim he does not have the money. The Master Salesman always takes this one with more than the proverbial grain of salt. If the salesman has accurately qualified his prospective buyer, he knows his financial status and can, therefore, tactfully meet this objection.
- The prospective buyer, if he is a man, may tell the salesman that he does not wish to decide until he talks the matter over with his wife, banker, or lawyer. If he hides behind his wife's skirt, the Master Salesman will tactfully invite him to permit him (the salesman) to talk to the two of them together. At this interview, the Master Salesman will analyze the wife and ascertain whether she is the real boss or a mere subterfuge for her husband. If she is the boss, he will direct his sales efforts mainly to her.
- The prospective buyer may claim he does not wish to reach a decision until he has had time to "think the matter over." That is an old one! The Master Salesman knows about how much thinking the majority of people do about anything. However, he will use tact in such cases, and will suggest ways and means by which he can assist his prospective buyer at his task of thinking. The Master Salesman permits his prospective buyers to believe they are doing their own thinking, but he takes care to see that they think with ideas and facts that he supplies.

All of this process of qualifying the prospective buyer must precede the attempt to close the sale. Practically every sale that is lost after the sales presentation has been made occurs for one of two reasons, namely:

First: Either the salesman has not properly neutralized the mind of his prospective buyer before making his sales presentation

or

Second: He has failed to qualify accurately the prospective buyer before trying to close the sale.

The Master Salesman never tries to close a sale until he is absolutely sure that he has painted in the prospective buyer's mind a picture that has created a strong desire for his wares. The prospective buyer must be able to buy. This is a point on which no guessing should be done. It is the Master Salesman's business to *know*, and if he does not know, he is not a Master Salesman!

Trying to sell a Packard automobile to a man who has only a Ford income and an Austin bank account is wasted effort. Accurate qualification prevents such waste.

The first thing a Master Salesman asks a prospective purchaser of life insurance is "How much insurance do you now carry, and what sort of policies have you?" Armed with this information, which is easily acquired from the asking, and knowing the prospective buyer's approximate financial status, the life insurance salesman knows what policy to offer his client.

The Question Method of Qualifying Prospective Buyers

Master Salesmen take the precaution of propounding an adequate supply of stock questions with which they acquire from their prospective purchasers such information, as they need to qualify them accurately. Most men will answer any reasonable questions that are asked them. Care and thought in the preparation and asking of these questions will enable the salesman to arm himself with all the information he needs to close a sale. Moreover, the information will be authentic and reliable because the prospect will supply it.

Let Your Prospect Talk Freely

When police officials arrest a man who is suspected of having committed a crime, they proceed, immediately, to induce the suspect to talk! Every word he utters, as well as his refusal to talk on certain points, places in the hands of the investigators facts from which they can easily make important deductions.

Until the point of actual presentation of the sales plan has been reached, every Master Salesman is, in reality, an investigator. It is his business to get the facts, and the best method of getting them is to induce the prospective buyer to talk! Some who call themselves salesmen spoil their chances of making sales by opening their mouths and closing their eyes and ears. The most successful salesmen manage an interview in such a tactful fashion that the prospective buyer believes *he* is managing it. When the sale has been closed, the buyer believes he has made a purchase rather than having been sold anything.

Stalking the Prospective Buyer

Master Salesmen make it a part of their technique to contact prospective buyers in advance of the time when any selling effort is made, for the purpose of qualifying them in an unobtrusive manner. One of the most successful life insurance salesmen in America specializes in the sale of life insurance policies to men with whom he plays golf. He takes great care, however, never to refer to his profession even briefly on the golf course. Moreover, he never tries to talk life insurance to his prospective buyers until after he has played golf with them at least three times, and even then he leads up to the subject through a series of cleverly prepared, tactful questions through which he induces his prospective buyers to ask him about life insurance. He calls himself a "life insurance counselor." It is his business, he tells prospective buyers, to go over their life insurance policies with them for the purpose of ascertaining whether they have the best form of insurance, the right amount, and so forth. Naturally, he chooses prospective buyers of insurance who carry large amounts of insurance and who, therefore, have many policies already in force. He has made hundreds of sales without asking his prospective buyers to take additional insurance, merely by analyzing their life insurance schedules in such a tactful way as to plant in their minds the thought that they need additional insurance of one sort or another.

Confidence is the condition of major importance that must be created by the Master Salesman in the minds of his prospective buyers. If he qualifies his prospective buyers accurately, he builds this confidence while doing so. No sale of note can be made without this element of confidence. Master Salesmen often "stalk" their prospective buyers for months while establishing confidence, meanwhile refraining from any attempt to make sales.

Methods of Qualifying

The skilled detective often plants stool pigeons where they can contact those who are suspected of crime, for the purpose of gaining information about the suspect. Here, again, the Master Salesman follows tactics similar to those used by criminologists, but the Master Salesman acts as his own stool pigeon and gets his information firsthand. The nature of his work makes stealth in acquiring information unnecessary.

Sometimes, however, Master Salesmen use skilled investigators. (They do not consider them to be stool pigeons.) These men are used for the purpose of gathering information about prospective buyers that the salesmen themselves cannot acquire in person. This practice is common among salesmen who sell to public officials where the personal habits of those who are empowered to do the buying is believed to be questionable. It is the Master Salesman's business, among other things, to know all about his prospective buyer. He must get the facts.

Lobbyists, whose number in Washington is legion, often serve those who employ them, more in the capacity of investigators than as salesmen. If they find anything in the private habits of a senator or a congressman that will not bear the spotlight of publicity, the discovery becomes valuable to their employers. The same tactics are employed with reference to other government officials whose cooperation sometimes is sought on the basis of coercion rather than persuasion.

This form of qualification is most reprehensible! Moreover, it is accompanied by great hazards to the one who uses it. This method of securing information is mentioned, not with the objective of recommending it, but for the purpose of showing how important it is for men who seek to persuade others, to have facts upon which to plan their sales presentation.

The salesman, who is too indifferent or too lazy to supply himself with sufficient facts to enable him to qualify his prospective buyers, deserves to fail, and he usually does.

Any man is nine-tenths beaten when his adversary gains possession of the motives by which he is most easily actuated and his major weaknesses, provided always that his adversary has the intelligence to use the information effectively. Master Salesmen possess this intelligence. Moreover, they become Master Salesmen largely because of their ability to gather facts and to qualify accurately their prospective buyers.

When police officials are called in to solve a murder mystery in which the motive for the murder is unknown, the first question they ask is "Where is the woman in the case?" Or they may seek to determine whether robbery was the motive. Unless the motive for the crime has been established, it is often difficult to apprehend the criminal and to convict him after he has been apprehended. These are facts from which the Master Salesman may profit. Find out the prospective buyer's major motives and his major weaknesses, and he is as good as in your bag before you begin.

10

Neutralizing the Prospective Buyer's Mind

AFTER the prospective buyer has been qualified or during the qualification process before a sale can be made, his mind must be emptied of prejudice, bias, resentment, and all other conditions unfavorable to the salesman. The prospective buyer's mind must be cultivated and prepared before the seed of desire can be successfully planted in it. A neutral or favorable mind of a prospective buyer should contemplate:

1. *Confidence.* The buyer must have confidence in the salesman and in his wares.
2. *Interest.* The buyer must be reached through an appeal to his imagination and interest, aroused in the commodity offered for sale.
3. *Motive.* The buyer must have a logical motive for buying. The building of this motive is the salesman's most important task.

No prospective buyer's mind has been neutralized and made favorable until these three conditions exist in his mind. The salesman's first duty is to create confidence in the mind of his prospective buyer. Obviously, this cannot be done by arousing any of the negative emotions. It can only be done by a careful analysis of:

1. The buyer.
2. The buyer's business or calling.
3. The obstacles that may face the buyer in the successful conduct of his business.

Nothing builds confidence more quickly than a keen, genuine interest in the buyer's business problems.

The salesman's second duty in preparing the mind of his prospect to receive favorably the seed of desire for his wares, is to arouse interest in those wares in the mind of the prospect. This may require the application of one or all of the "Qualities the Master Salesman Must Develop," described in a preceding chapter. To arouse interest in his wares, the salesman will at least find it necessary to use imagination, faith, enthusiasm, knowledge of his merchandise, persistence, and showmanship. A neutral mind will be of no advantage to the salesman who lacks the ability to plant in that mind the seed of desire for his merchandise. That seed cannot be planted without interest upon the part of the prospective buyer.

The salesman's third duty is to create an appropriate motive to induce the prospective buyer to purchase his wares. This will necessitate his having full and complete knowledge of the prospective buyer and his business or calling.

Failure to neutralize the mind of the prospective buyer is one of the five major weaknesses of the majority of unsuccessful salesmen. There can be no fixed rule to be followed in neutralizing the minds of prospective buyers, as each individual case offers conditions peculiar unto itself, and each case must be handled on its own merits. The salesman with imagination will not be slow to recognize the most appropriate methods of approach in neutralizing the minds of his prospective buyers. Some of the methods that have been used successfully for sales preparation or neutralization purposes are as follows:

1. *Social contacts through clubs.* It has been said that more business is done on the golf courses of America than is done in business offices. Certainly every supersalesman knows the value of club contacts.
2. *Church affiliations.* Here one may make acquaintance without the usual formalities, under circumstances that tend to establish confidence.
3. *Lodge and union affiliations.* In many lines of selling, the salesman will find it highly helpful to establish contacts through lodges and trade unions, where men naturally let down the bars of formality.

4. *Personal courtesies.* Dinner engagements offer favorable opportunity to break down the resistance of formalities and to establish confidence, a condition precedent to neutrality of mind.
5. *Personal service.* Under some conditions, salesmen are in a position to render valuable service and to supply helpful information to those with whom they intend to do business subsequently.
6. *Mutual interest in hobbies.* Nearly every man has a hobby or some form of interest outside of his business or calling. When discussing or pursuing his hobby, one is always inclined to step out from the defense behind which he hides in the course of his business routine.

Having neutralized the mind of the buyer and having established confidence, the next step in making a sale is to crystallize that confidence into interest in the salesman's wares. Here the salesman must build his entire sales presentation around a central motive that is appropriate and best suited to the business and financial status of his prospective buyer. The three subjects of confidence, interest, and motive having been attended to, the salesman has reached the point at which the sale may be closed.

Salesmanship Resembles a Stage Play

Scientific salesmanship involves principles similar to those upon which a successful stage play is based. The psychology of selling an individual is closely akin to that which is used by actors in selling an audience. The stage play that succeeds must have the advantage of a strong opening act and a smashing climax or closing act. If a play does not have these, it will be a flop.

Act I. Must grip the attention and arouse the interest of the audience.

Act II. Must develop plot or presentation: Though this be weak, it may yet go over providing the first act has been strong. The audience (or buyers) will be charitable, providing they gained sufficient confidence from the first act to arouse expectation of a strong climax.

Act III. Must realize the objective. This must be a knockout regardless of the first two acts or the play will be a flop. The third, or last, act is where the sale is closed or lost.

The approach in selling must be strong enough to establish confidence and arouse interest in the salesman and his wares. If he falls down in this first act, he will experience difficulty, if not impossibility, in making a sale. The sales presentation may be weak at many places in the middle without fatality to the sale, providing the opening and the close are strong and impelling. The art of scientific salesmanship may be described as a three act drama consisting of:

Act I ***Interest.*** (This must be created by neutralizing the mind of the prospective buyer and establishing confidence.)
Act II ***Desire.*** (Desire must be developed through the proper presentation of motive.)
Act III ***Action.*** (Action, or the close, can be induced only by the proper presentation of the two preceding acts.)

It is hardly necessary to suggest that the director (salesman) who presents successfully the three act drama of selling must possess and use imagination. The imagination is the workshop of the mind, in which is fashioned every idea, plan, and mental picture with which the salesman creates desire in the mind of his prospective buyer. Salesmen, whose imaginations are deficient, resemble a ship without a rudder—they go round and round in circles and finish where they started, without making a favorable impression.

Words alone will not sell!

Words, woven into combinations of thought that create desire, will sell. Some salesmen never learn the difference between rapid-fire conversation that does not end soon enough and carefully painted word-pictures that fire the imagination of the prospective buyer.

The sole object of neutralizing the mind of prospective buyers is, of course, to establish confidence. Where confidence has not been first built in the mind of the prospect, no sale can be made.

The 10 Major Factors on which Confidence Is Built

By careful observation of thousands of salespeople from whom I have learned all that I know about selling, I discovered that 10 major factors enter into the development of confidence. They are:

1. Follow the habit of rendering more service and better service than you are paid to render.
2. Enter into no transaction that does not benefit, as nearly alike as possible, everyone it affects.

3. Make no statement that you do not believe to be true, no matter what temporary advantages a falsehood might seem to offer.
4. Have a sincere desire in your heart to be of the greatest possible service to the largest number of people.
5. Cultivate a wholesome admiration for people; like them better than you like money!
6. Do your best to live as well as preach your own philosophy of business. *Actions speak louder than words!*
7. Accept no favors, large or small, without giving favors in return.
8. Ask nothing of any person without believing that you have a right to that for which you ask.
9. Enter into no arguments with any person over trivial or nonessential details.
10. Spread the sunshine of good cheer wherever and whenever you can. No man trusts a joy killer!

This list is well worth memorizing. It is also worth following.

A Master Salesman can sell a man anything he needs if the purchaser has confidence in the salesman.

He can also sell a man many things he does not need, *but he doesn't*. Remember, a Master Salesman plays the double role of buyer and seller. He therefore does not try to sell any person anything that he, himself, would not buy if he were actually in the position of the prospective buyer.

There is a well-known type of crook who is a Master Salesman. He is known as a *confidence man*. His sole equipment is his ability to build confidence in the minds of his victims. His thefts run into the millions, and his victims may be found among the shrewdest of businessmen, professional men, and bankers.

These crooks often stalk their victims for months, or even years, for the purpose of building a relationship of perfect confidence. When this foundation has been properly laid, the smartest men may be taken in. Men are without defense against those in whom they have perfect confidence.

If confidence can be used successfully as the sole tool of operation of the crook, surely it can be used with greater effect for legitimate business and professional purposes. The salesman who knows how to build a bridge of confidence between himself and his prospective purchasers may write his own income ticket, as all such salesmen do.

High-pressure methods, exaggerated statements of fact, willful misrepresentation, whether by direct statement or by innuendo, destroy confidence.

A little while ago, one of the biggest sales producers in the employ of a well-known automobile dealer was let out of his position peremptorily, at the end of the most successful sales month he had ever experienced. He was dismissed because a checkup of his accounts with the finance company disclosed the fact that more than three-fourths of his customers had lapsed in their payments. A further checkup disclosed the fact that this so-called salesman had high-pressured his buyers into signing orders by telling them that if anything happened that made it inconvenient for them to make their monthly payments promptly, they could skip a couple of months or so without jeopardizing their rights. The automobile agency for which this man worked lost prestige through his acts that it will never be able to regain.

Every successful business firm must have the confidence of its patrons. The salesman is the intermediary through whom this confidence is acquired, or he may be the medium through which it is lost. The Master Salesman, knowing as he does the importance of acquiring and holding the confidence of his buyers, bargains with them as if he were the owner of the business he represents. He deals with his customers exactly as he would want them dealt with if he were, in fact, the owner of the business.

Confidence is the basis of all harmonious relationships. The salesman who overlooks this fact is unfortunate; he can never become a Master Salesman. This means that he limits his earning capacity and circumscribes his possibilities of advancement.

In the city of Chicago, a Master Salesman conducts a chain of men's hat stores. Some 20 years ago, when these stores were first brought to my attention, they specialized in two dollar hats. The hats were sold with the guarantee that if the customer found his purchase unsatisfactory, he could bring back the hat, or any part of it, to the store and receive a brand new one in its place with no questions asked.

I was informed by the owner of the store that one man had been coming back twice a year, for more than seven years, and exchanging his old hat for a new one.

"And you permit him to get away with that?" I inquired.

"Get away with it?" the store owner replied, "Why, man alive! If I had a hundred men doing the same thing, I could retire from business with all the money I need, inside of five years. Never a day passes that we do not trace sales to the talking done by this man. He is literally a walking and a talking advertisement for us."

That statement threw an entirely different light on the subject. I saw that this hat store owner had built an enormous business upon an unusual policy that developed confidence.

There are two major occasions that cause men and women to talk, and, therefore, advertise favorably or unfavorably a business: when they think they have been cheated, and when they have received fairer treatment than expected.

All people are like this. They are impressed by the law of contrast. Anything unusual or unexpected, whether it impress favorably or unfavorably, makes a lasting impression.

11

The Art of Closing a Sale

THE climax, or closing of a sale, is said to be the most difficult part of the entire transaction. This is not true, however, if the groundwork preparatory to reaching the close has been properly laid. As a matter of fact, the climax of a sale is a mere detail *if* a sale has been properly prepared.

In almost every instance when a sale is hard to close, the difficulty may be found in some part of the transaction preceding the climax. Before trying to reach a climax, the Master Salesman prepares the way carefully, step by step, through proper attention to the following important details:

- He has taken care to neutralize the mind of his prospect to make it receptive to his sales presentation.
- He has made the mind of his prospect favorable by establishing confidence.
- He has qualified the prospect's mind accurately to make sure that he is dealing with a prospect and not a mere suspect.
- Above all, he has planted in the prospect's mind the most logical motive for buying.
- He has tested the prospect, during his sales presentation, and has made sure that the prospect followed his presentation with keen interest. This he has accomplished by keen observation of the prospect's facial

expression and his statements denoting a desire for the object of the sale.

- Last, but by no means least, the salesman has *made the sale in his own mind before trying to reach a climax!* He knows this by the *feel* of his prospect's mind. No one can become a Master Salesman without developing the ability to tune in to the prospect's mind through the sixth sense. This ability, more than anything else, is the distinguishing feature of a Master Salesman.

Having taken these steps satisfactorily, the salesman is now ready to reach terminal facilities or to close the sale. There are thousands of salesmen who can arouse interest, the first step in the actual process of selling; and create a desire for their wares, the second step; but at the third step they fall down because they lack the ability to close! Let it be remembered, however, that if the six detailed steps described in this book have been properly taken, the close comes easily and is nothing but a mere detail.

Suggestions for Closing a Sale

The following suggestions will be helpful, even to the seasoned salesman, in developing mastery in closing:

1. Do not permit your prospect to lead you away from your sales plan by engaging in argument over nonessentials or extraneous subjects. If your prospect insists upon breaking in while you are talking and tries to direct the conversation so as to build up a defensive alibi for not buying, let him go along until he exhausts himself; then tactfully switch him back to your own trend of thought the moment he hesitates. Go right along and develop your own thoughts to the climax. This is absolutely essential. Either the salesman or the prospect dominates. It makes a great difference to the salesman which one does the dominating.
2. Anticipate negative questions and objections that you feel exist in your prospect's mind, and beat him to it. Ask and answer these questions yourself. Never bring up negative questions unless you are sure that your prospect has them in his mind. In selling, it pays to let sleeping dogs lie.
3. Always assume that your prospect is going to buy, no matter what he does or says to indicate the contrary, and let him know by every word and every movement that you expect him to buy. If you weaken on this point, you are beaten at the outset because your buyer may be

shrewd enough to observe that you are not sure of yourself. If he does, he will use this as an alibi with which to give you a negative answer when you try to close. The Master Salesman *never* waivers for a moment and never shows the white feather, regardless of how clever the prospect may be at setting traps for the purpose of causing the salesman to weaken. Some of them are quite as clever at leading the salesman off the scent as the Master Salesman is at sticking to the trail of his argument. Be on the lookout for this sort of tactic, and be prepared to negotiate successfully through opposition of this nature.

4. Assume the attitude that your buyer is right; that he knows his business. Any suggestion that you may make by direct statement or by innuendo that you are smarter than he will be sure to antagonize him, although he may not show his antagonism openly. The majority of mediocre salesmen make the mistake of trying to impress their prospect with their superior knowledge. This is usually poor salesmanship. It has cost more than one salesman the opportunity of making a sale.
5. When naming the amount of the purchase, set the figure high. It is better to come down in the amount, if you find that necessary, than it is to set the amount too low and then find yourself with no margin on which to trade when closing time comes. It is far better to start high and compromise by coming down than it is to start low and then try to build up. Even if the figure you name is out of the prospect's financial range, your assumption of his ability to buy at the larger amount will not offend him. If, however, you make the mistake of underestimating his financial ability, you may offend. It has happened many times.
6. Use the question method to induce your prospect to commit himself on vital points out of which you intend to build your sales presentation. Then, refer to those points as his own ideas! This is among the most effective of sales tactics, since a man will naturally uphold any statement that he has made (or thinks he has made).
7. If your prospective buyer says he wishes to consult his banker or his lawyer or his wife or some acquaintance whose opinion he values, congratulate him on his good judgment and his exercise of caution, then begin at once to plant in his mind, through tactful suggestion, that while bankers may know the money-lending business, lawyers may understand the technicalities of the law, wives and friends may be well informed and loyal, the fact still remains that no one of them is apt to know as much about the wares you are offering as you yourself know. You have all the facts, while others have not and are not apt to take sufficient time or have sufficient interest to procure

them. Moreover, plant the thought in the prospect's mind that, after all, he knows his own mind and his own business better than any other person.

8. Avoid permitting your prospect to think the matter over unless he has a very logical reason for the delay. When he springs that sort of alibi, pin him down and help him do the necessary thinking right then and there. Remember, an ounce of persistence at this point is worth a ton of cure afterward. The truth is most sales that are lost could have been saved had the salesman been persistent for a few minutes longer.

When Is the Psychological Moment in Closing?

Much has been said about closing sales at the psychological moment, but experience has proved that the majority of salesmen do not know what the psychological moment is. The psychological moment is the time when the salesman feels that the prospect is ready to close. There is such a moment in every sale whether it be consummated or fails.

One of the major differences between a Master Salesman and a mediocre salesman is the Master Salesman's ability to sense what is in the prospect's mind, aside from what the buyer has expressed in actual words. The mediocre salesman is lacking in this keenness of perception through the sixth sense.

When you sense the psychological moment for closing, name the amount involved in the purchase and proceed to close the transaction right then. A delay of a few minutes, and often even a few seconds, may give the prospect a chance to change his mind. If you find, when you try to close your sale, that you have misjudged the psychological moment, go back over your sales presentation again, bringing in new closing arguments that you have saved for just such an emergency. You will need quite a stock of emergency arguments if you are to be placed in the category of Master Salesmen.

No Master Salesman ever uses all of his trump cards unless he is forced to do so, and even then, he does not use them all at one time. He holds some back in case he has to make a secondary sales presentation to get the order.

The psychological moment for closing is something that the salesman usually has to sense, although there are times when that moment is obvious, either from the statements of the prospect or from his facial expression. The salesman whose mind is negative or the salesman who is lacking in self-confidence often misses the feel of the psychological moment for closing, mistaking his own state of mind for that of his prospect.

On the other hand, this principle works in another way that is very advantageous to the salesman—the prospective buyer often mistakes the salesman's positive mind, self-confidence, and assurance of a willingness to buy for his own, and acts accordingly if the salesman insists upon closing the sale. If a salesman can transmit a negative thought to his prospective buyer (which he most assuredly can and does if he is not a Master Salesman), he can also transmit a positive thought, wherein may be found the real reason that the salesman should always assume an attitude both in manner and thought of belief that a sale will be consummated.

Eagerness to close a sale hurriedly, if observed by the prospective buyer, is generally fatal for the reason that eagerness to close is always accompanied by lack of confidence on the part of the salesman, who transmits the thought to the mind of his prospect, if, in fact, he has not already disclosed his state of mind by his words and facial expression.

If the prospect gets the impression (no matter how he gets it) that the salesman is eager to make a sale because he (the salesman) needs the profit that is to be made on the sale, the chance of making the sale is usually spoiled. A salesman who carries an air of prosperity and nonchalance, which reflects itself in his personal appearance and in the tone of his voice, is usually a successful closer! The reason is obvious.

A Master Salesman seldom asks the prospect if he is ready to close. He goes right ahead and, at the psychological moment, makes out the order, conducting himself in every way as if the question of the sale were settled. Asking the prospect if he is ready to close is the equivalent of expressing doubt that he is. But making out the order and handing it to the prospective buyer leaves no doubt as to the salesman's state of mind on this subject. The buyer usually acts favorably upon such a positive suggestion, provided, of course, that the sales presentation has been properly made and the desire to buy has been planted in the prospect's mind.

Remember always that the place for a salesman to close a sale is first of all in his own mind. The whole world stands aside and makes room for the man who knows exactly what he wants and has made up his mind to have just that. Let a man hesitate and by that hesitation express lack of confidence, and the crowd will walk all over his toes. The salesman who reflects the slightest sign of hesitancy or doubt when the closing time comes, may as well not ask for the order; he is almost sure to meet with a refusal.

This is the way men's minds work!

It is important that one be able to realize where a sale potentially exists and follow to successful conclusion situations that might not have been obviously declaring, "Here is a sale!"

Ray Cunliffe, the Baltimore distributor of the Cadillac automobile, told me of a typical case of a salesman who unwittingly tried to register a "no sale" that almost cost him the commissions on three expensive automobiles. The incident took place in the New York sales room of the old Locomobile Company.

Late one afternoon just before closing time (the five o'clock variety), a rather sportily dressed man walked into the sales room and told the floor man that he was interested in a Locomobile. Three new cars were standing on the floor. The man balanced himself on his cane and looked at all three cars for a few minutes, then asked the price. In a very indifferent attitude, the floor man told him, but made no effort to give his prospective buyer the "works." The price of the cars, as I recall it, was $12,000 each.

The sportily dressed gentleman stood and looked at the cars a minute or two. Then he said (pointing to each car as he spoke), "Well, I do not know whether I will take this one, or this one, or this one, or whether I will take all three of them."

That settled the matter. The man was a Broadway crank. Moreover, the salesman had a dinner appointment and was in a hurry to get away. Luckily, before his "no sale" mental attitude had had time to register in the prospect's mind, the man said, "I see you are anxious to get away, so I guess I will take this car," pointing to the one that stood in the middle of the floor.

"All right," the salesman replied, "I will get you to fill out an order.

"Oh, never mind about an order blank," the prospective buyer answered, "I will just give you my check for the car and you can send it out to my home tomorrow." Meanwhile, he took out his checkbook, wrote a check for $12,000, and handed it to the floor man.

As soon as the floor man saw the name on the check, his face turned three different shades of red. The signature was that of Charles Payne Whitney, who, as the floor man well knew, could have been *sold* all three cars just as easily as the one he purchased. Observe that I use the word "purchased"; no *sale* was made in that case.

Some time ago, I sent out word to several real estate men that I was in the market for property in the country and described in detail the sort of place I wanted. Salesmen came by the score. I never knew before how many men were trying to make a living by selling real estate. That they were all hungry for business was plainly indicated by their eagerness to "put me on the spot."

I said that scores of salesmen came. Perhaps it would be more in keeping with the facts if I said that *a* salesman came, for out of the entire lot there was but one man who understood the psychology of closing. Most of them described their property by showing me maps and the like. Some of them handed me printed literature describing it and asked me to look it over and let them know when I was ready to see the property. How did they know I was not then ready?

Not one of them had the initiative to invite me out to see their property with the exception of the one salesman who came. This man said, "We have just the place your letter described. We have been holding it for you a long time (winking to show that he was taking a slight liberty with my credulity). Jump in my car and we will run out and see your property. If it is not exactly what you want, I will buy you the best dinner in the city when we return." (He had enough imagination to observe that it would be about time for dinner upon our return.) "When you see this place," he continued, "you will look no further. I am sure it is just what you want."

By that time, I had begun to believe he knew what I wanted. He had caused me to do something I had not intended to do, namely, to inspect the property that day. His whole demeanor was so positive and assured that I found myself in his car before I had a chance to think of a good reason for not going. If he had hesitated in his approach, I could have put him off until the following day, but it was his business, doubtless, to strike while the iron was hot, so I was on my way in less time than it takes to tell the story.

On the way, this salesman described the place so accurately and so pleasingly that I almost felt myself the owner of it before I had seen it. Frankly, I would have been greatly disappointed to find anything wrong with it, because the salesman had planted the seed of desire in my mind so deeply that I was like putty in his hands.

The salesman took a contract with him and got my name on the dotted line before we left the property. It was one of the smoothest pieces of salesmanship I have ever observed. The moment this salesman sensed that I was ready to sign, he took out his contract and handed it to me with his pen. Seeing that I had nothing on which to rest the contract while signing, he rushed to his car and pulled out a brief case, saying, "Here, use this for a table, General!" Now, I am not a general, but the title was slipped to me so unobtrusively that I did not resent it.

And I signed!

This salesman handed me no literature to read over. He handed me the property instead. Master Salesmen always do something like that. It is one of their peculiarities.

Some of the other salesmen are still sending me printed literature *through the mail.* Now, if a country place was ever sold by printed literature alone, I should like to hear about it. The salesman who turned the trick must have been a miracle worker.

A few days ago, one of these salesmen came in to see me. He wanted to know if I had "made up my mind about that country place I was looking for some time ago."

"Bless your life, yes," I replied, "perhaps I should say, however, that I did not make up my mind to buy it. A very able salesman made it up for me the same day that you first came to see me and made the sale that very day."

"That's too bad!" the salesman exclaimed.

"No," I replied, "it is only one bad. It may be bad for you, but it was fine for me because I got just the place I was looking for."

With a look on his face that indicated that he vaguely suspected that I might be kidding him, this dilatory salesman turned and walked away without saying good-bye. He was obviously disgusted at my sense of humor or my credulity in buying a place the first time I saw it. I do not know which.

You cannot tell how far a frog can jump by counting the warts upon its back. No more can you tell, by merely looking at a prospect, whether you can sell him your wares. Give yourself the benefit of the doubt and give every prospect the works before registering a no sale in your own mind. It is the safest plan!

I once trained a sales army of 3,000 men and women for a Chicago firm. Efficiency had to be the watchword. We inaugurated a system from which I learned much about the possibilities of persistence! Before any salesman was permitted to become permanently allied with the organization, it was necessary for him to sell one out of the first five prospective buyers called upon. The instructions were to stick to these five prospects until a sale had been made. On many occasions salesmen called on those five prospects as many as a dozen times before the sale was consummated.

I recall that one salesman called on one of his prospects 18 times before he made a sale. The victim succumbed on the eighteenth visit and made a purchase out of self-defense. In the group of 3,000 salespeople, only 128 failed to qualify for permanent positions because they could not make a sale to the first five prospects called upon. We taught these salespeople that "no" seldom need be taken seriously. Moreover, we proved it!

It was also apparent that confidence must be manifested by the salesman as well as by the prospect before a sale can be effected. To make sure that our salespeople acquired confidence, we resorted to a very unique plan at the outset, that of setting up dummy offices, maintained by the company and managed by company employees. When we felt sure that a green salesman lacked only the quality of confidence in himself, we included in the list of the first five prospects the name of one of these dummy managers, who was instructed to give the salesman a hard battle, but to let him win by making a sale. These sales went through and commissions were paid on them. The effect was astounding, especially in the cases of salespeople who had never tried to sell before.

We usually had the salesman call on the dummy buyer last, after the four legitimate prospects had been called on. We found, too, by experimenting, that after making the sale to the dummy, the effect was so encouraging that we could then send him back over the list of the four who had not been sold, with the result that in some instances all four of them were sold, despite the fact that he had previously failed.

We discovered, from this experimentation, that the salesman's state of mind has more to do with determining whether a sale is made than the state of mind of the prospective buyer. It is an important discovery, as true today as when it was made.

Were I asked to give a summation to these varied and often detailed examinations of the subject of selling, I believe I could do it in one word.

There is a word that should stand out upon the horizon of every salesman's vision, like Mars blazing at eventide, always there to be seen, challenging, beckoning, urging, inspiring, commanding.

The word denotes that thing which dominates all great and able salespeople everywhere and it is a word that Edward Bok declared was the greatest in the English language. It is . . .

Service

We pass now to Part 2 of this book, devoted entirely to the application of the principles of marketing personal services to best advantage.

> If you are successful, remember that somewhere, sometime, someone gave you a lift or an idea that started you in the right direction. Remember, also, that you are indebted to life until you help some less fortunate person, just as you were helped.

II

The Use of Salesmanship in Marketing Personal Services

EVERY person who succeeds in any calling must understand and apply the principles of successful negotiation with others known as "salesmanship."

Part 2 of this book is devoted entirely to analysis of the principles of selling as applied in marketing personal services.

> Quibbling over salary to start with has lost many a man the big opportunity of a lifetime. If the position you seek is one that you know you can throw your whole heart into, take it, even if you have to work for nothing until you deliver a good sample of your "goods." Thereafter, you will receive pay in proportion to the quality and quantity of the work you perform.

12

Choosing Your Job

YOU have the privilege of choosing any position you desire, as an objective toward which to work! The making of this choice is the first step you must take in marketing your services effectively. Moreover, it is a responsibility that you alone must assume, as no other person can satisfactorily make the choice for you.

Before deciding what position or calling you desire, decide whether you merely want *a* position or *the* position for which you are best fitted by desire, education, temperament, and native ability.

The next decision to be made is that of determining whether you prefer a position that offers great opportunity in the future with modest pay at the start, or one that yields the maximum amount of pay but offers no promise for the future. In other words, you must decide whether you wish to start at the top or at the bottom of the ladder.

Upon this decision depends to a large extent the ultimate amount of your earning capacity, since it is obvious that one who starts at the top can move in only one direction.

Factors that Should Influence Your Choice of Occupation

Observe with profit the frequency with which the word "decision" appears throughout this book. The marketing of personal service, in an effective manner, calls for many decisions. The following are factors that enter into the marketing of personal services in connection with which you must reach decisions.

1. Decide which calling or occupation you like best. Careful analysis of many thousands of men and women has shown that one experiences the greatest and most enduring success when engaged in the work that one likes best. When one enters into that sort of work, it is with enthusiasm and zeal akin to that employed when playing a game. No person should voluntarily choose an occupation into which he does not feel he can throw his whole heart and soul.
2. Decide what type of employer you prefer. It is just as important for you to choose your employer with care as it is for the employer to choose his employees with care. In your choice of an employer, pick one in whom you have confidence and from whose example of conduct you may benefit. Choose one from whom you may gather useful knowledge connected with the occupation of your choice. Your employer should become, as he will in fact, your teacher. Be sure that the teacher is capable.
3. Decide the amount of money you intend to make your position yield year by year for the first five years. Then, proceed to render service that will justify the amounts upon which you have decided. Remember that the amount of your annual earnings is the equivalent of 6 percent of the capital value of your brains. For example, if your income is $6,000 a year, you have in your brain capital the equivalent of $100,000. Regard this capital as something that must be kept at work efficiently if you are to collect the income.
4. Decide—and this decision is most important—exactly the quality and the quantity of service you intend to deliver in return for the income you expect to demand and deliver at least that—no less! The majority of people devote more time to thinking about the money they want or need than they do to creating ways and means of earning that amount through an equivalent of service.
5. Decide to what extent you are handicapped by the major causes of failure and select an occupation that will be conducive to the elimination of that handicap. (These major causes are explained in the author's book, *Think and Grow Rich.*)

These five decisions must be made before you are ready to create a plan for marketing your services. They constitute five of the most important decisions you will ever be called upon to make. Reach them promptly, but with due thought and deliberation, because your whole future depends upon the sort of decisions you make.

If you are just starting out in search of your first position, it will be permissible for you to accept temporary employment such as you may need for living expenses until you have had time to gather the information required to make these five decisions intelligently. Do not make the mistake of permitting your temporary employment to become your lifework because of indifference or habit. Ninety-eight percent of the people of the world may be considered failures from the viewpoint of earnings and occupation. Also, 98 percent of the people holding positions have drifted into them and remained there because they lacked the power of decision to choose more suitable positions.

One of the most pathetic sights I have ever witnessed is that of a man who has committed himself to the wearisome treadmill of toil for his entire lifetime, where he must spend six days out of every seven at labor that he does not like. Such a man is in a prison to which he has sentenced himself for a term approximating six-sevenths of his life. Moreover, he is no less a prisoner than the man who is behind bars, the only difference being that he has a slightly wider scope of freedom one day out of every seven.

Performing labor that one does not like is one of the great tragedies of civilization. Stating the case conversely, voluntary choice of an occupation that one does like and into which one may throw himself wholeheartedly requires greater willpower and more force of character than the average person is disposed to exercise. Observe with significance that I did not say more force of character than the average person possesses. Possession of personal power and use of it are two different things.

The reason one should choose an occupation that one likes is obvious. Service rendered in connection with an occupation that one enjoys is never burdensome toil, because it is a form of labor that one enjoys. You get tired, not from overwork but from lack of interest in what you are doing.

Here is an appropriate place at which to reply to the person who asks, "How can I avoid engaging in labor that I do not like?" The answer is, you can avoid it by firmly *deciding* you will not become a prisoner for life in a prison of your own making. Or, if you find yourself temporarily in such a prison because of the necessity of living, you can release yourself by deciding that you are going to select another occupation and then follow that decision with action in harmony with the instructions described in this book.

The book was written with the primary idea of serving as a key by which men and women may release themselves from prisons of labor that they do not like. It will serve as such a key for all who follow it.

We are all creatures of habit!

We are where we are and what we are because of the habits of which we have become the victims, voluntarily or involuntarily. We are victims of the habits of thought and the habits of action. We can change our station in life—and this is the only way we can change it—by changing our habits.

You might as well know here and now that you cannot hope to market your personal services more advantageously without changing your present habits. If your habits were constructive, there would be neither the desire nor the necessity for you to concern yourself about marketing your personal services differently.

Something for Nothing

Life has no bargain counters. Everything has a price that must be paid in one form or another. No man is smart enough to cheat life. It has been tried by the smartest of men without success.

The price of success in marketing personal services is measured in a great variety of terms and equivalents, all of which have been plainly described in this book. Familiarize yourself with these price tags and decide if you are willing to pay the price.

If you are reading this book in the hope that it may explain some plan of hocus-pocus by which you may sell your services for more than they are worth, lay the book down right now. On the other hand, if you want money in greater quantities than you are now receiving and are prepared to give in return an equivalent of service, this book will guide you safely over the pitfalls and mistakes that even the most sincere sometimes make.

This is an age when the predominating tendency of man is to get without giving! That tendency toward avarice and greed is in the very air and you will become the victim of it by the example of others around you if you do not watch yourself.

I am trying to emphasize this for the benefit of young people who have not yet become the victims of this mad desire for something for nothing. I qualify my statement to apply to young men and women because I know that but few, if any, of the older ones whose habits have become fixed, will pay any attention to this warning.

Nature balances her books and asks for an accounting every so often. When the accounting time comes, as it always does, those who have been lucky enough to acquire temporary possession of something for which they have not paid full value are forced to disgorge.

This rule applies to the delivery of personal services just as to all other transactions. One may get by for a time by rendering services that are inadequate in quality and quantity, but nature's auditor awaits such a person just around the corner.

This chapter may appear to be a dry preachment on the morals of salesmanship of personal services because truth is often less romantic than fiction! To all who so consider this chapter, I would offer the suggestion that it conforms perfectly to the rules of conduct that have been followed, consciously or unconsciously, by every man who has accumulated and kept a great fortune.

The lives of all successful people are controlled and guided by rules of conduct that are exacting and often devoid of romance. Before leaving this chapter, make one more decision. Would you prefer instructions that are sound and helpful but free from fiction, or those that are optimistic, fictional, romantic, and unsound?

This book was not written with the purpose of describing how easy it is to receive big money by rendering inadequate service, but for the purpose of describing definite ways of earning money by rendering its equivalent in *satisfactory* service.

I am, by nature, an optimist! I would not rob labor of its romance if I could do so. To me, there is nothing more romantic in life than a man and a job that are suited to one another. Happiness is the ultimate height toward which every human being is striving. If life offers anything that will bring more happiness than the privilege of rendering useful service one enjoys, I do not know what it is.

Millions of people are out of employment and other millions realize from their labor barely enough for existence. Out of this experience have come many helpful lessons, among them the sure knowledge that there is one thing worse than being forced to labor. *It is being forced not to labor!*

No man can be happy without some form of occupation. Many have tried to find happiness in idleness. They have failed. Enduring happiness comes through serving. All other forms of happiness are transitory and delusive.

Happiness Comes from Aspiring, Not from Acquiring

No man can be happy in whose heart there is not the hope of achievement yet unattained. Men who have millions of dollars in wealth find no happiness in wealth. If they are happy, the happiness comes from aiming, hoping, creating, and building plans for future achievement. I know of no exception to this rule, despite the fact that I have a personal acquaintance with scores of men of great wealth.

I am trying, as you may have observed, not merely to show you how to market your personal services effectively, but how to find happiness through your efforts as well.

13

Selecting a Definite Major Aim as Your Lifework

SINGLENESS of purpose is a quality without which no one may attain outstanding success. This is an age of specialization. It is also an age of keen competition that does not favor the person who cannot excel in some specific occupation.

The Five Fundamental Steps to Success

There are five fundamental steps that must be taken by all who succeed. They are:

1. Choice of a definite goal to be attained.
2. Development of sufficient power to attain one's goal.
3. Perfection of a practical plan for attaining one's goal.
4. Accumulation of specialized knowledge necessary for the attainment of one's goal.
5. Persistence in carrying out the plan.

Every successful person follows, in one form or another, this five-step program. Some follow it unconsciously or by accident, while others follow it with a definite purpose and by design.

Some of the Advantages of a Definite Aim

Working with definiteness of purpose toward a single goal has many advantages, among them the following:

First: Singleness of purpose forces one to specialize and specialization tends toward perfection.

Second: A definite goal permits one to develop the capacity to reach decisions quickly and firmly.

Third: Definiteness of purpose enables one to master the habit of procrastination.

Fourth: Definiteness of purpose saves the time and energy one would otherwise waste while wavering between two or more possible courses of action.

Fifth: A definite purpose serves as a road map that charts the direct route to the end of one's journey.

Sixth: Definiteness of purpose fixes one's habits so that they are taken over by the subconscious mind and used as a motivating force (involuntarily) in driving toward one's goal.

Seventh: Definiteness of purpose develops self-confidence and attracts the confidence of other people.

The disadvantages that follow and blast the lives of those who have no clearly defined purpose are as "thick and numberless as the gay motes which people the sunbeams."[1] The purposeless lives and wrecked fortunes of a tragic host along the colorless shores of every sea whereon human endeavor has been launched, speak of millions without objective who have held to no fixed goal. Drifting people are like rudderless ships and "all the voyages of their lives are bound in shallows and miseries."[2]

Every cluttered tenement bears tragic evidence of this truth. Weak, pale, and undernourished children who have never stood straight-limbed and fair in God's sunshine convince us of this truth. Women, pinched of face,

---

[1] John Milton

[2] William Shakespeare

poorly clad and with worried eyes, who have not time to look up from their dismal drudgery, mutely tell us of husbands without purpose. Restless and scowling men are they who have not *one* great goal. Truth, naked and undeniable, points an accusing finger at the shambles of human figures who know not where they go nor why.

The North Star was not more fixed in the heavens than Caesar in his purpose. History is rich in the recital of men who have hitched their wagon to a star—a single star—and ridden it into the heights of great achievement.

Great men in ages gone have given us words to be used as symbols to guide us on our way, but no words should be graven so high in the sky, there to arrest the attention of young men and young women, challenge their consideration and bring them to a state of thoughtful reflection as these two words: *quo animo* (with what mind or intention).

Those who know where they are going usually get there. They do not dissipate their strength in aimless expenditure of time and energy, following first one course and then another, but concentrate their efforts upon a definite objective, exerting all powers to attain that end.

Brawn brings a daily wage. The price of it is fixed by the law of supply and demand. General services, rendered by one who has not specialized, brings but little more than brawn. Brains, when marketed through a definite aim, have no fixed price. The sky is the limit in the marketing of specialized talent. These are statements of obvious fact, yet 98 out of every 100 people fail all through life because they do not follow the principle of working with definiteness of purpose.

> Every failure will teach you a lesson that you need to learn if you will keep your eyes and ears open and be willing to be taught. Every adversity is usually a blessing in disguise. Without reverses and temporary defeat, you would never know the sort of metal of which you are made.

14

The Habit of Doing More than Paid for

THE habit of rendering more service and better service than one is paid to render is an absolute essential to the advantageous marketing of personal services.

In the previous chapter your attention was called to the importance of the word decision! In this chapter your attention is directed to the word *habit*, especially as it applies to the amount and quality of service rendered.

Among the many sound reasons for rendering more service and better service than expected are the following:

1. This habit turns the spotlight of favorable attention upon those who develop it.
2. This habit enables one to profit by the law of contrast, since the majority of people have formed and apply the opposing habit by rendering as little service as they can.
3. This habit gives one the benefit of the law of increasing returns and insures one against the disadvantages of the law of decreasing returns, thus eventually enabling one to receive more pay than one would receive without this habit.
4. This habit insures one preferred employment at preferred wages and permanency of employment as long as there is employment to be had. The person who practices this habit is the last to be removed

from the payroll when business is poor and the first to be taken back after a layoff.

5. This habit develops greater skill, efficiency, and also greater earning ability and tends to give one preference over others.
6. This habit makes one practically indispensable to one's employer because it is a habit not found in the majority of people, and because it induces employers to relegate greater responsibilities to those who practice it. The capacity to assume responsibility is the quality that brings the highest monetary returns.
7. This habit leads to promotion because it indicates that those who practice it have ability for supervision and leadership not found in those who follow the opposite habit.
8. This habit enables one to set one's own salary. If it cannot be obtained from one employer, it may be obtained from his competitor.

These are but a few of the major advantages of rendering more service and better service than one is paid to render.

If you render no more service than you are paid to render, then it is obvious you are not entitled to any more pay. This is a fact against which there is no argument!

Every business has either a potential or a real asset known as goodwill. While this is an asset not generally listed in the inventory as such, it is, nevertheless, an asset without which no business can grow and but few, if any, businesses can exist for any great length of time. An individual who renders more service and better service than paid for may also have a goodwill asset that will insure him opportunities and advantages in connection with the sale of personal services that are not available to the person who does not practice this habit. This goodwill asset is generally known as one's *reputation* for efficiency. It is an asset without which no individual can market his personal services to best advantage.

The strongest and most attractive selling feature any individual may have, in marketing his personal services, is the habit of rendering service that is greater in quantity and superior in quality.

The habit of rendering more service and better service than one agrees to render for a stipulated sum is one of the most important principles through which businesses grow to huge proportions and businessmen accumulate great fortunes. The principle works on behalf of an employer just as it does on behalf of an employee, a fact that a few employers have discovered.

Men become harmonious, loyal, and cooperative in their efforts because of motive. Men who achieve outstanding success, whether as individuals or as the heads of business enterprises, understand how to attract the qualities of harmony, loyalty, and cooperation through appropriate motive.

Every individual who works for a salary naturally wants more money and a better position. Not every such individual, however, understands that better positions and greater pay come as the result of motive and that the greatest of all motives with which these desirable benefits may be attracted is that of rendering more service and better service than one is paid to render.

Your Greatest Opportunity May Be Right Where You Are

It is man's inherent nature to seek what he believes to be greener pastures in the distance. When a man begins to look for a better position and more pay, he usually seeks opportunity in the distance with some other employer. Sometimes this may be necessary, but changes in employment, while they may bring advantages, always bring some disadvantages, the most outstanding of which is the fact that one is never as efficient in a new position, a new environment, and among new associates, as he is where he is familiar with the details of his work and has the confidence of his associates. Moreover, the changing of positions deprives an individual of much of the goodwill value built around himself through long association with an employer.

Before deciding to change employers, be sure that you have exhausted the possibilities of your present position. Take inventory of your job and ascertain in what ways you can make yourself more valuable to your employer. Follow this practice until you have made yourself as nearly indispensable to him as possible, remembering meanwhile that indispensability is the only thing behind which you can successfully hedge when you ask your employer for a better position or more pay.

If your employer is a successful businessman, he is probably also intelligent. He has the ability to approximate your value to his business. Before you make demands for more pay, or seek opportunity elsewhere, be sure that you are worth more by having first practiced the habit of rendering more service and better service than your employer has expected or demanded of you. If you have followed this habit long enough for your employer to have observed that it is a habit, you are in a position to ask him to discuss readjustment of salary. You are not likely to suffer if your employer is successful and intelligent.

People sometimes outgrow both their positions and their employers. More often, however, the reverse proves true.

Before deciding to change employers, take inventory of your employer and his business. Ascertain whether or not they offer you a future commensurate with your ability. If the analysis shows that an adequate opportunity exists where you are, develop that opportunity. You already have your foot inside the door. You have your employer's confidence or you would not be where you are. Capitalize this opportunity by making yourself indispensable, and very soon the law of increasing returns will begin to reward you.

Every competent farmer understands and makes use of the law of increasing returns. He puts this law into operation in the following manner:

First: He selects soil that is appropriate for the crop that he expects it to yield.

Second: He then prepares this soil by plowing and harrowing and perhaps by fertilization, so it will be favorable to the seed he plants.

Third: He plants seed that have been carefully selected for soundness, knowing that poor seed cannot yield a bountiful crop.

Fourth: He then gives nature a chance to compensate him for his labor through an appropriate period of time. He does not sow the seed one day and expect to reap a harvest the next.

Having taken these four steps, all of which have been in advance of his reward, the farmer knows that he will profit by the law of increasing returns when harvest time arrives and that he will get back from his labor not merely the amount of seed he planted in the soil, but a greatly increased quantity.

Marketing personal services effectively involves this same principle. Prepare carefully the soil in which you intend to plant the seed of service by selecting an employer who is intelligent and successful. Then, cultivate that soil and prepare it through conduct that is *harmonious* and *cooperative*. Plant in the soil the finest seed of service and be sure to plant an abundance of that seed, as not all seed will germinate and grow. Do not expect to harvest a crop of pay before you have sown the seed of service. After the seed has been sown, do not become impatient if you do not reap your reward immediately. Give the seed time to germinate. Meanwhile, you are making yourself indispensable to your employer and insuring permanency of employment.

If, after you have done your part, your employer does not show his appreciation, do not stop sowing the seed of service, which is right in both quality and quantity. Keep right on sowing because it will provide you with the evidence of your capacity to render useful and desirable service if you find it necessary to seek employment elsewhere.

The habit of frequent changing of positions places an individual under the disadvantage of the law of *diminishing returns* because no employer wants to permit a rolling stone to become a factor in his business. This is worthy of application before you decide to change employers.

You are a merchant. You have the equivalent of a commodity to market. That equivalent is your personal services. Use the same principles of sound judgment in marketing your services that a successful merchant uses in marketing his merchandise. You know, of course, what happens to the merchant who short-weighs his customers or cheats them at trade. He pays by loss of business. You know, on the other hand, what happens to the merchant who builds confidence by rendering service and delivering merchandise that measure up to or exceed the customer's expectations.

John Wanamaker, Marshall Field, and Sears-Roebuck built businesses that have become landmarks in American merchandising. Their motto is: "The customer is always right," and they go to great extremes to make this motto mean what it says, even permitting some of their customers to take advantage of them in order to put teeth into that policy.

No person may be sure of success, no matter what may be his calling, without applying this principle of giving before trying to get! Failure to apply this principle will render practically useless every other principle for the successful marketing of personal services.

Emphasis of this principle seems doubly necessary because of the prevailing tendency that obtains all over the world at this time to seek a harvest in wealth without first sowing the seed of service. The Depression that began in 1929 was a most impressive example of the existence of the law of diminishing returns. People went money mad and tried to get without giving through the law of chance. That law is tricky. It permits you to win just often enough to lure you on to sure destruction.

Every person whose major source of capital is his capacity to render personal services should remember the lesson taught by the Depression and profit by it. From that experience came a worldwide demonstration that "He profits most who serves best."

During prohibition, I visited a small town just across the border of Southern California in Mexico. I witnessed the spectacle of 40,000 men and women who had come across the line to patronize saloons and gambling halls. Except for the Depression, I have never witnessed so huge a demonstration of man's lack of understanding of the futility of gambling. The experience aroused my curiosity and caused me to investigate for the purpose of understanding and ascertaining how well Lady Luck favored those 40,000 go-getters who were looking for something for nothing.

The government authorities in charge informed me that, by conservative estimate, fewer than 300 of the 40,000 people who visit the town every Sunday go back over the borderline with more money than they brought with them. The officials also estimated that the net value to the saloon keepers and gaming proprietors of a Sunday's business averaged about $10 per person or $400,000! They estimated that the 300 who were lucky enough to go away with more than they brought, took away not to exceed $20 each, or a total of $6,000. Compare these two sums and you have about the percentage of opportunity one has of winning when one tries to get without giving!

The odds against the person who tries to get without giving an equivalent apply to the person who attempts to collect pay before delivering adequate service, just as they do to people who gamble. Those who try to harvest before sowing generally believe themselves wise enough to beat the game. It cannot be done. The business depression proved conclusively that the strongest men living, just like the small fry, fall and are crushed by this unsound belief.

Every person whose income is derived from the sale of personal services has occasional opportunity to cheat by delivering a shortage in quantity or deficiency in quality, but the cheater only cheats himself because this form of default is a mild method of stealing, and those who practice it write the results indelibly into their own characters to be heard from later on.

Most men can cheat others occasionally without detection. But no man can cheat others without observation by his own *conscience*, and that conscience is an official recorder of one's acts and thoughts. It writes the record of every thought and deed into the fabric of one's character.

A clear conscience is an asset comparable to no other!

You will discover this to be true when you come to the time when you wish to negotiate for the readjustment of your pay.

Master Salesmanship, regardless of the wares one may be selling, is based upon absolute faith in the thing one is offering for sale. Remember this when you bargain for the sale of your services.

E. M. Statler became the most successful hotel man in the world by rendering more service and better service than his guests were asked to pay for.

15

A Pleasing Personality

A major portion of your responsibility, regardless of your calling, is that of being able to negotiate your way through life with a minimum of friction between yourself and other people. To negotiate with others without friction is a rare ability. It is a necessity in marketing personal services effectively.

A pleasing personality is an asset without which it is difficult to market personal services or to keep them marketed. Andrew Carnegie rated this quality at the head of the list of qualifications for success and went so far as to say that personality could often be substituted for brains. Perhaps Mr. Carnegie did not mean for that statement to be taken literally, but used it merely to emphasize the importance of a pleasing personality in marketing personal services.

Anyway, it is well worth thinking about.

The person who markets his or her services effectively must be an able salesman. A pleasing personality is an essential quality in salesmanship. Let us approach the study of this subject on a common ground of understanding by defining pleasing personality as follows:

A pleasing personality is one that has flexibility and adaptability sufficient to permit an individual to harmonize with any environment, and the necessary magnetism to dominate through attraction.

A pleasing personality consists of a blending of many qualities, the more important of which are:

1. Good showmanship. An efficient showman is one who understands and applies the art of catering to the masses. He appeals to people through their imagination and keeps them interested through curiosity. A good showman is quick to recognize and to capitalize on other people's prejudices, biases, likes, and dislikes at the psychological moment.
2. Harmony within self. No one may enjoy a personality without first developing harmony and control within his own mind.
3. Definiteness of purpose. The procrastinator who drifts through life without plan or purpose can never be pleasing to others. To have a pleasing personality, one must at least be definite in developing relationships of harmony with others and in adopting a major goal at which to aim as a life work.
4. Appropriateness of clothing. The person with a pleasing personality dresses in clothing that is appropriate not only to himself but also to his calling. First impressions are lasting. Inappropriate wearing apparel creates a prejudice that is difficult to overcome. Clothes may not make the man, but they give him an advantageous start, if selected with taste.
5. Posture and carriage of the body. One does not have to be a character analyst to be able to judge other people by the way they walk and the general posture of their bodies. Alertness in posture and carriage of the body indicates alertness of the brain and keenness of perception.
6. Voice. The tone, volume, pitch, and general emotional coloring of one's voice constitute important factors of a pleasing personality. A high-pitched voice is never pleasing; it is often offensive.
7. Sincerity of purpose. This quality needs but little, if any, explanation. Without it, one may not have the confidence of others.
8. Choice of language. The man with a pleasing personality expresses himself in language appropriate to his calling and avoids the use of slang and profanity.
9. Poise. Poise is based upon self-confidence and self-control. Lack of it irritates and annoys other people.
10. A keen sense of humor. Perhaps no other quality is more essential than this. Without it, one's life is a series of ups and downs—mostly downs!
11. Unselfishness. Selfishness and a pleasing personality are never found together. No one is attracted to a selfish person.
12. Facial expression. Facial expression is an accurate medium for the interpretation of one's moods and thoughts. It is the character

analyst's barometer, by which he may measure accurately how one's mind functions.

13. Positive thought. Negative thoughts and a pleasing personality do not make good bedfellows because the vibrations of thought are picked up by others. Be sure, therefore, to release only such thoughts as will be pleasing to other people.
14. Enthusiasm. People who lack enthusiasm cannot arouse others. Enthusiasm is an essential factor in all forms of salesmanship, the sale of personal services included.
15. A sound body. Poor health does not attract people. Moreover, one cannot be enthusiastic without health and vigor. A bottle of citrate of magnesia or an internal bath would have saved many persons the loss of their positions.
16. Imagination. Alertness of the imagination is one of the most essential factors of a pleasing personality. Without it, people are generally referred to as dumb.
17. Tact. Lack of this quality has cost many men their positions, to say nothing of their greatest opportunities. Lack of tact is usually expressed through loose conversation and boldness of expression.
18. Versatility. A general acquaintance with the important subjects of current interest and the deeper problems of life and living is a quality conducive to a pleasing personality.
19. The art of being a good listener. Train yourself to listen attentively when other people are speaking and do not show ill breeding by breaking in and taking the conversation away from others. Give your ears a chance! Your tongue will take care of itself.
20. The art of forceful speech. No single factor of a pleasing personality is more important than this. Forceful speech is the salesman's greatest asset. Without it, he is sunk before he begins to swim. It is an art that may be acquired by practice. The instructions for making an interesting speech are: Have something to say that is worth listening to and say it with all the enthusiasm at your command.
21. Personal magnetism. This term has reference to *controlled* sex energy. It is the only factor of a pleasing personality that may not be acquired. One is either born with it or does not have it. Most people have it, but do not control it! It is the major asset of every great salesman and every great leader in all walks of life. Its importance as a factor of a pleasing personality entitles it to appear at the head instead of the foot of the list.

This may appear to be a rather formidable list of qualities that one must possess in order to have a pleasing personality, but there is encouragement in the fact that the majority of these qualities may be had through practice plus definite determination to possess them.

As a part of your preparation as a salesman of your personal services, you should check yourself carefully against this list of factors of a pleasing personality, find out in which you are deficient, and begin at once to correct those deficiencies. You will find more explicit instructions for making this analysis in the chapter on Personal Analysis. You want all that your personal services can be marketed for, but you have no reason to expect your services to yield more than they are worth. Make them *worth* more. You can begin by rebuilding your personality. It is almost certain that you will find in this long list of factors that constitute a pleasing personality, some in which you are deficient. That is the place for you to begin rebuilding yourself!

A Few Who Have Achieved Success through a Pleasing Personality

It may be helpful if you are reminded of some of the men who have risen to high places in life, not because of their superiority of education, but because they understood the art of selling themselves to advantage.

William Jennings Bryan kept himself sold to a large proportion of the American people for more than 30 years, almost solely upon his ability as an orator. Bryan was not a really great thinker. He was popular because of his ability to reach people through an appeal to their imaginations. The tone of his voice was responsible for much of his popularity.

Theodore Roosevelt kept himself well sold to the American people, in the highest position any American can hold, through almost two terms as president of the United States and just barely missed a third term. He was a great showman and an appealing public speaker, dynamic, energetic, powerful.

Will Rogers converted a pleasing personality into a huge fortune, through clowning. He was not a great actor but he acquired the ability to please people.

The late Knute Rockne developed the Notre Dame football team into the most popular team known to the American people. He was an able showman and possessed the ability to inject his personality into his players.

The Influence of Personality on Atmosphere

Every human being carries with him what is known as an "individual atmosphere." This atmosphere is but the sum total of an individual's reflection of the factors of a pleasing personality, plus any of the factors of a negative personality that the individual may possess. This atmosphere is contagious.

Every business and every place of employment has also a distinctive atmosphere that consists of the combined personalities of those who work there. A person with a dominating personality of a pleasing nature may so color the atmosphere of the place where he works that the spirit of the entire place will also be pleasing. On the other hand, one person who has a dominating personality of a negative nature may transmit that personality to everyone in a place of business so that the atmosphere of the place becomes displeasing and unpleasant.

Emerson had this truth in mind when he said, "Every business is the extended shadow of one person."

Remember that you are contributing through your personality to the atmosphere of the home in which you live and the place of business where you work. The feeling one gets when one walks into either the Marshall Field Store in Chicago, or the John Wanamaker Store in Philadelphia, is pleasing and attractive because of the positive atmosphere found in them. Every home carries an atmosphere that indicates clearly whether there is harmony or friction as the dominating factor of the home.

The positive or pleasing atmosphere value of a place of business, while it is an intangible asset, is one of the greatest assets any business can have. Such an atmosphere may be had only through a combination of positive individual personalities.

The man or woman who carries a grouch into his or her place of employment does almost as much damage to his or her fellow employees and to the business as might be done if poison were placed in the drinking water. Employers who understand this principle—and some of them do understand it—watch very carefully to see that only people with pleasing personalities work in their establishment.

The Major Factors of a Negative Personality

We come now to examine the qualities that constitute a negative personality. Analyze and check yourself carefully to make sure that you are not unconsciously carrying around with you an atmosphere that causes people to dislike you. The list is as follows:

1. Disloyalty. There is no substitute for loyalty! The person who lacks loyalty is poverty-stricken, regardless of his other qualities or worldly possessions. Such a person cannot possibly market his personal services effectively because the market for those services will play out as soon as that quality is disclosed.
2. Dishonesty. There is no substitute for honesty! It is the keystone to the arch of character. Without sound character, no person can market his services effectively.
3. Greed. A person who is cursed by greed is never liked by others. It is a quality that cannot be kept under cover. It will assert itself so clearly that all may observe it and shun the person who reflects it.
4. Envy and hatred. These qualities make a pleasing personality an impossibility. Like attracts like. The person who hates people will, in turn, be hated by people, regardless of company manners or attempts to cover this disagreeable trait.
5. Jealousy. This is a mild form of insanity. It is fatal to a pleasing personality.
6. Anger. Whether passive or active in form, this is a quality that arouses antagonism and makes one disliked by others.
7. Fear. This quality repels people. It never attracts. There are six basic fears against which every person must guard. These are negative states of mind that must be eliminated before one may develop a pleasing personality. Fear never pleases and it never attracts anything except its counterpart. (See the author's book, *Think and Grow Rich*.)
8. Revenge. A revengeful person cannot be pleasing to anyone.
9. Fault finding. The person who has the habit of finding fault with others or with conditions cannot please. Such a person might more profitably spend his time looking within for faults.
10. Peddling scandal. The old saying that "a dog that will fetch a bone will take one back" is true. People may listen to the scandal-monger because they cannot avoid it, but they will not like the person.
11. Uncontrolled enthusiasm. Too much enthusiasm is as bad as none. Enthusiasm, controlled and directed, is generally more effective than that which is expressed too freely. No one is attracted to the person who starts his tongue wagging and then goes off and leaves it.
12. Prevarication. The untruthful person is *persona non grata* in every household and in every place of business. With some people

prevarication is a habit. It destroys confidence and sets up antagonism.

13. Escaping responsibility for mistakes through alibis. The alibi artist is never pleasing to others. It is better to assume responsibility for mistakes you do not make than to form the habit of trying to place responsibility for these mistakes on others.
14. Exaggeration. It is better to understate a truth than to overstate it. Exaggeration causes loss of confidence.
15. Egotism. Uncontrolled egotism is one of the most damaging of traits. There is but one form of egotism that is acceptable. It is the habit of expressing one's ideas in deeds helpful to others, not in words. Self-confidence is one of the most desirable and necessary traits, but it must be controlled and directed to definite ends, through methods that do not antagonize others. All forms of self-praise are easily recognized as evidences of inferiority complexes, therefore one's motto should be "Deeds, not words."
16. Obstinacy. The person who is obstinate, stubborn, and self-willed is never pleasing. A certain amount of determination and the ability to stand by one's opinions is, of course, essential, but these qualities should not become a blanket policy.
17. Selfishness. No one likes a selfish person. This quality attracts opposition in every conceivable form.

These are not all of the negative qualities of personality, but they are, on the whole, the ones that do the most damage. Somewhere in the list you may find the cause of opposition that you may have experienced from others. You cannot have a pleasing personality until you put your foot upon the neck of every one of these signals of danger! Be merciless with yourself when you check yourself against this list, remembering that an enemy discovered is an enemy half conquered.

This chapter deals with subjects of a highly intimate personal nature. Remember when you step before the mirror of your own conscience, as you will if you derive real benefit from this chapter, that this book was not written as a sop to the vanity of any reader. It was written as a means of helping people to market their services effectively by first understanding and improving what they have to market.

Keep this thought clearly in mind and be your most severe critic as you read, if you wish to avail yourself of the benefits that await after you have mastered the principles described in this book. A pleasing personality is a self-acquisition asset with but few exceptions. Its acquisition calls for self-control and a willingness to change destructive habits.

This book has been written with the object of helping people to convert their personal services into wealth without violating the rights or arousing the antagonism of others. This will, of course, require effort. Through your personal conduct, you are establishing the limitations of your life. Just as surely as a criminal is in the penitentiary as the result of conduct through which he reflected a very negative personality, so is every reader of this book where he is because of his personality as reflected through his conduct.

With these two important statements this chapter will be closed:

1. A pleasing personality will help one to market one's services effectively.
2. Sound character will help one to keep one's services marketed permanently.

16

Cooperation

COOPERATION is a quality without which no person can hope to market his personal services effectively! It is a quality that must become a habit with all who make themselves indispensable to their employers.

The late Andrew Carnegie said inability to cooperate stood at the head of the list of the causes of failure. Moreover, he emphasized the fact that lack of cooperation was one deficiency that he would not tolerate, no matter how well equipped in other ways a man might be. He amplified his statement by the explanation that a man who lacks the ability either to cooperate with others or to gain cooperation from others is a disturbing element whose influence spreads with disastrous results. He then stated his point conversely by saying that a man who not only cooperated with others but who had the personality to induce others to cooperate with him, served as a powerful influence through which coordination of effort or teamwork could be produced.

He should know: He made cooperation pay.

Through a series of tests made by the late Dr. Alexander Graham Bell and others, it was discovered that one person of the fault-finding type in an organization of a thousand people would have the effect of coloring the mental attitude of everyone around him, thereby creating friction and dissatisfaction.

Success is achieved through power!

Power is developed through organized and intelligently directed knowledge. The intelligent use of knowledge calls for cooperation. Woe unto him who fails to understand and apply the principle of cooperative effort.

The larger corporations have already learned that cooperation among their employees and executives is their greatest asset. It was the lack of this sort of cooperation that placed business at the mercy of labor racketeers.

It is only a question of time until every well-managed business will have a system by which it may discover lack of cooperation among its employees. Friction among employees has been one of the greatest evils of the past in industry and business. The well-managed business of the future will insist upon an *esprit de corps* among its employees, such as business management of the past has not demanded. Those who are capable of managing business successfully have learned that no business can succeed without this spirit of *harmonious* cooperation. Moreover, the cooperative effort must be in spirit as well as in deed. This point is important so bear it in mind.

I am stating these facts very plainly because I am convinced that no person can market himself effectively in the future without understanding and applying the principle of harmonious cooperation! Observe with profit the emphasis upon the word *harmony*. Cooperation, to be effective, must be more than tentative. It must be real and it must be based upon perfect harmony.

Indigestion, a bad liver, and auto-intoxication are a few of the causes of inability to cooperate. Grouchiness will turn out to be "ouchiness." This statement applies to the owner of the business as well as his employees. The public has learned to expect and demand efficient and pleasant service.

> Your position is nothing more than your opportunity to show what sort of ability you have. You will get out of it exactly what you put into it—no more and no less. A "big" position is but the sum total of numerous "little" positions well filled.

17

How to Create a Job

KEEN imagination is essential in all forms of salesmanship. Imagination is of two forms. One is known as synthetic imagination and the other is known as creative imagination.

Synthetic imagination consists of combining or bringing together two or more known ideas, principles, concepts, or laws and giving them a new use. Practically all inventions are created through the faculty of synthetic imagination because they consist merely of a new combination of old principles and ideas, or of giving old ideas or principles a new use.

Creative imagination consists of interpretation of basically new ideas, plans, concepts, or principles that present themselves through the creative faculty and whose source is outside the range of the five senses of perception.

Imagination can be cultivated; it is a fascinating pursuit, rich with rewards.

We are concerned at this time mainly with the principle of synthetic imagination because it is the keystone to the arch of selling either personal services or commodities of any description.

The faculty of imagination becomes more alert through use! In this respect, it responds like any organ of the body or group of cells.

Some people have the mistaken notion that the imagination is complicated and that only geniuses make effective use of it.

Through the use of his imagination (while working as a telegraph operator), James J. Hill saw that the East should be connected with the

West by a dependable railway system. His ability to see this was imagination that enabled him to build and operate the Great Northern Railway System. Any other man could have done it.

Organized imagination brings the highest price of any form of ability. It always has a market and it has no limitations as to value. Business depressions do not destroy the market for imagination; they merely increase the need and extend the demand for imagination. The world stands in need of men who will use their imaginations.

The most desirable and highest paid positions are those that men of imagination create for themselves. Business is stagnant all over the country. Use your imagination and discover ways and means of stimulating business, even in a very small way, in any line, and you may name your own salary. The country is faced not by the necessity of solving one problem, but by the necessity of solving hundreds of problems. Pick out any one of these problems and work out, through your imagination, its solution and your problem of acquiring money will be solved.

Not all of the new ways of doing business nor the best ways have yet been found. The future will call for still more new ways. This need is your opportunity. Use your imagination and convert that opportunity into fortune.

Take inventory of the shortcomings of the business in which you are employed and use your imagination for the purpose of eliminating some of them. Or, if you are not employed, use your imagination to create some plan by which you may improve some part of any business with which you may be familiar, and you will soon find a place for yourself. Positions can be made to order.

This is an age of rapid-fire change in business! It is an age that was made to order for men who have and use imagination. Because business is stagnant, businessmen will try almost anything. Create some new, unique idea that is sound and sell it to them!

If you are employed and find yourself worrying about the possibility of losing your job, convert the time you have been wasting on worry to a better use by creating some plan that will improve your work or add to your employer's business. You can make yourself indispensable in this way. Indispensability commands a high price and permanency of employment at all times.

18

How to Choose an Occupation

INSTRUCTIONS have been offered for aiding those who wish to choose jobs intelligently. These instructions were not entirely adequate for the needs of young people who have just finished their schooling but have never held positions or chosen a vocation.

Decision in connection with the choice of a life work is one of the two most important decisions that young people have the responsibility of making. The other is the decision in connection with the selection of a mate in marriage.

These two decisions determine largely whether one's life shall be blessed with happiness and fortune or cursed with misery and poverty!

A decision as to a vocation suited to his or her needs is a very difficult matter for any inexperienced young person. Had I chosen my vocation at the end of my high school training, I would have become a telegraph operator since this was the work that most appealed to my imagination at that time. Fortunately, a former schoolmate who had been away attending business college came home for the Christmas holidays and, before returning, sold me on the idea of going with him. My decision to take business training proved to be one of the most important decisions of my life. In the first place, this training prepared me to earn a living. In the second place, it brought me into intimate contact with some of the greatest business and industrial leaders the country has ever known.

In the capacity of secretary, I literally went to school to the men for whom I worked, and I am happy to acknowledge this part of my schooling was worth more than all the other schooling I received. I am convinced that every young man and woman should take a business course and gain some experience firsthand in many lines of business before selecting a vocation. This gives one an opportunity to weigh and to consider the possibilities available in various fields of business and to make a choice of vocation that is based upon actual knowledge of the details of the chosen work.

Business training not only gave me the opportunity to go to school to some of the most able men in America, but that training proved to be a veritable source of insurance against catastrophe on more than a score of occasions during the 25 years of effort when I found it necessary to stop my research and earn money. There was never a time when I could not market the knowledge that I gained in business school for more than enough to take care of my living expenses.

Because of my business training, I was privileged to work for the late Dr. Elmer R. Gates and the late Dr. Alexander Graham Bell, inventor of the long distance telephone. From both of them I received knowledge of a priceless nature. Through this training, too, I was privileged to work for a doctor from whom I received much of the biological data I needed and for a noted lawyer from whom I gathered a knowledge of law and legal procedure, which has been most helpful to me.

Training in business brought me the knowledge through which I obtained every promotion I ever had while working for a salary. To it I also owe the selection of my life's work, for it brought me into contact with Andrew Carnegie, Thomas A. Edison, Henry Ford, and most of the others who have been so helpful to me in the building of this philosophy.

Every young man and woman ought to be able to: 1) operate a typewriter efficiently, 2) take shorthand notes speedily, and, 3) keep a set of books accurately, before selecting a vocation. Knowledge of these subjects is of vital importance in the successful conduct of any business or profession.

The modern business college is a sort of missing link between the public schools and colleges and the field of business because the business college specializes in a form of training that is inadequately handled by the public schools. The public schools and colleges, although they should prepare young people for efficient service in business, do not. Moreover, I have learned from my experience in employing many young people, some of whom were graduates of commercial departments of high schools and others who were graduates of modern business colleges, that the business college graduate is far superior to the graduate of the commercial departments of high schools.

A business college training is an absolute necessity to the person who aspires to a position as an executive in the field of business today for the reason that executives must have understudy experience of a nature that can be acquired only through business college preparation.

The modern business colleges of today have had the foresight to see the dawn of a new era of business ethics that has grown out of the Depression and are preparing their graduates to adapt themselves to the new standards.

The public schools on the whole have not seen this need, or if they have seen it, they are doing nothing to equip students to meet it.

This chapter is intended solely for young people who have not yet selected a life work. If you are in that category, defer your decision as to a vocation until you have taken a complete business training and have applied that training for at least two years. Your decision then will be more sound than any you could make at this time, for it will provide an opportunity to go to school to successful men who will pay for the privilege of training you!

Business training, in my case, was the result of a chance or accidental decision. Your decision to market your services through the aid of a business college training should not be accidental; it should be by design.

There is no way of determining the actual value of the training I received in business college, first, because I am still in the prime of life and have before me what I consider the best part of my career, and second, because I have found through my business training the vocation that I like best and in which I am happy. Happiness and contentment cannot be measured in terms of bank balances alone. Were I forced to set a monetary value on my business college training, however, I would estimate it at no less than $1,000,000. Its total cost was approximately $500 in money and a year's time. The investment has yielded me more than adequate returns.

There is a certain atmosphere about a business college that is most helpful to young people because all of the students in attendance are thinking and talking in terms of rendering useful service. In the public schools and colleges of today, the atmosphere often takes on an entirely different tone that savors more of play than it does of work.

The best results cannot be obtained in this way.

Mindful of the fact that some readers may wish to go from high school to college for the purpose of preparing themselves to take up a profession, I would particularly recommend that they take a business college training first. The competition in the professions today is very keen. Only those who understand the business foundation on which every profession must be conducted will survive. The large percentage of fatalities in the professions is due mainly to the fact that so many professional people know nothing about the fundamentals of business organization. Such knowledge is essential.

Moreover, the business-college-trained student can easily earn his way through college. I know many successful college graduates who paid their way through college. The person who can operate a typewriter efficiently and who can take shorthand notes rapidly, can get much more out of college than the person who lacks these skills.

Young women usually begin to think in terms of marriage about the time they complete their high school training. While marriage is a lofty ambition, it brings responsibilities and creates emergencies that call for wise thought and action. The woman, who has been schooled in a business college and who has had some experience in a business office, is much better prepared to assume the practical responsibilities of a home than one who has had no such training. She not only is in a position to cooperate with her husband in a spirit of sympathy and understanding in connection with his problems of earning a living, but if occasion demands, the married woman who has had business training may go back to it and earn a living. Business training, therefore, becomes a sort of insurance against dependence.

Use Wisdom in the Selection of a Business College

No statement in this chapter should be interpreted as a blanket endorsement of all business colleges. Happily, most of the business colleges in the United States are efficient and their management consists of men and women who are conscientious. But, as in all other fields, there are some that are better equipped than others to render practical service. The first thing to be looked for in the selection of a business college is age. The college that has survived a long number of years must have adequate equipment and competent teachers or it would not have lasted. The next thing to be considered is the business and ethical standing of the owner. The school whose practice or teaching is unethical cannot be long-lived. The third thing to be considered is the question of the competency of its teachers.

A Suggestion for Financing Yourself through Business College

Usually the young people who pay a portion or all of their expenses while taking a business or college training get more out of their training than those who do not pay any part of their expenses. I have delivered lectures to many groups of students. The students who work their way through college are the first to arrive and they occupy the front seats, while those whose expenses are paid by their parents usually arrive late and select seats well toward the rear of the auditorium where they can make a quick getaway as soon as the lectures are finished. Those who work take copious notes on the lectures, while those who do not work usually take no notes. I have no doubt that if I could follow these young men and women into the business world, I would find that the students who worked their way through college had much less difficulty in earning a living than those who did not.

I believe you'll agree with that statement.

The urge of necessity is a great blessing to most people. It forces them to do the things they should do, but too often would not do without the pressure of necessity. One reason business college graduates usually find less difficulty in marketing their services is the fact that most of them are attending business college because they come from families who know from experience the urge of necessity.

This is an age of unprecedented opportunity due mainly to the great need for leadership in practically every calling. Opportunity will be greatest for those who have had thorough business training. This is an age that accepts young blood in positions of responsibility.

These greater opportunities of today call for greater efficiency than was acceptable 25 years ago. This machine age of efficiency in production has brought with it a demand for greater efficiency in manpower. The principles through which efficiency may be attained have been described in the pages of this book. Not one of these principles is difficult to develop or apply.

In closing this chapter, your attention is called to a principle that I believe to be the factor, more than any other, which determines whether one succeeds or fails in any calling. The principle to which I have reference is so simple that its importance may be underestimated by many, especially by the young person inexperienced in business.

The principle may be described as "the faith and persistence to accept defeat as being nothing more than an experience from which something of value may be learned." Most people give up or let their ambition be killed when serious obstacles are met.

Life is filled with obstacles that must be surmounted. Only those who have the stamina and the willingness to fight can win. Others must take the count. Do not expect that you will be one of the fortunate who never meet with serious opposition in life, for you will be no exception to the general rule. Everyone meets with opposition. Opposition should be accepted as a signal to put everything you have into its mastery.

It has been my privilege during my public career to know many men and women of great achievement. Some of them I have known intimately. All of them had met with opposition that necessitated struggle and persistence.

When defeat comes, as it will, accept it as a hurdle that has been placed in your way for the purpose of training you to jump higher! You will gain strength and skill from each hurdle that you surmount. Do not hate people because they oppose you. Thank them for forcing you to develop the strategy and imagination you will need to master their opposition.

This is a beautiful world and life is stocked with an abundance of everything you need, including riches and happiness, which you may have, provided you do not overindulge in the things you like best, nor permit yourself to be suppressed by the circumstances and things you do not like.

Accept both the bitter and the sweet of life's cup like a real sportsman, remembering all the while that a well-rounded life requires some of each. Success without defeat would lead to autocracy and a consequent boredom. Defeat without the counteracting effect of success would kill ambition. Be willing to accept your portion of each, but do not expect success without temporary defeat, for there is no such possibility.

Now, let us see what a popular writer says.

Ed Sullivan, the noted Hollywood newspaper columnist, wrote the climax of this chapter for you. He wrote out of an abundance of opportunity to observe what helps people to sell their way through life successfully. His counsel may be of great value to any young person who thinks for a moment that one can crash the gates at Hollywood or any other place without paying the price of success.

> **A few days ago, a Boston professor urged the graduating class to forget their ambitions and go on relief. The class orator at New York University sounded the same refrain. Now, I've seen a lot more of life than either of these two speakers, have traveled wider, met more varieties of people, observed life much more intimately, so let me say something to you who have just graduated from high schools and colleges.**
>
> **Five hundred thousand were graduated from American colleges this month. Are the odds 500,000 to 1 against you, then? Certainly not. Fifty percent of that total will disqualify**

themselves by laziness, lack of ambition, refusal to accept responsibility, because I've found that half of the world is as intent on not succeeding as the other half is intent on success. So your opposition is sliced in half. Sickness, temperament, liquor, gambling will cut heavily into the remainder.

The best dramatization of what I'm telling you is the Kentucky Derby. Last year, 110 horses were nominated for the derby. These nominees were well trained and coddled in every possible way that great trainers could devise. Of the 110 horses, only 10 of them went to the post. It's the same in everyday life. The odds are always less when the chips are on the lines.

So don't worry about the opposition and competition that will be offered you. It will be much less than you expect. And don't worry, either, if you won't be able to go to college, now that you have finished high school. University of Southern California recently conferred a degree of master of science on a boy who never even finished high school: Walt Disney.

It wasn't so long ago that Disney and his brother, Roy, didn't have enough money to eat decently. They'd go into a restaurant and order one dinner with two sets of knives, forks, and spoons.

You'd think, from the present goings-on, that these days are so extraordinary that the present generation should have medals struck off in their honor. It's not so. The successful men and women of this motion picture industry all had to work their way up from poor homes. Times always have been tough for the poor.

Paul Muni was a poor boy. Sam Goldwyn was a glove salesman. David O. Selznick is the son of a rich man who went broke. Louis B. Mayer, power at M. G. M., recalls when his family didn't have enough to eat. Disney was ridiculed, and shoved around by shrewder businessmen.

Had any of them been quitters, you would not know of them today. They had ambition and courage. They were tenacious. Nobody shoved them upstairs. Nobody created jobs for them, or told them how to hang on once the job was secured. Just as nobody can tell you what to do or how to do it. You've got to learn that yourself; you've got to adapt yourself to conditions, and that is a personal issue.

If you listened to the radio in recent years you heard the broadcast of two fights, the Joe Louis-Max Baer fight, and the Henry Armstrong-Barney Ross fight. Baer quit, and you heard the referee count him out while Baer rested on one knee. In the Armstrong-Ross fight, Ross took a terrible lacing, but refused to let his handlers or the referee stop the fight.

In life, you can take the count on one knee as Max Baer did, or you can imitate Barney Ross. You can quit or you can carry on. I'll let you decide which to emulate.

You are living in an age that is distinguished for the greatest liberalism that ever has been focused on the American scene. Legislators are occupying themselves with the problems of the poor, which didn't happen years ago. There are Civilian Conservation Corps camps and the Works Progress Administration; the world is interested in relieving distress in much greater measure than ever before. Governments actually tell off dictators and speak on behalf of weaker nations. All of these things are encouraging.

So, to all of you kids who are starting out, don't be too overwhelmed by surface indications. The weather forecast still is weather clear, track fast, and the rewards are greater than ever before. Don't ask too much of life, that's all. In the final analysis, if you get just a little success, and a lot of love, they'll hold up your hand as the winner.

19

How to Budget Your Time

BEFORE you can market your personal services effectively, you must lay out a program for yourself based upon an appropriate budget of your time. Nothing will be of greater assistance than compliance with this suggestion, a fact that will be surprising when you begin to make up your first-time budget; surprising because of your discovery of the amount of time you have been wasting through lack of a budget. All well-managed businesses are operated on a budget system. The marketing of your services is a business. Moreover, to you it is the most important business in the world. It is a business that you can conduct efficiently only by organizing the hours at your disposal, so they will yield a greater return than you could get from them without a budget.

Experience has proved that the following schedule is one that the majority of people can easily follow. It has also proved that it is an efficient schedule.

8 hours for sleep
8 hours for one's vocation
4 hours for recreation and health
2 hours for study and preparation
2 hours for extra service for the benefit of others, without pay

---

24 hours

Take inventory of yourself before creating any plans for marketing your personal services effectively and budget your time as nearly as possible to conform to this schedule.

Your attention is called emphatically to the last two periods of two hours each. These are the most profitable hours because the use that you make of these hours will determine more than any other factor whether you market your services effectively.

You will observe that this schedule calls for two hours a day that must be devoted to study and preparation for greater efficiency in connection with your occupation. The majority of people have no such provision in their time budget—if, in fact, they have any budget.

You will also observe that the schedule includes two definite hours that must be devoted to rendering extra service for which one is not paid. This fixes approximately the time that one must put into one's work in following the habit of rendering service that is greater in quantity than one is paid for. The proportion is one-fourth of the time allotted for one's vocation. If you follow this schedule, you will find ways and means of doing approximately one-fourth more work in the future than you have been doing in the past. The majority of people can easily follow this part of the schedule. It does not mean that one must be on duty 12 hours a day instead of 8. It means that one should accomplish in 8 hours as much as one has heretofore been accomplishing in 12 hours.

These additional 2 hours of quantity of service may be rendered in many ways other than by merely being on the job 2 hours longer. For example, the equivalent of 2 extra hours may be delivered by:

1. Greater cooperation with fellow employees and management.
2. Personal conduct that constitutes a more pleasing personality.
3. Greater skill in connection with one's efforts.
4. Working with a definite goal or amount of work to be performed, as salesmen work on definite sales quotas
5. Working in a spirit of enthusiasm and genuine interest.

The following schedule represents fairly the budget actually followed by the average person because of indifference:

The Time Budget One Should Not Follow

8 hours for labor that is performed with one eye on the time clock and one's thoughts on quitting time

8 hours for sleep

8 hours for miscellaneous dissipation of one's energies, ranging all the way from gin parties and habits of intemperance in eating, drinking, and sex indulgence, to even more destructive habits

———

24 hours

Check this schedule carefully and compare it with your use of time. This will constitute a most important part of your self-analysis. Check yourself against this schedule with courage and frankness. Do not make the mistake of giving yourself the benefit of all doubts. Reverse the rule and analyze yourself with merciless accuracy. Remember again that you are where you are and what you are because of your own conduct. Find out if your conduct is lifting you up the ladder of success or lowering you to failure.

By the time you are through with this self-analysis, you may catch a glimpse of some of the habits that have been standing between you and the station in life you would like to attain. Also, you may reach the conclusion that there is something which you must do for yourself in marketing your personal services effectively. Unless you are an unusual person, this analysis will bring to your attention many changes of habits that you must make before you can hope to market your personal services effectively.

You cannot be successful without paying the price of success!

The price that must be paid has been clearly described. Not the least important part of this price is definitely outlined in this chapter.

Before any reputable physician will undertake to prescribe a remedy for the ills of a patient, he will insist upon making a thorough diagnosis to ascertain what are the patient's ills. Diagnosis is the most important part of the physician's work. The same is true of the person who markets personal services effectively. He must begin by ascertaining what his weaknesses are and when they have been discovered; he must form habits that will either eliminate or bridge those weaknesses so they will not work against him.

This book will probably be of little value to all who, through either neglect or indifference, fail to follow the plan of self-analysis here described.

Before leaving this chapter, I feel impelled to ask the reader to analyze the last eight-hour period of the time budget one should not follow. I have helped a large number of men and women to emancipate themselves from misery and want by aiding them in making an analysis of this eight-hour period of the day, which constitutes the pivotal point of one's life at which failure may be turned into success, or success into failure, as the result of the way these eight hours are used.

Let it be clearly understood that I am not a reformer, nor have I any bill of complaint against those who wish to relax through play that may not be entirely conventional, because play and relaxation are just as important as labor and study. That which I have to say to the readers of this book in the subsequent paragraphs of this chapter is intended as a warning to those who devote the entire eight-hour period to what they call relaxation and play.

This is a swing age which has been keyed up to the highest pitch of action. If it is stepped up much higher, the insane asylums will be filled with those who have cracked up. Millions of people, who ought to be seriously interested in marketing their services effectively, have been caught in this maelstrom of speed that is whirling them around ever faster and faster until they have completely lost balance.

These pleasure bound unfortunates not only use up eight hours in the mad whirl, but they cut in on the eight-hour period allotted for sleep and use up from two to six hours of that period. This has the effect of cutting into the eight-hour period allotted for work and robbing it of two to six hours through lowered efficiency!

I know a great number of young people still in their 20s who look old and have far too little endurance. These young people are shortening their own lives and robbing themselves of the most vital asset they possess in marketing their services effectively.

The human body is so organized that it requires eight hours of complete relaxation in sleep out of every 24. Human society is so organized that at least 8 hours out of every 24 must be devoted to rendering useful service in one form or another. These two eight-hour periods cannot be whittled down or robbed for other purposes without a price that means failure. The third period of eight hours is the only period that one can afford to gamble with under any circumstances!

This third eight-hour period holds the key to one's future because the manner in which it is used affects for weal or for woe the other two eight-hour periods. It is the period that requires the closest attention because the freedom it provides often serves as an invitation to indulge in the attractions being indulged in by others. We are all more or less the victims of habit.

The two eight-hour periods allotted to work and sleep by their very nature more or less force one to acquire sane habits. If a person chooses to steal time from the eight-hour sleep period, Nature steps in sooner or later and stops the practice temporarily by sending him to the hospital. If a person misappropriates a part of the eight-hour work period, the law of economic necessity steps in and calls a halt, as one must have food and clothing and a place to sleep.

The third eight-hour period, however, is a freelance period that may be either wasted in dissipation or used as a period of preparation for greater efficiency and greater earning capacity, as one elects.

Watch your habits during this eight-hour period because those habits hold the secret of your future, no matter who you are or what may be your calling in life. This period offers the only hope available to the person who is poverty stricken but desires riches. It is the starting point of the person who aspires to a position of independence and freedom.

When you come to analyze yourself for the purpose of discovering how many of the causes of failure are standing in your way, you will discover that most, if not all, of those disclosed by your analysis have grown out of your habits of waste during this eight-hour period.

If you work for others and desire promotion and larger income, you will find the answer in this eight-hour recreational period. You will find it nowhere else!

We are all victims of the power of suggestion. Most of our habits are acquired through the influence of other people around us. This is an age of wasteful, destructive habits and the price of escape from these habits is eternal vigilance. It is a price that must be paid by every person who markets his personal services effectively.

Gin parties are very exciting. To some, they are very interesting. To all, they are destructive! If you have not the willpower to resist the temptation to join your friends in parties of this kind, you had better look for new friends whose habits will tempt you in a more profitable direction. These parties, so popular in this age, collect a heavy toll in two ways from all who indulge in them: Their victims pay in loss of efficiency, which means loss of earning capacity, and they pay sooner or later in loss of health.

Young people can, because of the endurance of youth, make tremendous inroads upon their vitality without apparent effects. There comes a time, however, when these debts against one's health must be paid. Nature attends to this! She keeps a set of books in which every item is recorded. Moreover, she forces the individual to become his or her own bookkeeper. The charges compiled through the indiscretions of youth are collected through the infirmities of old age. A little while ago, I was called to a hospital to visit a former schoolmate whose habits of youth have piled up a huge account against his old age reserve. He had not yet reached old age, but his account had been so grossly overdrawn that Nature brought him into the debtor's court for settlement. He was suffering from partial paralysis of the brain! In plain English, he was on the road to insanity.

All this may sound like a prohibitionist's preachment against drink. It is more than that. This acquaintance had cut himself down through excesses in eating, drinking, and sexual expression for over ten years, using up his eight-hour recreational period and making serious inroads upon the other two. I went to see him at the hospital for the purpose of helping him out of his financial difficulties. Excesses take a financial toll as well as a physical toll.

I have never desired to be a reformer or a preacher! This is a book on the subject of marketing personal services effectively. Nothing can be marketed *effectively* unless the product to be marketed has value. It has been my aim throughout these pages to describe what constitutes valuable services. It is hoped that some suggestion or statement may throw light upon your own situation and point out the way to a more effective marketing of your personal services.

During my public career, I have observed the methods used by thousands of successful men in selling their way through life. Space does not permit a description of the methods used by all these men, but I have chosen from the group one man whose principles of selling himself are described in detail.

The man chosen is Henry Ford, known the world over for his ability to get whatever he wants without violating the rights of his fellow men. I have chosen Ford for my analysis of men who successfully sell their way through life, because he has used the same principles every successful person must use.

I have chosen Ford for the reason that I have had the privilege of closely observing him over so long a period of years that I feel sure I understand the principles underlying his success.

Do not browse through the Ford analysis or read it hurriedly. It is worthy of slow reading and careful analysis, because it conveys the material of which you may easily build your own successful life. The story has not been included to glorify Ford. The sole purpose in publishing it is to place in the hands of every reader an accurate outline of the plans and principles that have made America's most successful businessman the success that everyone knows him to be.

You are especially requested to study carefully the rating given Ford on the Principles of Individual Achievement. After you finish reading this book, come back to the Ford analysis and take inventory of yourself, measuring yourself honestly and frankly by these principles. If you do this faithfully, you may discover what the major points of difference are between you and Henry Ford. The discovery, if accurately made, may both shock and benefit you!

It is well worth trying.

This book on personal promotion would hardly be complete without a description of the methods by which the world's leading industrialist lifted himself from poverty to plenty. As you read the analysis of Henry Ford's astounding achievements, you should remember he was no outstanding genius at the start, had but little schooling and was a pioneer in a new industry at a time when the entire country was unfriendly toward him and his "horseless buggy."

Do not make the mistake of assuming that Ford began in an age blessed with greater opportunities than those available at the present. The truth is just the opposite, and coincidental as it may seem, Ford's influence on civilization has actually had much to do with creating the more extensive opportunities that exist today. His influence has helped to bring the country and the city dweller into closer contact because of the wonderful system of good roads that belts the entire nation. He has provided employment for more people than any other man living. He has proved that an American citizen may start from scratch, without pull or financial backing, and accumulate a vast fortune without violating the rights of others; and I wish to emphasize one truth above all others, namely, the principles employed by Ford in his climb to opulence are understandable and usable by any person who has the ambition to appropriate them.

Did you ever think of that?

Ford is a self-made man in the true sense of the term. If ever a man sold his way through life successfully, with his own brain and his own ideas, that man is Henry Ford. His story has been included in this book because his entire life represents one of the finest jobs of selling the world has ever known. There has been no scandal connected with the Ford methods of selling. He has helped everyone whom he has influenced. Every dollar of his fortune is being used constructively. He has established an all-time high standard of business ethics that every other individual might do well to emulate.

I have begun my analysis of Ford by describing the one principle which, more than all others, has been responsible for the stupendous success he has achieved, the principle of singleness of purpose. That was all Ford had as an operating capital to begin with, but it was enough. Remember this, you who wish to emulate Ford, and remember, too, that you are reading an analysis of the number one citizen and successful businessman of the entire world.

> Here's a good joke to play on your employer: Get to your work a little earlier and leave a little later than you are supposed to. Handle his tools as if they belonged to you. Go out of your way to say a kind word about him to your fellow workers. When there is extra work that needs to be done, volunteer to do it. Do not show surprise when he gets on to you and offers you the head of the department or a partnership in the business, for this is the best part of the joke.

20

The Master Plan for Getting a Position

THERE is a definite, surefire method by which anyone may procure any position for which he is qualified. I will describe the method in detail, but first take notice I did not say that this plan would enable anyone to hold any job he might procure. Getting a job is one thing; holding it is something else. Inasmuch as the major portion of this book has been devoted to a description of the principles by which people hold jobs, I will not here repeat what I have stated on that subject.

I have been asked often, "How did you manage to interview all those successful men who helped you to organize the Law of Success philosophy? How did you induce them to give up so much of their time?" My answer is, "It is simple to get the opportunity to talk with men if you approach them through some subject in which they are interested, and do most of your talking about *them*!"

I might say the same thing in connection with procuring a position. It is easy to get any position one wants, providing one has the ability to fill it and makes the right sort of approach in applying for the position.

Through the pages that follow, I am addressing men and women who are interested in procuring some sort of a position, or some form of personal contact requiring the cooperation of one or more other people. The advice I offer is intended solely for the general guidance of anyone seeking to get the cooperation of others. The details should be changed to fit the particular needs of each individual, and should not be copied verbatim from this book. Your own judgment will tell you what to do.

Let us assume you are desirous of procuring a position with the Standard Oil Company; that you are willing to start anywhere the company wishes to place you, your major desire being an opportunity to demonstrate what sort of services you can render.

Very well, here is a step-by-step outline of the approach which, if changed to fit your particular personality, could hardly fail to get you the desired opportunity.

First: Decide what particular position with the Standard Oil Company you desire, then make a complete list, in writing, of all your qualifications to fill that position. If you feel the list of your capabilities is inadequate after you have placed it on paper, go to work and prepare yourself through study and observation of some other person who is filling a position similar to the one you want, until you are sure you are ready for the position.

Second: Write out a list of the following 17 principles of success and grade yourself accurately on each, the grade running from zero to 100 percent on each principle. Under each of the principles state in detail why you believe you are entitled to the credit you have given yourself, what definite proof you have to offer that your grading is accurate.

		(Grade Yourself Anywhere from 0 to 100%)
A Definite Major Aim in Life	Under this heading describe your major purpose in life, and show that it is connected with the position you are seeking with the Standard Oil Company. If the particular position you wish is only to serve as a stepping-stone, and you are aiming for a higher place, say so and give your reasons for believing you can advance to the better position.	_____%

Self-confidence	State your reason for the grading you give yourself on this principle, and clearly indicate that you know the difference between self-confidence and egotism.	______%
Initiative	Under this heading give illustrations of occasions on which you have acted without supervision, on your own initiative, and state to what extent this procedure is a habit with you.	______%
The Habit of Saving	Under this heading make it clear that you have formed the habit of budgeting both your time and your income, and that you recognize the necessity of this sort of self-discipline as a means of attaining the object of your Major Aim in life.	______%
Imagination	Give illustrations of occasions on which you have used your imagination. The best possible method by which you can do this impressively will be to indicate to what extent you used imagination in familiarizing yourself with the requirements of the position you are seeking.	______%
Enthusiasm	State to what extent you have your enthusiasm under control, and indicate your knowledge of the difference between passive and active enthusiasm. Indicate that your greatest enthusiasm is associated with your desire to procure and fill the position you are seeking with the Standard Oil Company, giving your reasons for your enthusiasm.	______%

(*continued*)

Self-control	Give your reasons for your grading on this principle, and state definitely how you make application of the principle as a means of striking a balance between your head and your heart, or in other words state to what extent you use self-discipline to help your head manage your emotions. Above all else, indicate that your self-control is sufficient to enable you to avoid becoming involved in controversies of other people; that it is sufficient to enable you to think for yourself, without the aid of self-appointed leaders or propagandists.	_____%
The Habit of Doing More than You Are Paid to Do	Here is your big opportunity to land the position you are seeking. Give a detailed statement of why you have formed the habit of doing more work and better work than you are paid to do. This is the most important of the 17 principles as far as the procuring of a position is concerned. Moreover, it is the principle of major importance in connection with the holding of a position after you procure it; therefore, make a strong statement as to your reasons for observing this principle as a part of your philosophy of life.	_____%
A Pleasing Personality	In explaining your reasons for your rating on this important principle, give at least five definite illustrations of qualities you have that entitle you to rate as having a	_____%

	pleasing personality. Above all, give a detailed statement of your personal attitude toward others, whether it is at all times friendly and cooperative, and describe your disposition in negotiating with friends, relatives, and business associates.	
Accurate Thinking	Make it clear that you are grading yourself on this important principle only as it applies to your relationship to the position you are seeking. Give your reasons for believing you can think accurately in connection with the position you are seeking, and be sure they are based upon facts easily discernible from your statement.	______%
Concentration of Effort	State clearly your reasons for your grading on your ability to concentrate your mind upon any given task and keep it there until that task has been completed. Be sure, also, to indicate the extent to which you have formed the habit of concentrating your willpower upon the attainment of your Major Aim in Life.	______%
Cooperation	Clearly describe your reasons for following the habit of working with other people in a spirit of harmony, and explain that you do this not merely on occasion but as a matter of continuous habit.	______%
Profiting by Failures	No one is expected to be infallible, therefore state frankly that you make mistakes, but indicate to what extent you try to avoid duplicating, and be sure to	______%

(*continued*)

	describe how you manage to profit by your own failures and the failures of other people. Indicate, also, that you know the difference between failure and temporary defeat, and say that you never accept defeat as anything more than an inspiration to make a fresh and a more determined start.	
Tolerance	In explaining your grading on this important subject, clearly indicate that you understand tolerance to mean "an open mind on all subjects, toward all people." Be sure to describe the extent to which you practice tolerance.	______%
The Golden Rule Applied	Grade yourself on your application of this great law of human conduct, and explain why you follow the habit of placing yourself in the other fellow's place when reaching decisions that in any way affect him.	______%
The Habit of Health	In explaining your grading on this subject, be sure to indicate that you do not suffer with imaginary symptoms of illness, that you follow the habit of attending to your diet, exercise, and elimination, and be sure to indicate clearly that you do not have a bad disposition due to your failure to keep your sewer system cleaned out.	______%
The Master Mind Applied	The Master Mind is a principle through which one or more people may coordinate their efforts in a spirit of perfect harmony for a definite purpose. Indicate	______%

definitely that you understand the value of such coordination of effort, that you follow the habit of observing this important principle, and explain how you believe you can make use of it in connection with the position you are seeking.

After you have graded yourself on the foregoing 17 principles of personal achievement, write the following letter, or some modified form of it, and mail the letter to the manager of the department of the Standard Oil Company in which you are seeking a position:

Mr. Walter Teagle, President
Standard Oil Company
New York City

My Dear Mr. Teagle:

With this letter, I am sending you an accurate statement of the reasons why I deserve the position of ______with your company, and with this statement, I am sending also an accurate grading of myself on each of the 17 principles of success, together with a detailed explanation under each principle as to why the grade was given.

Now, here is the condition under which I ask you to give me the position I am seeking:

Let me work in the position for one month without compensation. At the end of the month if I have not demonstrated, beyond all question of doubt, that I have the sort of material in me that any great corporation such as the Standard Oil Company would naturally be seeking, I will step aside, but before doing so I will pay your company a reasonable sum to reimburse it for the actual cost of the supervision given to me during the month's trial. (Omit this last offer, if you choose.)

If you want the trial period to go beyond one month, that will be satisfactory with me. All I ask during the demonstration is that you allow me to put into my work the hours and the sort of effort I believe to be necessary to prove that I am not merely just another person seeking a job. What I am really seeking is not a job, but an opportunity to earn a place as ______ in your company.

Will you give me this opportunity?

Very cordially,______________

Have the letter neatly typed, and also have your grading on the 17 principles of achievement and your statement of reasons why you believe yourself qualified for the position you seek typed.

If you desire to apply for a position with several different firms, send a similar letter, with the grading and the statement of your capabilities, to each firm, but be sure to take the time to investigate each different firm's methods of doing business, its problems, and so forth, so you will be in a position to make your application fit the job you seek.

In grading yourself on the 17 principles, use your own imagination and so word your explanations of your grading that the person to whom you are applying for a position will quickly see that you are familiar with the requirements of such a position.

Remember, as you prepare your application for a position, that you will be practically sure to get a favorable hearing if you so word your letter and your grading that you definitely convey the impression you are willing to prove your ability before asking anyone to purchase your services.

Remember, also, that you will not receive encouragement unless you choose some position in which a person of your personality, education, and experience is needed. Do sufficient advance investigation to convince yourself the position for which you apply really needs you, then go after it and sell yourself to the man who has the yes or the no over the job.

Do not make the mistake of grading yourself too high on all the 17 principles. Grade yourself down on at least a few of them, and explain why your rating is not higher. I once knew a young man who applied for a position through this plan who was so lacking in modesty that he graded himself 100 percent on each of the 17 principles. It might have helped him had he known that not even Henry Ford could accurately grade himself that high.

If you do a good job of grading yourself, and go into details to show how you arrived at your rating, you will have a marvelous sales letter that will interest the right person in your services in the grading alone. Remember, as you explain each of your grades, that your explanation is in fact your strongest selling argument on your behalf.

The day that you mail your application, send the following telegram to the person to whom you send the application, and do not forget to prepay the message:

Walter Teagle, President
Standard Oil Company
New York City

In today's mail, I am sending you an important letter that I hope your secretary will deliver to you promptly.

Attach a good, unmounted photograph of yourself to your letter—one that has been recently taken.

Send with the letter the names and addresses of five references, preferably people engaged in established businesses or bankers.

State your age, nationality, and schooling.

If your application is properly prepared and you select with care the firms to whom you send it, you can safely count on procuring a position if you include at least 10 different firms on your list. In other words, you will be practically sure of finding what you want by seeking it in 10 different directions.

Let me emphasize that you should use your own imagination and initiative when it comes to the actual writing of the letter of application. The only thing you should not change is the policy of offering your services for one month, or longer, strictly on trial. Everything else in the letter may be altered to suit your personality, or to make the letter fit your needs to better advantage.

If you follow these instructions carefully and fail to get the results you desire, you may send the author a copy of your letter and your personal grading on the 17 principles of success and he will determine wherein you have failed. Be prepared, however, to back up all you promise in your letter, in the event that you are given a trial. Any lack of sincerity on your part will be quickly detected if you are given a position, and this will not help your case.

I may as well tell you, here and now, that there always has been a place, and there always will be a place, for a man or a woman who has ability and sincerely follows the habit of rendering more service and better service than that for which he or she is paid. No matter how many business depressions may come and go, there will always be a place for the person willing to render such service. Moreover, the rendering of service in this spirit is the surest way to promotion.

If you grade yourself accurately on each of the 17 principles of success and discover after completing your grading that your percentage is too low on any of the principles, you will have made a valuable discovery about yourself which, if acted upon, will enable you to prepare yourself to bridge whatever weakness you may possess. This grading should prove to be a profitable checkup on yourself, and it might well turn out to be the most important turning point of your life, providing it brings you face-to-face with yourself and portrays your personality as it really exists.

You need this self-analysis, whether you wish to use it to procure a position or not. Everyone needs such a checkup, and especially during these times, when so many people are trying to get something for nothing, and thousands are killing off their initiative, self-confidence, and definiteness of purpose to go on government relief. If you are willing to throw yourself on charity and live without rendering useful service, this analysis will do you no good. It is intended only for the person who wishes to be self-determining and who truly is willing to earn whatever he demands of life.

After preparing the copy for your letter of application and your personal grading on the 17 principles, if you have a feeling that your case has not been properly prepared, you may send a copy of your letter and grading to the author and either he or one of his assistants will look over your work and offer such suggestions for its improvement as may seem to be needed. Under no circumstances, however, will the author or his assistants undertake to write the copy for these documents.

You now have in your hands, in this simple plan, the finest of all possible methods of selling yourself into any position for which you are qualified. The psychology back of the plan has been tried in thousands of cases, and I have never known it to fail to produce the desired results. The *spirit* of the plan is far more important than the mere wording of the application. Let me emphasize this important truth: It is so seldom that any person applies for a position on this sort of basis, that those who do so benefit by the law of contrast. Not one executive out of a hundred would refuse to investigate the merits of a person offering to work on the basis of demonstrating his ability before trying to collect pay. Why, do you know that some of the largest corporations in the world have regularly employed talent scouts out searching for young men and young women with just such a spirit of willingness to render service as the one here described? When such a person is found, he or she is quickly employed, and the gates to quick advancement are eternally left ajar.

One final word: If you find the 17 principles helpful in procuring an opportunity to demonstrate your ability, think how much more helpful they may be if you make intelligent application of these principles after you get your foot inside the door! In other words, do not stop by using these universal principles of success to induce someone to give you a position, but go further and so use these principles that you can collect whatever you want or demand of life, as effectively as Henry Ford has used them. Read the grading of Henry Ford on the 17 principles, as given in another chapter, then compare yourself with Ford on each of these grades and you may discover wherein you differ from Ford. The chances are a thousand to one that the difference between you and Ford is not so much one of intelligence or education, as it is in application and use of these 17 principles of success, and the chances are equally great that you could so apply these principles in your chosen calling that you may go as far in your field as Ford has in his.

> There are no lazy men. What may appear to be a lazy man is only an unfortunate person who has not found the work for which he is best suited.

It is well worth remembering that the customer is the most important factor in any business. If you don't think so, try to get along without him for a while.

III

What You May Learn from Henry Ford

EVERYONE has heard of Henry Ford, and most people know that he began at the bottom in poverty and illiteracy and by his own efforts climbed to the top. But few know, however, of the principles by which the great industrialist gave himself spiritual and economic freedom. Part 3 of this book has been devoted to a complete analysis of Ford and the method by which he became self-determining. The story has been used as a simple explanation of one of the greatest selling achievements in the history of our country. It tells not only how Ford sold himself into power and plenty, but also how he has managed to remain in that enviable position despite subtle and powerful attempts to dethrone him.

> The educated man is the man who has learned how to get everything he needs without violating the rights of his fellow men. Education comes from within; you get it by struggle and effort and thought.

21

Singleness of Purpose

21

Singleness of Purpose

FOR more than a quarter of a century, I have watched the rise of Henry Ford from poverty to wealth and affluence. At the suggestion of Andrew Carnegie, I adopted Mr. Ford as my teacher many years ago.

Once every year for 20 years, I analyzed Mr. Ford carefully, point by point. I believe I have made discoveries about him through these annual analyses that have never been mentioned by any of his biographers. I shall describe these discoveries.

Henry Ford has been the source of more useful knowledge than all the other men whom I have ever met. I am no hero worshipper, but I am appreciative of the opportunity of observing the efforts of the most successful industrialists of America and especially those of Henry Ford, because his activities have been so extensive that he has encountered and conquered the majority of obstacles that obstruct the path of human beings.

Mr. Ford has been my "Exhibit A." Through his achievements, I tested the fundamental principles of success that went into the building of my success philosophy. Without the privilege of observing and studying him in his stupendous industrial operations, my work on the philosophy would have required at least another 25 years, if, in fact, it could have been completed at all.

This statement is made in explanation of the credit given Mr. Ford as being the man from whom I have acquired more useful knowledge than from all others combined. Mr. Ford is not my idea of a perfect man, but his fine qualities and business acumen far outweigh his defects.

Henry Ford has taught me the value of selecting a definite major purpose as a life goal at which to aim and to which all other aims and purposes are subordinated.

Mr. Ford has worked with a central purpose mind for more than a quarter of a century. That purpose is to manufacture and sell a dependable automobile within the price range of the farmer and the working man.

Everyone who has ever heard the name of Henry Ford knows what his definite major purpose is and what it has been for the past 30 years. Not everyone, however, has interpreted correctly the part that the selection of this definite purpose has assumed in the accumulation of the Ford fortune. Few have endeavored to emulate Mr. Ford by selecting and pursuing persistently a single purpose as he has done. I shall be eternally grateful to Mr. Ford, because this one lesson alone has yielded me the fundamental basis of a sound philosophy of success.

Had I not been influenced by Henry Ford, I would probably never have paid the price in struggle and hardship and sacrifice necessary for the completion of my research. All down the years during which I was engaged in building that philosophy, Henry Ford's outstanding tenacity of purpose served as a mighty influence, forcing me on, when I would, otherwise, have quit.

Such useful service as may be rendered by my writings should be, in the main, credited to the influence of Henry Ford because he contributed more than all the other men of achievement whom I have observed.

Mr. Ford was responsible for my meeting Dr. Alexander Graham Bell, Dr. Elmer R. Gates, Thomas A. Edison, and Luther Burbank, who, in turn, led me to the discovery of the vast possibilities that lie hidden in the subconscious mind. Through many years of experimentation, both independently and in collaboration with these men, I made discoveries about the potentialities of the subconscious mind that enabled me to understand to a certain extent the workings of that mysterious power. Such help as I may be able to render other people can be traced directly to what I have learned from Henry Ford, and especially to his influence upon me in the matter of adopting and persistently following a definite central purpose in life.

It seems to me more than a mere coincidence that I should have been led to the discovery of facts of vital importance in connection with the psychology of singleness of purpose, as the result of having acquired such a purpose through observation of Henry Ford. This fact has caused me to recognize the truth that every great discovery and every noteworthy achievement of man may be traced to the influence of some other person. Sometimes, we neglect to give credit where credit is due; at other times, we fail to interpret the cause of achievement, and again we prefer to salve our own ego by choosing to believe that we are the great creators!

In my own case, I prefer to state frankly that whatever useful knowledge I may possess was acquired from other and more brilliant people.

The Psychology of a Definite Central Purpose

As briefly as possible, I wish to describe what takes place in the mind when one adopts and follows a definite central purpose, viz:

1. A definite purpose, when mixed with faith in one's ability to achieve the object of that purpose and held as a dominating desire in one's conscious mind, is picked up by the subconscious mind and used as a pattern or blueprint by which that purpose is transmuted into its physical equivalent.
2. The medium through which a definite purpose is picked up by the subconscious mind is autosuggestion or self-suggestion. A strong, burning purpose, held persistently in the conscious mind, will induce action by the principle of autosuggestion.
3. The subconscious mind is the intermediary by which the thoughts of the finite mind of man are communicated to and mixed with infinite intelligence.
4. Infinite intelligence, through some strange principle that has not yet been isolated by science, has a tendency to transmute into its physical equivalent any desire that is transmitted to the subconscious mind and mixed with the emotion of faith.
5. A definite central purpose when transmitted to the subconscious mind with the emotion of faith is worked out or transmuted into its physical equivalent through the same principle by which prayer is realized (when it is realized).
6. The subconscious mind is the medium or intermediary through which mental processes of prayer may be, and sometimes are, transmuted into their spiritual equivalent and by infinite intelligence transmuted into their physical equivalent.
7. A definite central purpose when mixed with faith in its attainment is the equivalent of prayer!
8. No thought or prayer will be recognized or acted upon by the subconscious mind, except those that have been mixed with emotion or feeling. Thoughts produced through cold reason or will are not recognized or acted upon by the subconscious mind.

In these eight paragraphs have been described as briefly as possible the sum and substance of what I have learned about the working of the subconscious mind. These discoveries I owe, indirectly at least, to the influence of Henry Ford. I am convinced that Mr. Ford's stupendous achievements are due to his understanding and application of the principles I have here described. I have as evidence of this fact his own word, as well as my observations of his efforts and the results he has obtained. Henry Ford's financial achievement has not been due to luck or accident. Nor has he done anything that cannot be duplicated by any other man of reasonable intelligence through application of the same principles he has used.

Biologically, Henry Ford has no advantage over any other man of average intelligence. His superior achievements have been due entirely to his knowledge and use of superior principles with which the average man is not familiar. I am convinced that no man can attain to noteworthy success in any calling without consciously or unconsciously organizing his efforts and working with definite plans toward a definite goal!

Singleness of purpose is essential for the efficient organization of one's efforts. Division of attention, purpose, and effort render one's efforts fruitless and ineffective. This is where many people fall down but don't know the reason why.

The very act of definitely reaching a decision in one's own mind to attain a definite objective renders the attainment of that objective comparatively easy. A firm decision to reach a definite goal brings that goal within the range of attainment. Knowledge of this great truth has been priceless to me. That knowledge was acquired from my observation of the methods used by Henry Ford. In my observation of Mr. Ford's methods, I have not been alone. Thousands of people have made the same observation. Perhaps only a few of them have interpreted it the same way I did. My different interpretation is due to the fact that I am a student of life and of men. Most of my time has been devoted to studying effects by analyzing their causes. Thousands of people have observed that Mr. Ford has made himself fabulously wealthy. Few have looked for the underlying reason. Thirsty for knowledge, I sought and found the cause of the acquisition of that fortune.

> If you have tried and met with defeat, if you have planned and watched your plans as they were crushed before your eyes, just remember that the greatest men in all history were the products of courage, and courage, you know, is born in the cradle of adversity.

22

Persistence

HENRY Ford has taught me the value of persistence!

I have watched him start from scratch and fight his way through opposition and past obstacles that would have floored the majority of men in the very first round of battle. I have seen him whip poverty, illiteracy, and ignorance. Without persistence, he would never have surmounted these grave difficulties.

In all my observation of men who have made enviable places for themselves, I do not recall having heard of a man who planned his work and worked his plan as persistently as Henry Ford has done.

His persistence is not of the ordinary brand. It is of the quality that knows no such possibility as defeat!

I have never known a man who could make decisions more quickly nor stick to decisions more persistently than Mr. Ford. While visiting in the home of George S. Parker, the manufacturer of the famous Parker fountain pen, I met one of Mr. Parker's neighbors who was formerly chief engineer in the Ford plant at Detroit. He told me of an incident that is typical of Mr. Ford's bulldog persistence. The engineering staff drew up and reduced to blueprints elaborate plans for improving the rear axle construction of the original Model T car. After the plans were ready, Mr. Ford was invited into the engineering room to look them over.

One by one, the engineers explained their reasons for the change. Mr. Ford listened without saying a word until the last man had his say, then, walking over to the table, he tapped the blueprints and said,

"Gentlemen, you know that we are now selling more cars than we can possibly deliver. We are working 24 hours a day. As long as this condition lasts, we are not going to make this or any other change in the Ford automobile."

The meeting was at an end. Mr. Ford turned and walked out of the room without further ceremony. That was typical of Henry Ford's way of following through with his definite central purpose.

In later years, competition began to cut in on the Ford business so keenly that a change in body design and other changes became imperative. With great reluctance, it is said, Mr. Ford gave orders to his engineering department to begin work on plans for improvements. Out of those plans grew the Model A, which was the first car Ford built that had any semblance of beauty. He made that change very slowly. In fact, he made it too slowly, because competition had taken such strides that he has not yet fully recovered the ground lost by the delay.

Later, it became obvious that the public wanted still further improvements. This time, Mr. Ford moved more rapidly and turned out the present model, with the eight-cylinder feature and other improvements in design. When Henry Ford changes his plans, he usually does so with great deliberation. It is a part of his nature to work his plans with such persistence that they succeed, even though more practical plans might be devised. Mr. Ford is not the type of man who yields to opposition, nor is he easily moved by criticism. Persistence—to the degree that he carries it—may be a fault, but too little or no persistence is a far graver fault.

Persistence requires courage, especially if it is used as the foundation of a new idea. Most people do not accept new ideas quickly. Moreover, most people discourage men who undertake to create anything new. Without persistence, the average man is apt to yield to criticism and quit before his plans have been matured.

In 1908, I watched the Wright Brothers through three days of tenacious effort to get an airplane off the ground. They finally got it into the air. It circled around two or three times and came down with a crash. An old man, who was sitting on the running board of my car, emptied his mouth of tobacco juice, looked up at me and said, "It is just as I expected. If God Almighty had intended for man to fly, He would have given him wings. They'll never make them thar things fly." The old boy saw nothing but failure for the airplane. I saw only temporary defeat. Even at that early date, observation of Henry Ford's persistence had profited me.

The majority of the people of the United States criticized Theodore Roosevelt when he began the Panama Canal program. General opinion held that it was a fool's mission. It was pointed out that two unsuccessful attempts had been made to build the canal, and the prophecy was that the United States government would waste a lot of money and the venture would end in failure. Under the able direction of General Goethals, the plans for the Panama Canal were carried through with persistence. The investment proved to be one of the best ever made by this country.

The bankers of America criticized the late Woodrow Wilson when he asked Congress to pass the Federal Reserve Banking Act. They prophesied catastrophe for the banking business if the bill passed and fought it to a standstill. Now, only a few years later, the service that this system has rendered the banking fraternity has proved itself invaluable. Wilson's persistence proved to be worth more than the bankers' skepticism.

Persistence is one of the attributes of great leadership. Without it, enduring leadership is impossible. Persistence is enduring and stubborn. The persistent man with a poor plan stands a better chance of winning than the man with a perfect plan who hesitates and wavers in carrying it out.

Persistence is one of Ford's most prominent qualities! He applies it almost to the point of obstinacy. And because of this quality of persistence, Ford recognizes temporary defeat, but *does not* accept it as failure! All men who have the quality of persistence have also the advantage of being able to distinguish the difference between temporary defeat and failure. They know that temporary defeat can be made to serve as a stepping-stone to a higher rung on the ladder of achievement. Men who lack persistence have not this knowledge. They quit at the slightest provocation, even before reaching the stage of temporary defeat.

23

Faith

HENRY Ford has taught me the value of faith!

Without faith, one is apt to be lacking also in persistence. Faith is the very foundation of persistence.

What Is Faith?

Faith is a state of mind that enables one to visualize one's central purpose or one's minor plans and purposes as achieved even before beginning their pursuit.

Faith is a state of mind that can be induced through intensity of desire backed by persistent suggestion to the subconscious mind that the object of that desire shall become fully realized and attained.

Faith begins to take the place of doubt when one recognizes the existence and availability of infinite intelligence.

Faith multiplies itself through use! The more one relies upon it, the more pronounced it becomes.

Faith is nature's elixir through the use of which nature enables man to transmute the impulse of thought into a skyscraper of riches or a hovel of poverty.

Through his demonstration of faith, Henry Ford has taught me to work with whatever tools were at hand and not to wait until the time is right, before beginning to translate my desires into their physical equivalent. I have discovered that the right time in the fullest and most literal sense of the term never comes to any person. If we wait until all conditions are just right before beginning to translate our central purpose into concrete form, we will never begin!

The time to start is *now*.

Analysis of Mr. Ford shows that he believes in, and practices the habit of, starting where he stands. During the early days of his experience in the automobile industry, he was forced to follow this habit. The time was not just right when he began to experiment with his horseless buggy contraption, but he went ahead with it anyway. In fact, he followed the habit so literally that it once cost him his position while he was working during the day and experimenting with his automobile at night. Mr. Ford was cramped for money during the early days of his career but he substituted faith for money and, miracle of miracles, he discovered that the substitute worked!

During the early days of my experience, my path was beset by enemies who tried with enduring persistence to undermine my reputation and destroy my chances of completing and taking to the world my success philosophy. I discovered, as the result of the influence of Mr. Ford, that persistence is no match for faith. I went ahead with my labor, looking neither to the right nor the left, never stopping to reply to my critics nor to explain to my friends, relying entirely upon my faith in the soundness of my plan to take the place of explanations. I have not been disappointed.

Beginning in 1929, a great calamity overtook the people of the world through what is commonly known as the Depression. Banks closed their doors by the thousands. Men were thrown out of employment by the millions. Great fortunes faded into nothing by the scores. Leaders in business and finance, industry, politics, and religion showed the white feather and went into seclusion by the thousands. Chaos and pandemonium prevailed and continues to prevail on a widespread scale. Through all this demonstration of fear, Henry Ford was one of the few leaders who stuck to his post and went ahead with faith in the future of America. While others were talking about the return of prosperity, Mr. Ford was digging in and demonstrating prosperity. When other automobile manufacturers were laying off men by the thousands, Mr. Ford took them on in similar proportions. Only faith can carry a man through in times like those experienced in 1931 and 1932.

Mr. Ford was not in the least disturbed by the Depression. While thousands of small-minded men and women were madly rushing to the banks and drawing out their money, forcing the banks to close their doors, Mr. Ford, who had as much money in banks as any thousand men, let his money remain there and went about his business as calmly and as confidently as if nothing unusual had been happening. That required faith. Henry Ford has faith and, because he has it, he also has a fortune.

Faith is the master of all obstacles that beset the path of man with the lone exception of death. Perhaps even death might be conquered by faith! Who knows? Who is willing to trust faith far enough to find out what are its limitations or if it has any limitations?

The tenets of the greatest religions are all grounded in faith. Jesus Christ in performing the miracles credited to him, did so solely through faith. If faith is the hub of religion, if it constitutes the sum and substance of Christ's philosophy, should not this fact serve as a tip to men who are concerned about ways and means of succeeding in business?

We all have hopes and wishes, but these do not and cannot take the place of faith!

If Henry Ford had only hoped or wished to translate his central purpose into reality, he would have gone the way that hundreds of other automobile manufacturers have gone since he started in business. He has succeeded in the face of more obstacles and opposition than the average man has ever known because he has had faith!

Every year, some wiseacre predicts that Ford will overstep himself; that Wall Street will take his business from him. Meanwhile, Ford continues to follow his own course and build new plans.

Mr. Ford *knows,* and knows that he knows, that his faith will carry him through any business emergency with which he may meet. Consequently, he rides on the waves of emergency instead of being submerged by them.

The intelligentsia belittle Henry Ford because he is not "educated." Few, if any of them, have accumulated a billion dollars. Ford knows how to get whatever he wants of a monetary or material nature, or its equivalent, without violating the rights of others. That is more education than that of which 99 percent of the people of the world can boast. Ford can get whatever he wants because he has faith! Others could do the same if they had Ford's capacity for faith!

An educated person is one who knows how to get everything he wants without violating the rights of others. What more than this could a man with six degrees after his name accomplish? No one who knows Mr. Ford will question the statement that he is well qualified to acquire every material thing he wants. He has a definite central purpose and has succeeded in achieving that purpose. What more than this could the faculty of Yale, Harvard, Princeton, or any other university accomplish?

Any fool can ask questions that the best informed man cannot answer, but no fool can whip poverty and illiteracy and ignorance and accumulate a fortune of a billion dollars by rendering useful service.

Mr. Ford is a man of education. He has learned by meditation, thought, and experimentation that man has no limitations, within reason, beyond those that he sets up in his own mind. Mr. Ford has achieved more than most men because he has removed the limitations by which most men permit their minds to be bound.

Henry Ford was reared on a farm. He laid the foundation for his abiding faith by observing the orderly, organized fashion in which nature moves. Looking up into the sky, he saw the millions of stars and planets moving in space with order and precision. He gathered from what he saw the conclusion that nature works always with a purpose, producing from the soil everything that man needs and that the production is abundant and efficient.

When the Depression got underway, Mr. Ford observed, as any other man who thinks might have done, that there was no depression in the realm of nature. He saw the same sun shining down on the earth warming the roots of the grass and causing the seed in the ground to germinate. He saw that nature went ahead with her business in 1930 and 1931, precisely as she had done prior to the Wall Street crash. From these observations Mr. Ford deduced the fact that business depressions are man-made. From past experience he knew that whatever man makes he can unmake. Because he saw and believed, Henry Ford went right ahead with his business, knowing that the storm of the Depression would pass and that harmony would come out of the chaos when men had regained their sense of balance.

And we all know that he guessed right:

It is impossible to defeat the man who has an abiding faith!

If one plan fails, he will create another to take its place, knowing that it was only the plan that had failed. The man who has this faith is educated, no matter if he never saw the inside of a schoolhouse. Henry Ford knows, as few men know, that all success is based upon confidence and faith! He also knows that the prolonged business depression grew out of man's loss of these two prerequisites of success.

Those who criticize Henry Ford might well spend their time studying and emulating him instead, despite the fact that he has many short-comings. There was a time when I, like others, was inclined to criticize him. Now, I am trying in my humble way to apply to my calling some of the principles that have made Henry Ford one of the most conspicuous figures in the entire history of American industry. Of all the men who have accumulated great fortunes in America, I know of none from whose record of achievement one may learn more than from Ford. To me, he is one of the two most interesting men in the world, the other being Mahatma Gandhi, the East Indian patriot.

Incidentally, Mr. Ford and the Mahatma have many qualities in common, among them abiding faith. Through his great capacity for faith, Gandhi has induced over 200,000,000 people to coordinate their minds in a spirit of enduring harmony. That is an achievement the world has never before seen.

Faith is a rare quality. All who have it are worthy of study and emulation.

More than once during his career, Mr. Ford has had to match talents with men who represented combined power through wealth. Every time, he has come out on top. His faith has always proved to be stronger than other men's cunning. Some of the Wall Street bankers have had occasion to remember this from their experience with Mr. Ford. He has held his own, despite the efforts of shrewd men to rob him of his business, because he had faith in his ability to do so. Henry Ford has met with defeat many times, but always he has armed himself with the knowledge gained by defeat. Out of that knowledge he has constructed a bulwark of self-defense which, so far, no man or group of men has been able to penetrate.

> Any man may become great by doing the commonplace things of life in a great spirit, with a genuine desire to be of helpful service to others, regardless of his calling.

24

Decision

HENRY Ford has taught me the value of prompt and definite decision!

By comparing his methods with those of other men, I have observed that men who are slow to reach decisions and quick to modify them if and when they are made, seldom achieve noteworthy success in any calling. I have learned from Mr. Ford's methods this axiom:

"When in doubt, do something, even if it is no more than to walk around the block and think what to do."

Inspired by the stupendous activities of Henry Ford, I have learned that indecision is one of the major causes of much of the misery that people experience; that indecision leads to disappointment and self-imposed punishment, which one experiences from no other cause.

Indecision in the time of emergency destroys whatever capacity one may possess for leadership. Shortly after the Depression began, I saw signs of indecision among leaders in practically every business and profession. Men, who under normal circumstances would act quickly and definitely, pulled the covers over their heads and quaked, doing nothing. They apparently adopted as their motto, "When in doubt, do nothing."

The man who reaches decisions quickly probably makes more mistakes than the man who reaches them slowly. He certainly makes more mistakes than the man who never reaches a decision. Let it be remembered in his behalf, however, that the man of quick and definite decision can make mistakes in 9 out of every 10 decisions and still accomplish immeasurably greater results in the tenth decision than the man who either reaches no decision or permits others to decide for him.

What is a decision? It is a completed thought! Men of decision are of necessity men who think. The act of reaching a decision involves the principle of accurate thought, a process of which the majority of people are wholly ignorant.

One of the strangest discoveries I have made about people is the extent to which people will go to avoid reaching decisions for themselves. Most people will work much harder to avoid thinking than they would have to work by thinking.

The man who understands how to reach decisions intelligently is not only the master of his own destiny, but he may also control the destinies of many others. Let us, therefore, analyze the principle through which decisions may be reached intelligently, viz:

1. Before reaching a decision, be sure you have at hand *all* the facts available in connection with, or affecting that decision.
2. Learn to distinguish the difference between facts and mere hearsay, even though some effort may be required to separate the two.
3. Learn to make a distinction between important and unimportant facts.
4. When it is impossible to avail yourself of all the facts you need in making a decision, use your past experience and your commonsense and supply theory for the missing facts. All decisions reached in this way should be made with mental reservations and should be subject to immediate change if later it is discovered that the assumed facts were not correct.

These four simple rules will, if followed as a habit, be helpful not only in reaching decisions promptly, but in reaching them intelligently as well.

Decisions based upon guesswork, when facts are obtainable, are inexcusable. Henry Ford does practically no guesswork deciding! The same might be said of any man who thinks for himself.

Opinions are the most plentiful and the cheapest things on earth. Everyone has a flock of them. Moreover, practically everyone gives them away freely. No one has a right to an opinion on any subject unless that opinion has been reached by careful thought and analysis of facts or that which one believes to be facts. Most opinions are worth just what is asked for them by those who give them out: *nothing!*

Every normal person has been endowed by nature with the power of reason. The reasoning faculty provides man with the capacity to separate facts from fiction. In the majority of men, this faculty becomes practically atrophied through disuse. In Henry Ford, it has developed and grown strong and accurate through use!

Some readers will want to remind me of some of Mr. Ford's inaccurate decisions. Practically all who read this book will probably want to call my attention to his attack on the Jews and his famous "Peace Ship" journey during the World War. A few will be inclined to ask, "What have you to say about these decisions?"

I have a lot to say about them. In fact, I have more than space will permit me to say. In the first place, Mr. Ford's attacks on the Jews proves that he is one of those men who has the courage and the sense of fairness to reverse decisions that have been found to be unsound. There is no guarantee of good judgment in every decision; every human must run the risk of errors and poor judgment.

So far as the Peace Ship decision is concerned, I am not so sure that it was as weak as some believe it to have been. It did not "bring the boys out of the trenches by Christmas" as it was intended to do, but it probably had the effect of causing millions of people to stop, think, and wonder what the war was all about, and if it did this, it was more than justified. Perhaps that was all Mr. Ford really intended it to do.

Suppose both of these decisions were weak and ill-advised, what of it? Two weak decisions out of the thousands of decisions a man of Mr. Ford's achievements must have made is not a bad record, is it? Henry Ford is not infallible. No man is! We all make mistakes, but the main trouble with most of us is that we do not make enough mistakes, because we neither think nor act until we are forced to do so. Personally, I would rather try and fail a thousand times than to fail by never trying!

The immortal Emerson said, "Consistency is the hobgoblin of small minds." Mr. Ford may not always have been consistent; I am sure that he has not been, but he has whipped poverty and accumulated a fortune without violating the rights of others. In addition, he has made some huge fortunes for those associated with him and employed at top wages hundreds of thousands of men. These are facts, and they are the soundest evidence that Henry Ford is an accurate thinker. Sound thinkers are always men of decision!

25

Sportsmanship

HENRY Ford has taught me the value of good sportsmanship! For over a quarter of a century, I have watched Mr. Ford master fear of criticism by accepting defeat as graciously as he has accepted success. I have never heard of his striking back at his enemies or complaining in any way about their conduct toward him. In his disagreement with the Dodge Brothers, he extricated himself from an embarrassing business situation with the least possible damage to his foes. If he ever gave out any press interviews about that transaction, I have never heard of it.

Many men went into the Ford enterprise during its infancy either by investing a few thousand dollars, or their personal services, or both, and came out later with huge fortunes. Mr. Ford did not try to stop them from leaving when they were ready, nor did he try to stop them from taking out of the business wealth far out of proportion to anything that they put into it. From the start of the business, Henry Ford has shown himself to be a real sportsman, remarks about his cold-bloodedness notwithstanding.

Sometimes, I hear some former Ford agent or salesman or employee speaking about Mr. Ford's ruthlessness toward his men. So far as I have been able to obtain the facts, his ruthlessness has consisted of his having worked out ways and means of making men become efficient despite themselves.

I am sure that before the saturation point was reached in the automobile industry about 1930, Mr. Ford kept his distributors stepping faster than some of them wanted to move. Perhaps many of them needed this sort of discipline, as, in fact, most of us do. In fairness to Mr. Ford, it should be remembered that competition in his class of automobile became very keen about the time the Chevrolet attained its peak of distribution. Mr. Ford knew that increased activity on the part of his distributors was necessary to meet this competition. It should also be remembered that any plan Mr. Ford inaugurated to step up his distributors helped them as much or more than it did him. Obviously, the more cars he forced them to sell, the more profits they made. Far from being evidence of cold-bloodedness, his efforts to produce and distribute cars with efficiency should have been accepted by his distributors as a real service.

Mr. Ford is not the hail-fellow-well-met type of man. He does not have a flexible personality and his disposition is decidedly unyielding and firm in carrying out his plans, but with it all he is a sportsman because he has had uppermost in mind the thought of building and selling a car that would serve the average man efficiently at a price within his means. I have never heard Mr. Ford called dishonest; I doubt that anyone else has. The most that his enemies have said about him is that he is ruthless. When one stops to consider the scale on which Mr. Ford operates his business, it can be easily understood why he cannot grant every demand made upon him. Efficiency presupposes a definite business policy and definite plans for carrying out that policy. Mr. Ford has always operated under such a policy and plan. Had he not done so, he would not have been the success he is today.

At almost the very outset of his business career, Henry Ford saw, as but few others have seen, the stupid inefficiency of men who manufacture and sell merchandise. He made up his mind not to become a victim of this sort of stupidity. He realized that he was operating in the midst of a machine age in which the law of the survival of the fittest had to prevail. He knew, of course, that fitness meant efficiency of every man and with remarkable success he created plans through which that fitness was obtained.

None of the elements of good sportsmanship are lacking in such a policy. When a firm carries 150,000 on its payrolls and its purchases of raw materials run into the millions of dollars annually, either efficiency must be obtained or failure will soon overtake the business.

Many men who were considered better sportsmen than Mr. Ford did not survive the Depression. From this I feel safe in drawing the conclusion that there is a certain laxity that sometimes passes for good sportsmanship which is, in reality, inefficiency.

Mr. Ford has always paid the top scale in wages. On the other hand, he has managed to get value in services. There is nothing unsportsmanlike about that unless I have totally misjudged the meaning of the word.

Professional charity workers have been heard to berate Mr. Ford on the ground that he would not give to charity! I suspect that an element of selfishness entered into such complaints. A man who gives profitable and regular employment to as many thousands of men as Henry Ford has done, at wages and under working conditions superior to the average, is doing directly and efficiently what professional charity workers are trying to do through direct gifts. Mr. Ford believes that the best form of charity is not to destroy a man's self-respect by giving him something, but to place a man in the path of opportunity to be self-determining through his own labor. That, in my opinion, is the most practical form of charity. It is also good sportsmanship.

As a matter of fact, Mr. Ford has become fabulously rich by helping other men to earn and to accumulate more through his methods of efficiency than they could possibly have earned or accumulated without his aid. His efficiency has, in turn, become the efficiency of those who profit by distributing his automobile or working in his factories.

In all this talk about Henry Ford's ruthlessness, I suspect that envy has had its part. It is the nature of man to envy and to express his envy toward the man who succeeds.

I believe the business world has reached the stage at which it must and will pattern after Henry Ford in many respects rather than criticize his methods. The successful business of the future is going to be managed in a manner similar to Henry Ford's policy of giving the consuming public the utmost possible for its money. To do this, the merchant and the manufacturer must eliminate waste and the high costs of poor management.

Not only business and industry can learn from Henry Ford; educators might profit by observing his methods. His business policy could, if applied to education, shorten the years now spent in schoolrooms in the study of abstract subjects that are of no practical value to the student.

Politicians also might well afford to study and to apply the Ford methods of efficiency. It has been said and, I believe, conservatively, that Henry Ford could run the United States government at a saving of no less than $500,000,000 a year, if he could be given a free hand. If he were the manager of the exchequer, I have no doubt he might cut out at least half of the red tape and the overlapping and sometimes totally unnecessary positions. Of course, those on whose toes he stepped would put up a howl, but it is safe to say that no complaints would be heard from the taxpayers who support the government.

When you hear someone berating Henry Ford for lack of sportsmanship, make careful inquiry into the complaint. It is probable that it comes either from one who has been pinched by Mr. Ford's efficiency or one who is not in sympathy with any plan that forces people to give value received.

26

Budgeting of Time and Expenditures

HENRY Ford has taught me the value of budgeting my time and my expenditures.

By observing Mr. Ford, I discovered that men who become financially independent achieve this desirable end by organizing their time to make it yield a greater income. I am convinced that no man who works for wages can become financially independent merely by saving a portion of his wages. The majority of men waste more time out of every 24 hours than they efficiently devote to labor. This is particularly true of the so-called white collar or salaried type of man and the small businessman.

Since the close of the World War, the waste of time upon the part of men in these two classes has been stupendous. The waste often takes the form of intemperance and takes count of its victims not only in terms of money that they do not earn, but in health as well. Wasted time takes a yearly toll in America in astounding proportions. There are some who will complain that they must have time for relaxation for their health's sake. To these, I would offer the suggestion that Henry Ford maintains good health without wasting time in dissipation of the kind mentioned.

Mr. Ford takes time to relax. The major difference between Mr. Ford's method of relaxation and that of the average time-waster is that the latter's dissipation results in deleterious effects on health and mind, while

Mr. Ford finds relaxation through sources that enrich his mind and make no inroads upon his health.

I am neither Mr. Ford's biographer nor his propagandist. I am merely one who has observed his habits and his business policy for over a quarter of a century and profited by them.

Self-discipline, through an appropriate and strictly enforced budget of time and expenditures, is an essential for financial independence. It is a price that the majority of men will not pay. That may, in part, account for the overwhelmingly large number of people who never attain financial independence. Most of us prefer to look at Henry Ford in the hour of his triumph and say, "How lucky!" Few of us have the stamina to follow the course that he has taken, even if we take the trouble to analyze the cause of his "luck." I have made it my business to analyze him as closely and as accurately as circumstances would permit and have made discoveries about his methods of living and his business policies that have been most helpful to me.

Several pages of the manuscript for this book are being written during a very hot day in June. Just a little while ago, an acquaintance called and offered to take me for a boat trip. I was tempted to go with him, but on the wall in front of me hung a copy of my daily time budget plainly indicating that I could not go. Was I disappointed? Not in the least, because I like the work in which I am engaged and make it serve in the place of many forms of recreation in which I might indulge. Instead of worrying because my habit of self-discipline often deprives me of a fine opportunity to waste time, I look out into a world that is peopled with men and women who need the sort of practical inspiration which, it is hoped, may be found in my writings and return thanks once again to Henry Ford for having caused me to discipline myself thus through a strictly enforced budget of my time.

Not only am I as happy now as I was before I began to budget my time, but I am far more contented because I have learned that enduring happiness comes from rendering service that is helpful to other people.

Therefore, a rigidly enforced time and expenditure budget not only leads to financial independence, but, more important, it leads to happiness.

> No man can rise to fame and fortune without carrying others along with him. It simply cannot be done.

27

Humility

HENRY Ford has taught me humility of heart!

His habits, his style of living, his attitude toward other people are the same today as they were when he was bound down by poverty. Success has not gone to his head. That which may appear to be austerity on his part is no more than his lack of flexibility of personality.

Many important men are like that.

Mr. Ford has no false notions about his importance! He leads a simple life and is not above association with those who are less fortunate financially. He is not a fluent conversationalist. In fact, he is just the opposite and for this reason has unjustly earned the reputation of being frigid and self-centered.

I think, too, that Mr. Ford has attained some of his shyness toward people from a sort of necessary system of self-defense behind which he has had to hide from those who have sought conferences with him since he came into prominence. The fact that annually more than 30,000 people write him, begging for financial help in one form or another, gives some little idea of why he has found it necessary to shut himself in a shell. But these letters are not entirely wasted. He has them baled and sold as old paper!

By and large, Mr. Ford has proved himself to be a man of unusual poise. Nothing discourages him and nothing unduly elates him.

His humility grows out of his understanding and use of the intangible laws of nature. His close association with Thomas Edison, Luther

Burbank, John Burroughs, and others of their caliber, indicates with what reverence he considers men who deal with the laws of nature. I think perhaps it was in a large part his association with these scientists and naturalists that is responsible for his humility.

Henry Ford knows that there is an infinite intelligence that permeates every atom of matter and every unit of energy and fills all space throughout the universe. He knows, too, that this intelligence may be induced to aid man in the solution of his problems, if, and when, man adapts himself to it. Because Mr. Ford has remained humble in heart, he has not found it difficult to tune in on the forces of infinite intelligence. Because of that humility, he has never been fettered and bound by the thing called pride, which frequently spoils the usefulness of men. Infinite intelligence and pride cannot be found together. Many men who have attained financial power have learned this truth too late in life. Pride is often only conceit! If Mr. Ford has any conceit in his makeup, I have never heard anyone speak of it nor observed any evidences of it. Conceit usually demands its chance to be heard. Conceit and humility are opposites. Where one is predominant, the other is conspicuous by its total absence.

Perhaps not all who will read this book have analyzed Mr. Ford as a humble man. Adverse propaganda concerning his activities has misled many people as to his true nature. His own attitude of aloofness and silence has not helped correct this impression.

All men who have a keen understanding of nature's laws are humble at heart. I had the privilege of knowing the habits and tendencies of John Burroughs and Thomas Edison even better than I knew those of Mr. Ford. Each of these men was blessed by humility of heart. Men who know, and know that they know, are always more humble than those who have but a smattering of knowledge.

> Make excuses for the shortcomings of others if you wish, but hold yourself to a strict accountability if you would attain leadership in any undertaking.

28

The Habit of Doing More than One Is Paid to Do

HENRY Ford has taught me that it pays to render more service and better service than one is paid to render.

I have learned this great truth from others as well as from Mr. Ford, but he has proved its soundness in more different ways than any other person whom I have had the privilege of observing. Moreover, Mr. Ford has proved that this principle may be applied by an employer in his dealings with his employees, just as effectively and profitably as it can be applied by an individual who works for an employer.

Mr. Ford's first serious major disagreement with his business associates grew out of their lack of understanding of this principle. Back in the early days of his career before the famous Model T made its appearance, some of Mr. Ford's associates wanted him to build a much larger and more expensive type of car, pointing out to him what they believed to be the advantage of a larger car in bigger profits per car. Mr. Ford saw the situation from an entirely different viewpoint. His notion was then, and has remained so ever since, that the utmost value should go into a small car that could be sold at the lowest possible price. On that policy he has built the Ford reputation and the Ford fortune.

When other automobile manufacturers raise the price of their cars, Mr. Ford lowers the price of his. When other employers lower wages, Mr. Ford usually raises them. His business policy is about as perfect a contradiction of that of other businessmen as one could find. The soundness of his policy can be measured by the degree of success he has enjoyed under its application.

In analyzing financial reports on the automobile industry, I have noticed that most of them contain a notice at the bottom to the effect that "the above report is exclusive of the Ford operations." It would be hard indeed to make up any sort of financial report in which would be included the operations of Mr. Ford; his method of doing business is entirely different from that of other industrialists. He is the proverbial exception to the rule in practically every walk of life. Mr. Ford is unorthodox and original in his business methods. He refuses to follow, parrot-like, any method upon which he can improve.

I have observed a few other men who, like Henry Ford, follow the habit of rendering more and better service than they are paid to render. Every one of them is successful to a noteworthy degree. Also, every one of them is free from the orthodoxy of business procedure, having found newer and better ways of doing business than others in their lines.

The late William Wrigley, Jr., was one of those who made this policy yield him a handsome fortune. The late E. M. Statler followed the same principle profitably in his management of the Statler Hotels.

Mr. Ford takes the attitude that if a man does no more than he is paid to do, he has no valid ground upon which to seek promotion or more pay. Moreover, if a man does no more than he is paid to do, he is, obviously, being paid for all he does. He proves that he believes in the principle of rendering more and better service than one is paid to render by practicing it in his relationship with his own men and in his dealings with the public.

All over the world, big businessmen and little businessmen alike view the Ford achievements with surprise, wondering how he did it! They know that he began in poverty. They know that he was handicapped by lack of schooling. They know that he had insufficient capital during the early part of his career when he most needed it. Despite these handicaps, they have seen him master obstacles that floor most men and rise to stupendous heights of financial achievement. They envy his success without realizing that his success has been the result of strict adherence to principles that would work just as well for others. Moreover, the principles upon which

Mr. Ford's fortune has been built are comparatively simple and easy of application. Perhaps this may explain why so few people have adopted the Ford method of doing business. His methods are simple and unorthodox. Most men are afraid to try a new idea. Mr. Ford goes out of his way to discover new ideas.

Already, he has learned that most of the business methods used by American business are obsolete and inefficient.

The late Elbert H. Gary once told me that the United States Steel Corporation spent several million dollars annually trying to eliminate friction and disagreement among the members of its staff. Mr. Ford has found through new methods how to reduce friction among his men to a minimum. He has proved that his methods are sound because they work. Everyone, in fact, who knows anything about the Ford operations, knows that his methods work. His most severe critics claim that his business efficiency methods work too well! They claim that he kills individuality in men by his efficiency methods. I doubt this. I am sure even from my limited knowledge of the vast Ford operations that he has thousands of men on his payrolls who are earning wages that they could not command anywhere else.

Don't overlook that important fact.

Strictly speaking, it is not Mr. Ford's responsibility to send men into the homes of his workers to see that they conduct their homes efficiently and under sanitary conditions that contribute to health and happiness. Following his habit of going the extra mile and rendering more service than he is paid to render, he does, however, maintain supervision over the homes of many of his employees, with the result that they are worth more to him and more to themselves. Other employers take the attitude that their workers' homes are no concern of theirs, with the result that those homes in many cases are not fit places for human beings.

Some people are so indifferent or slovenly in their personal habits that they require some form of outside control for their own good. Where such discipline seems necessary among the Ford employees, they get it. There is nothing impractical or idealistic about this. It is simply a part of the Ford policy of making his men worth more to him and to themselves.

Henry Ford is an exceedingly practical man. He knows men and he knows life. He applies his knowledge in a way that is advantageous to himself and to his men. I can see nothing about this to justify criticism; on the contrary, there is much to justify his action.

I have watched the Ford policy and the Ford methods for over a quarter of a century, and I have yet to observe the first incident in which Mr. Ford inaugurated any policy that affected unfairly either his own men or the public he serves. No matter how radical or unorthodox his methods may be, upon close and unbiased analysis, they will prove clearly that he has uppermost in his mind the rendering of better service.

Some automobile manufacturers literally rob their patrons in connection with the sale of automobile parts and on repair work. Ford was the first to establish a new precedent that guarantees every Ford owner uniform service at a reasonable, uniform price. More than one Ford dealer has lost his franchise for trying to gouge the owner on service and parts. These are facts that I fear the public at large has not understood.

Many a business concern could well take note of this particular principle.

Analyze any part of the Ford business policy and you will find it based upon this habit of giving the public the utmost service for the least possible cost. Moreover, this policy was inaugurated at the very outset of Mr. Ford's career. Failure to sympathize with it has cost more than one Ford sales manager and executive his position.

Mr. Ford has succeeded because he has deserved to succeed! Many of those who fail in business do so because they deserve to fail. Of course, those who fail are not expected to admit this truth. Most of them look everywhere for the cause of their failure, except the one place where it is to be found—in themselves.

There is nothing mysterious or miraculous about the Ford success. Henry Ford will tell you so if you ask him. He does not attribute his success to superior brains and certainly not to superior advantages. He knows that his success is attributable to the application of definite sound principles that will work as successfully for one person as for another. It has always been astounding to me to observe how few people profit by Mr. Ford's example. Automobile manufacturers have come and gone by the score since Mr. Ford started his business. Their failure for the most part has been due to their indifference and lack of observation of the Ford policy.

Once in a great while, some man with imagination and the power to analyze the Ford policy adopts it in some other line of business and rides to success. One of these was Mr. Whalen who founded the United Cigar Stores. Another was the founder of the Atlantic and Pacific Tea Company. John D. Rockefeller, Sr., discovered and applied the Ford policy long before Mr. Ford's rise to fame and fortune. The Standard Oil Company is a leader in its field despite powerful competition. Its business policy is the nearest approach to the Ford policy that I can call to mind at the moment. The Standard Oil Company set all of the other oil companies a merry pace in the matter of rendering more and better service than the customer expected, evidence of which may be found at any Standard Gas Station.

Marshall Field and John Wanamaker built two of the greatest retail merchandise establishments in America by applying the Ford policy of rendering more service and better service than the customer was in the habit of receiving elsewhere. There is no patent right on the policy. Anyone may use it.

Fortunate is the person who has learned that the most certain way to get is to first give through some sort of useful service. I try to practice, as well as preach, the principle of rendering more service and better service than I am paid to render. Preaching is cheap. Many people have a decalogue of principles that are preached more than they are practiced. It is my policy to follow the principles that I have learned from Mr. Ford because I have observed that they have served him advantageously.

We are entering an age favorable to all who follow the habit of rendering more service than is expected. In fact, this is an age that demands that kind of service. In the future, those who are unwilling to render such service or are indifferent about it will have the unhappy experience of seeing their opportunities taken over by their more progressive competitors.

The small independent merchant is rapidly becoming only a memory. He is being crowded out by men whose greater imagination has foreseen this stupendous change that is taking place in the demand for greater service, and who have organized themselves to deliver that sort of service.

The man who renders more service and better service than he is paid to render is repaid in proportion.

> Some men are successful as long as someone else stands back of them and encourages them, and some men are successful in spite of hell! Take your choice.

29

Ford the Master Salesman

HENRY Ford has taught me the principles of Master Salesmanship. Within the short period of 30 years, I have seen Mr. Ford belt the earth with the product of his definite central purpose! No one but a Master Salesman could have accomplished this astounding result.

Salesmanship consists very largely in *knowing* and in *showing* the prospective buyer the real merits of the goods or service you are trying to sell.

I am convinced that men who achieve noteworthy success in any calling must become Master Salesmen. This conclusion has been reached not only by observing Henry Ford, but by analyzing other men who have accumulated great fortunes.

The Qualities that Make Henry Ford a Master Salesman

I am convinced that Henry Ford has no more brains than the majority of men. I am equally convinced that his success has been due to more efficient use of his brains. I feel certain that I know no less than a hundred men who, had they followed the principles employed by Mr. Ford, could have equaled or even excelled his financial achievement. Let us examine these principles through which Mr. Ford has accumulated a billion dollar fortune.

Henry Ford's Rating on the Fundamental Principles of Success		
1. A Definite Chief Aim	Men, who have aspired to mastery in selling, always work with definite quotas toward definite goals.	100%
2. Self-confidence	No salesman can become a master of this science without possessing an abundance of self-reliance. Mr. Ford has met and surmounted myriads of obstacles because he knew the difference between temporary defeat and failure. Most salesmen never learn this difference and, because they do not learn it, they go down in defeat instead of using it as a stepping-stone on which to climb higher.	100%
3. The Habit of Saving	From the very outset, Mr. Ford adopted the habit of budgeting both his time and his income. Through this habit, he pyramided cash reserves sufficient to absorb the shock of all his mistakes and experiments.	100%
4. The Habit of Health	Mr. Ford has not been a hard worker. He has been an intelligent worker. This means that he has learned to relax by emptying his mind systematically through contact with other men from whom he learned much that he needed to know. He has been temperate in all of his habits. He has eaten sparingly of plain food. He has not been the	100%

	victim of hypochondria or symptoms. He has made his mind serve him instead of scaring him.	
5. Imagination	A keen imagination is the greatest asset of the Master Salesman. Mr. Ford has developed such an imagination; he has developed it the only way that the imaginative faculty can be developed, through systematic use.	90%
6. Initiative and Leadership	The man who waits for others to build him a plan, and then waits for others to help put the plan into action, never develops mastery in selling or in any other calling. Mr. Ford conceives his own plans through his imagination and translates them into action through his own initiative. He does not wait for a sales manager to furnish him with leads.	100%
7. Enthusiasm	Enthusiasm is of two varieties: active and passive. Mr. Ford's enthusiasm has been a mixture of the two. He has expressed his enthusiasm more through action than through words. His has been the type of enthusiasm that kept his imagination at work when it was not obvious, because of his silence to outsiders.	60%
8. Self-control	Mr. Ford has maintained an even keel in most of his activities because he acquired the ability to counterbalance the emotions of his heart with the reasoning power of his head. For a man of his stupendous activities and achievements, he has been remarkably free from tangents and fundamental errors.	100%

(*continued*)

9. The Habit of Doing More than Paid for	Mr. Ford has been outstanding in his practice of this habit. He reversed the order of application of this rule when he adopted his famous $5.00 a day minimum wage scale, thereby practically making each workman his own supervisor. Instead of paying more for services by this policy, he actually paid less than other employers because his policy insured his receiving service greater in quantity, more efficient in quality, and more harmonious in spirit than he had been receiving at the lower scale.	100%
10. A Pleasing Personality	Mr. Ford's lower rating on this principle has been offset by his exceptionally high rating on the majority of the principles. Despite his low rating, he has shown himself to possess sufficient personality to induce other men to follow his leadership with loyalty and harmony.	30%
11. Accurate Thought	There are but few men in America qualified to rate as high as Mr. Ford on this principle. His high rating on this subject is largely responsible for the accumulation of his great fortune. He has made but few mistakes in thought that he has not erased through thought.	90%
12. Concentration of Effort	Mr. Ford's most prominent quality is that of his ability to stick to a plan until he has made it work. He makes decisions quickly and changes them, if at all, slowly. He has persistently followed his definite chief aim for 30 years and is still following it.	100%

13. Cooperation	Teamwork is essential to selling. Mr. Ford has built and maintained the greatest automobile distributing agency in existence. No matter what his critics may say about his iron hand, he has held his organization together and helped himself to make money by helping others to do so. Mr. Ford's greatest asset is his sales distributing force.	70%
14. Profiting by Failures and Mistakes	Mr. Ford has made some huge mistakes with which the public is familiar and, perhaps, many mistakes that the public has never heard of. But he has profited by those mistakes, as indicated by his efforts to mitigate the damage they did.	100%
15. Tolerance	Tolerance means "an open mind on all subjects at all times." Mr. Ford's mind has not always been open, but he has not been long in opening it when he has discovered it closed.	90%
16. Applying the Golden Rule	Some have criticized the rating given Mr. Ford on this principle, believing it to be too high. It will be found to be an accurate rating if analyzed on the basis of Mr. Ford's business policy as a whole. His operations are stupendous in scope. For this reason, he could not survive if he permitted himself to be influenced by policies that favored individuals, instead of following the broader policy of working by plans that offer equal advantage to the masses who are affected by his operations.	90%
17. The Master Mind	The Master Mind principle is the basis of Mr. Ford's stupendous power. It means, "Coordination of	100%

(*continued*)

effort in a spirit of harmony."
Mr. Ford has built one of the most powerful Master Mind groups known to the industrial world. Units of his Master Mind alliance are located in practically every nation on earth. Mr. Ford has shown himself to be an educated man by surrounding himself with men who could do anything he wanted done. That which he may have lacked personally in connection with any of these principles of success, he has provided through the units of his Master Mind group.

Henry Ford is America's first go-giver type of salesman.

More than 200 go-getter automobile manufacturers have come into the picture and faded out of it again since Mr. Ford's start. When other automobile manufacturers put their earnings into expansion programs, Ford usually puts his earnings into a reserve fund. Point by point, when compared with other automobile manufacturers who have failed during the past 20 years, Mr. Ford is an almost direct antithesis.

Throughout the long years of my research, I had the privilege of testing each of the principles of this philosophy by observing Henry Ford. He is the finest living example of the soundness of the philosophy because he has used it as the basis of one of the greatest fortunes ever accumulated by an American businessman.

I had the privilege of testing the principles of success through observation and analysis of the work of other successful men, but Mr. Ford was more helpful to me than any of the others because of his unorthodox habit of blazing new trails and doing things through experimentation.

Study carefully Henry Ford's rating on the fundamental principles of success. It tells, briefly, the story of his astounding financial achievements. There are two facts which, to me, are more than mere coincidences. One is well known to the entire world: that Henry Ford has accumulated a huge fortune. The other is the fact he rates the highest of any living man on the fundamental principles of success with the exception of the Mahatma Gandhi. These two facts are rich with significant suggestion!

30

Accumulation of Power

BY observing Mr. Ford, I have discovered that great power can be accumulated only through the Master Mind principle. I have already stated that Mr. Ford is a Master Salesman. He came by that mastery not through magnetism of his personality but through his ability to coordinate the efforts of other men in a spirit of harmony. This achievement is possible only through understanding and use of the Master Mind principle.

This principle was first called to my attention by Andrew Carnegie who attributed to its application his entire fortune. Incidentally, it was he, also, who first brought Henry Ford to my attention and suggested that I observe Mr. Ford carefully if I wanted to analyze the methods of "a man who would, one day, dominate the entire motor industry."

How right he was in that prophecy!

My discovery of the Master Mind principle came about as the result of my first interview with Mr. Carnegie at which I asked him what he considered the major cause of his success. After asking me to define my understanding of the term "success," which I did by indicating that I believed money to be the concrete evidence of success, Mr. Carnegie said, "I can tell you in a very few minutes how I accumulated my money, if that is what you call success."

"To begin with," said he, "I did not accumulate my money. It has been accumulated through the efforts of my Master Mind group, consisting of about 20 executives." He named each member of the group, telling what part each had taken in carrying out the Master Mind principle. He emphasized the fact that harmony in both spirit and action is essential in applying the Master Mind principle. He called attention to the fact that discord, even though it may exist only in the subconscious mind of a single unit of a Master Mind group, will destroy the power of the Master Mind principle.

Watch out for this important point.

Since that first interview with Mr. Carnegie, I have studied the methods of many hundreds of successful men and discovered that the Master Mind principle is interwoven throughout the business policy of every man who has attained noteworthy success in any calling.

The Master Mind principle is the very hub of Henry Ford's astounding achievements. He has two major Master Mind groups; one is responsible for efficient production of automobiles, the other is responsible for the efficient distribution of his product. The Master Mind group charged with the responsibility of distributing Ford automobiles—his agency force—is the most efficient sales organization in the world. Through the organization of this force, Mr. Ford has provided himself with a definite market for his product. Moreover, through his close contact with that organization, he knows approximately how many automobiles he will sell annually long before he purchases the raw materials needed for their manufacture. It is, therefore, little wonder that Mr. Ford can manufacture a better car for less money than his competitors.

For a great number of years, Mr. Ford, through the cooperation of his Master Mind group, was able to determine very accurately the number of cars each of his dealers had to distribute, based upon a careful analysis of the population in each dealer's territory. The dealer's sales quota was fixed in the Ford offices at Detroit. Once it had been established, the number was set and each dealer had to sell that number. Alibis and excuses did not go. The dealer either sold his allotment or made room for another who could.

It was this policy that gave Mr. Ford the reputation of being ruthless toward his dealers. It was this policy, also, let it be remembered, that made many of his dealers wealthy! I suspect that his dealers as a whole were very well satisfied with Mr. Ford's business policy.

It was Mr. Ford's dealer Master Mind group through which he, years ago, successfully sidestepped an attempt by Wall Street bankers to gain control of the Ford business. Fortunately for Mr. Ford, this incident occurred at a time when the automobile market was still flexible enough to permit sales quotas to be increased and successfully reached by sales pressure.

Recall what he said about his electric push buttons during the trial of his case against the *Chicago Tribune* and you will understand that the use of the Master Mind principle was not accidental. There have been many men who accumulated great fortunes through accidental application of the Master Mind principle. Mr. Ford was not one of them. He applies this principle with purpose aforethought. I have never asked Mr. Ford how or where he first discovered the possibilities of this principle, but I have reason to believe that he discovered it through his association with Thomas A. Edison. I have heard Mr. Edison speak of Ford's achievements, and always when doing so he referred to Mr. Ford's understanding of the Master Mind principle. He understood, as Mr. Ford also understands, the psychic as well as the economic phase of the Master Mind principle.

Success, let me repeat, is achieved through power!

Power is accumulated through organized and intelligently directed knowledge. Organization and intelligent direction of knowledge require coordination of effort in a spirit of harmony between two or more minds. Surely, the intelligent reader will catch the significance of what has been said on this subject and will see clearly that great achievement, regardless of its nature, must take place through application of the Master Mind principle.

I have heard some men express the opinion that the Ford enterprise would eventually collapse and that he would lose his fortune more quickly than he accumulated it. That is not likely to happen unless the automobile industry should fail. Even if it did, Ford would quickly recoup his losses through redirection of his talent along some other line of endeavor.

31

Self-control

HENRY Ford has taught me the value of self-control! He has not taught me to apply the principle of self-control. This is one thing each individual must teach himself.

Over a long period of years, I have observed Mr. Ford maintaining a marvelous state of poise that might well be the envy of any man. Even when he was being attacked by a subsidized press, by inspired writers whose reasons for their scathing denunciation of Mr. Ford were best known to themselves, he kept an even temper and made no reply. Men with less self-control than him would have struck back with vengeance.

I have seen evidence of Mr. Ford's self-control in his dealings with men who went into his business with a few thousand dollars and came out with many millions of dollars. One by one he paid them off when harmony no longer prevailed, but as far as I have been able to learn, he did not vilify or denounce them after they had gone. That is more than can be said of some who became wealthy through Mr. Ford's efforts and for one reason or another left his business.

Mr. Ford's most exemplary demonstration of self-control in my opinion has been in connection with his simple style of living. He has never indulged in any ceremony for the purpose of impressing the public with his financial strength. He conducts himself now pretty much as he did in the old days when he was working on his first horseless carriage in an old shop in Detroit. He has demonstrated self-control in the rearing of his son to appreciate the glory of labor.

He demonstrated remarkable self-control when graft-seeking labor organizations were trying to alienate the Ford workers some years ago. Instead of posting men armed with rifles at the gates of his factories to keep the labor organizers out, Mr. Ford used brains in the place of bullets and placed insurmountable obstacles in the way of those organizers by voluntarily providing working conditions and wage scales, such as no labor union could possibly hope to secure for its followers.

Mr. Ford has consistently exercised remarkable self-control by living his own life in his own way and by preserving his right to think for himself. Most men prefer to yield to popular opinion and throw themselves upon the side of the herd in both their thoughts and their deeds.

Mr. Ford has demonstrated remarkable self-control by gaining and maintaining mastery over his emotions. The majority of men are ruled by their emotions. Mr. Ford has emotions but they are under control always. It is a form of self-control that most men never attain.

It has already been stated in a preceding chapter that Mr. Ford has an abundance of faith in himself, in other men, and in Infinite Intelligence. In view of some rather disconcerting experiences he has had with his fellow men who are inclined toward avarice, his faith in men could have been maintained only through great self-control. Despite his experiences with some men who have proved themselves untrustworthy, Mr. Ford steadfastly refused to place all men in the same category. It is a well-known fact that he has given employment to scores of men who had been unfortunate enough to have served prison terms. One ex-convict who applied to Mr. Ford for employment started to explain that he had served time. Mr. Ford stopped him, saying, "Never mind about that. Start where you stand." Nothing more was ever said about the incident. The man later had to be let out, but he was not blacklisted among other employers.

Mr. Ford has shown unusual self-control by remaining at his post and continuing to shoulder the responsibilities of his huge enterprise at an age in life when most men who were financially independent would have retired. He has learned the rare art of playing at his business.

These are but a few of the ways in which Henry Ford has demonstrated his amazing self-control. By observing this habit, I have been inspired over a long period of years to mend some of my ways very profitably. During the earlier days of my experience, I frequently gave way to my feelings. By following Mr. Ford's example, I have discovered that it is more profitable to put one's best thoughts and efforts into one's definite central purpose, looking neither to the right nor to the left, than it is to permit one's self to be baited into striking back at those who criticize.

By studying Henry Ford, I have discovered there are more men in the world who can tear down than men who can build something constructive. Moreover, I have discovered that the destroyers are, sooner or later, destroyed by their own thoughts and deeds.

> Think well before you speak because your words may plant the seed of either success or failure in the mind of some other person.

32

Organized Effort

HENRY Ford has taught me the value of organized effort!

Early in life, Mr. Ford chose a definite central purpose. He has devoted his entire time to achieving the object of that purpose. He has managed to employ both his time and his fortune profitably in one major line of highly concentrated effort. He has ably demonstrated the wisdom of this principle.

Division of effort is one of the major weaknesses of those who do not succeed. I learned this from the analyses of over 25,000 men and women who were classed as failures.

At the very outset of his career, Henry Ford recognized the advantages of organized effort. He knew that an average lifetime is entirely too short to justify one in trying to be a jack-of-all-trades. That reminds me of a statement made by Andrew Carnegie during one of my interviews with him, nearly 25 years ago. "Put all your eggs in one basket," he said, "and then watch the basket to see that no one kicks it over." He emphasized the importance of concentration of effort regardless of one's calling.

I have often endeavored to determine which of the lessons taught by Henry Ford has been of the greatest service to me, and while I have found it difficult to reach a decision, I am of the opinion that his example of organized effort has been more valuable, perhaps, than any of the others.

I have devoted the better portion of my life to gathering, classifying, and organizing into a simple philosophy, the factors that enter into the achievement of success. The task has been stupendous. I have had to read and assimilate the contents of many, many books through which I have informed myself on the subjects of biology, chemistry, astronomy, geology, economics, religion, business, philosophy, and many related subjects.

I felt the necessity of becoming familiar with the discoveries of other men on all subjects that were related directly or indirectly to the subject of financial achievement. To accomplish this end, I read every book I could find dealing with all forms of mind stimulants, from the fragmentary records of what has been recorded of the discoveries of Socrates down to the philosophy of Emerson.

While conducting this laborious research, I felt the necessity also of studying and analyzing the methods of practically every man of great financial achievement known to the American public during the past quarter of a century for the purpose of ascertaining by what means he came by his wealth.

After the necessary data had been gathered, organized, and classified, I had to test it for soundness, a task that required years of tedious effort.

All of this labor required organized effort! Moreover, my labor during the early days was of such a nature I could not convert it into money, except in a few isolated instances.

At times, I became discouraged, and except for the lessons I had learned from observation of Henry Ford's philosophy of business, I am sure I would never have completed my task.

I recall that Andrew Carnegie cautioned me that no less than 20 years of concentrated, unprofitable labor would be required to complete the task I had begun. He suggested that I might never live to enjoy the fruits of my labor since recognition comes late to most philosophers.

Mr. Carnegie's suggestion did not tend to help me in concentrating my efforts upon a task that, from his viewpoint, might never be profitable or helpful to me. It has always been a profound mystery to me how I gathered the courage to carry on my labor in the face of the multifarious obstacles that I have had to surmount.

Whatever the correct answer may be, the fact remains that the influence of Henry Ford was my major inspiration in carrying on a highly organized form of concentrated effort until the philosophy was completed.

The map of the world has seen major alterations since I began. The customs and habits of the people have changed with almost unbelievable rapidity. The world has caught on fire and all but burned itself to death in a form of wholesale murder dignified by the name of war, the effects of which are still apparent everywhere. Prohibition has been instituted and repealed with the subsequent rise and fall of various rackets. Crime has mounted the saddle of civilization while justice has been forced to walk on bare feet. The Machine Age has reached its apex. Churches have lost much of their hold on people. Politics and statesmanship have practically become rackets.

And last, but not least, Mother Nature has turned the whole world over her knee and given it a good spanking through depression and recession.

These are some of the major changes in human history that I have seen pass before me, since I started delving into *causes* and *effects* that make or unmake men and women.

It never occurred to me before my first interview with Andrew Carnegie that I would spend over a quarter of a century of my life in building a philosophy of success. His influence upon me was so great that I began the long trek in quest of the knowledge that was necessary for the building of such a philosophy.

Mr. Carnegie not only planted in my mind the seed that finally germinated and grew into my life's work, but suggested a study of Henry Ford, the man who was destined to exercise a much more vital and helpful influence upon me than Mr. Carnegie.

Practically every one of the men of outstanding achievement who collaborated with me not only gave me the full benefit of his own experience, but introduced me to some acquaintance with whom I made contact and from whom I gathered useful data.

It may be a great surprise to Henry Ford to learn that he has been my most helpful teacher over a period of a quarter of a century. I trust any shock he may experience will be mitigated by the fact that his student has endeavored, and shall continue to endeavor, to be a credit to him.

My greatest wish and hope is that I may be as efficient in releasing men and women from the limitations they have set up in their own minds as Mr. Ford has been in producing and marketing automobiles. If I fall short of this aim, the fault will be entirely with me. I as an individual may fail in the application of the Ford principles, but the principles cannot fail because they are a part of the phenomena of nature's laws.

> It is a peculiar trait of human nature, but it is true, that the most successful men will work harder for the sake of rendering useful service than they will for money alone.

33

Personal Initiative

THE definite chief aim to which Mr. Ford has devoted the better portion of his life was created and matured through his own individual initiative.

Early in life, Mr. Ford took inventory of his present and his future and discovered that many obstacles stood between him and success. No one helped him take this inventory and no one suggested that he do so. The idea was entirely his own.

His self-analysis disclosed many weaknesses that had to be eliminated or bridged. He began, from the very outset of his career, to correct such weaknesses as he found in himself.

Mr. Ford's early analysis of himself and his environment disclosed the fact that he was without a definite central purpose. He immediately set about the task of creating one. Being naturally inclined toward machinery and vehicular conveyances, he began to experiment with a buggy that could be made to run without horsepower. This idea was suggested to him by his observation of a portable threshing machine outfit, which moved on its own wheels by steam power.

Bear in mind this fact: Mr. Ford began his experiment at a time when such experiments were considered the work of a crank. Thus, he had to have sufficient initiative to buck public opinion. Farmers objected strenuously to the presence of Mr. Ford's horseless carriage contraption on the roads because it frightened their horses. Moreover, they registered their objections in no uncertain terms. This is the point at which men with less initiative than Henry Ford would have yielded to opposition and criticism.

From my own experience, I know how many detours invite one to leave the main highway of one's definite central purpose. Every crossroad serves as a place to quit, unless one is gifted with or has acquired initiative in abundance.

Every obstacle with which one meets in any undertaking serves as an alibi for quitting! Most people yield to obstacles because they lack the persistence and the initiative to give battle. Initiative and persistence are two of Mr. Ford's most prominent qualities. They are, I believe, the two qualities that have been largely responsible for his astounding achievements. Include with these two qualities singleness of purpose and concentration of effort and I am sure you will then have the four qualities that have made Henry Ford the richest man in America.

When analyzed, it will be readily seen that through these four qualities Mr. Ford has whipped poverty and illiteracy and ignorance, three of man's most stubborn enemies. Through these four qualities he has evolved, viz:

1. By knowing exactly what he wanted.
2. By creating definite plans for acquiring that which he wanted.
3. By persistently following those plans, or some modification of them.
4. By concentrating all of his efforts and resources behind his definite central purpose.

Those four short paragraphs describe the outstanding qualities through which Henry Ford has become the mystery man of the entire business and industrial world. In reality, there is nothing mysterious about him. Of all the thousands of people whom I have had the privilege of analyzing, I have found Mr. Ford to be the easiest to analyze. He moves always with frankness and in the open. He has no personal secrets. His entire life is an open book that all may read at will.

Henry Ford understands cause and effect. When Mr. Ford suffers defeat, he finds out immediately what caused the defeat. When he succeeds, he notes carefully the cause of his success. Some other successful men whom I have met have not been as painstaking and accurate as he in this respect.

My interpretation of Henry Ford's achievements is now in your hands. It is my earnest hope that you may find it helpful as I have found his example helpful. The world is passing through a very trying period during which millions of people have experienced temporary defeat, disappointment, and, unfortunately, loss of faith.

To all whose burdens seem heavy, I offer the consoling thought that they are not alone in their hour of despair. Others walk with them through this modern Garden of Gethsemane.

Many centuries ago, a Persian philosopher, who was poet and private counselor to His Majesty King Cyrus of Persia, offered the king a very sound bit of philosophy. He said, "I am reminded, O King, that there is a wheel on which the affairs of men revolve, and its mechanism is such that it prevents *any* man from being *always* fortunate."

There is indeed such a wheel. It is intangible, to be true, but it is real and it is powerful. However, this wheel of fortune is eternally turning. While it prevents any man from being always fortunate, by the same rule it also prevents any man from being always unfortunate!

Millions of people have been and still are facing the flat side of life's great wheel of fortune. Have patience! Have faith! Be persistent and carry on, knowing that the wheel is still turning albeit the revolutions may seem slow.

Some day it will turn in your favor.

Humility of heart is a marvelous and desirable quality. Nothing creates humility as quickly as poverty and want. Perhaps the wheel of fortune has been slowed purposely so that its flat side, which brought the business depression, may impress the world with humility.

As the work on this book is being completed, the country is suffering from a form of business stagnation known as a business recession. The condition began immediately after Franklin D. Roosevelt launched his fruitless attack on the United States Supreme Court, following his second term in office.

Because of the widespread effects of the president's unfortunate move, I feel impelled to close this chapter with a statement of what I would do if I were in the president's place. This statement is a fitting climax because the statement contains a detailed analysis of a principle essential to every person who sells himself through life successfully.

No book on the subject of marketing personal services would be complete, with conditions as they are in the world today, without an analysis of the astounding principle here described and recommended as the foundation upon which all enduring success must be built.

The chapters that follow are particularly appropriate as a climax to my analysis of Henry Ford, for the reason that they suggest the widespread adoption and use of a principle that, more than all others, has been responsible for his ability to sell himself so soundly that he has kept himself in the favor of the people for more than 40 years.

It is a striking coincidence that "American" ends with "I can."

Until you have learned to be tolerant with those who do not always agree with you—until you have cultivated the habit of saying some kind word of those whom you do not admire—until you have formed the habit of looking for the good instead of the bad there is in others—you will be neither successful nor happy.

IV

A Rule for Winning Friends that Has Stood the Test of More than 4,000 Years of Time

THE remainder of this book describes a principle so important in all human relationships that it was chosen as the only fitting ending for the book.

Before you read the description, I want you to be reminded that it was mainly due to his scrupulous observation of this principle that Franklin D. Roosevelt became the idol of the American people during his first term in office.

After you have finished reading the analysis of this principle, I wish to call your attention to the fact that his neglect in application of this principle during his second term in office is costing the president much of the gains he made during his first term.

Stating the facts in another way, the president sold himself into the hearts of the American people—one of the finest and ablest pieces of selling on record in the history of this country—by subordinating all his political and personal privileges for the benefit of the people as a whole. Had he continued serving the people in that same spirit of unselfishness through his second term in office, he would without doubt have gone down in history as one of America's greatest personalities!

As you read the concluding chapters of this book, it will be beneficial to you if you carefully study and weigh both the records of Henry Ford and Franklin D. Roosevelt. If your analysis of the two men is sound, you will be forced to the conclusion that Ford, despite his handicap of a lowly beginning in poverty and illiteracy, has sold himself into a position of power from which he can never be removed by literally following the principle described in the closing pages of this book. You will also be forced to the conclusion that the president, despite his privileged advantages of wealth at birth and his 100-point personality, has met with a decline in popularity due to his neglect of this principle. A comparison of the records of the two men will be helpful to all who are trying to sell their way through life successfully, no matter what may be one's leanings toward or against both Roosevelt and Ford.

34

If I Were President!

IF I were the president of the United States at this time, I would serve the people of America with an idea that might change the entire nation from chaos and conflict into harmony and understanding. I would take the idea to all the people, by radio and the public press. My radio speech would begin in these words:

> **My friends, the time has come when we should speak plainly and think clearly. With your permission, I shall set an example of plain speech by saying we have come to the crossroads of civilization at which we must choose, because we have the choice of many roads.**
>
> **Today, our indebtedness amounts to almost $40 billion, and the amount is growing bigger every day. I hardly need to remind you that we have just passed through the worst economic crisis this country has ever known, and that this experience leveled us all down substantially to the same financial and spiritual foundation. To recoup our personal fortunes and eventually pay off our huge public debt, we must awaken anew our spiritual forces, subordinate our political and economic differences of opinion, and all pull together, and by this I mean that we must cooperate in both spirit and deed, each of us recognizing the fact that we are our brother's keeper whether we like it or not.**

It is time we understood the truth that we can remain the richest and freest people on earth, only by that form of cooperation which inspires hope and faith and trust in one another. *It is time, also, we realized the need for a nationwide spiritual renaissance, without which mere business recovery will do us no permanent good.* It is time we stopped talking about business recovery, and began talking of spiritual recovery, for it must be obvious to the most humble citizen of our country that we are *spiritually bankrupt!*

Before we concern ourselves with the sins of other nations, with their impending wars and internal conflict, let us put our own house in order. We should begin by bringing about a better spirit of understanding between employers and their employees, who are now engaged in a form of warfare, that will, if they are not stopped, destroy not only the individuals directly engaged in the conflict, but more than 100 million innocent bystanders—men, women, and children generally known as the public.

This nation is still a republic and we are a free people, with the right to help establish and maintain the political and economic principles that must support this and all other republics. I feel sure that no true American wants this nation to come under the control of one man or any form of minority rule.

I feel sure that you will be willing to put your shoulders to the wheel of destiny, all of you, and help to keep it turning so that we may remain a free people.

I have come to you through this personal appeal because I have a plan to offer for your approval, a plan that I know to contain the solution of our joint problem. The plan is no invention of mine, but it has the advantage of more than 4,000 years of testing that has proved, beyond room for doubt, it is practical.

The plan is in no way connected with politics. It works no hardship on any human being. To put it into action calls for no personal sacrifice from anyone. It violates no man's religion. It offers immediate and definite financial and personal advantages to every citizen of our country. It will wipe out the conflict between capital and labor overnight. It will give every church in our land a new transfusion of spiritual energy as soon as it has been put into operation. It will establish a fine example for the

people of other nations to follow, an example that might easily bring to them the same widespread freedom and economic benefits that we expect of it for our people. It is no exaggeration to state that the proposed plan is so laden with promise that it might easily wipe out all this rattling of swords and threats of war that now plague many of the countries of Europe.

The sum and substance of this plan is a joint promise of the people of this nation, to be made in writing in a new Declaration of Independence, that they will return to the original principle on which this nation was founded, and that they will adopt and henceforth use the Golden Rule as the basis of all their business, professional, political, and personal relationships.

Do not be alarmed, my friends, at the simplicity of this plan, for therein lies its strength. The plan is so simple that the most humble person can adopt and use it. It is within reach of both adults and the youths of the land. It is available, equally, to people of every race and creed. Use of the plan requires the consent of no one, and no one who adopts and uses it can be cheated of the benefits it provides, *because those benefits are spiritual as well as economic in nature.*

To put this plan into practical operation, as quickly as possible, I shall ask the specific and hearty organized cooperation of the governors of all the states and the churches of all denominations. I feel privileged to call upon the churches for their cooperation because they will benefit greatly by the spiritual quickening of the people who commit themselves to live by the Golden Rule.

For the purpose of simultaneous adoption of this plan, I hereby set aside one week, starting on the twenty-fifth of December and ending on the first of January of each year, to be known as "Golden Rule Week," and I ask that during our first Golden Rule Week, each and every person sign a pledge to adopt and use this universal law *as the basis of all human relationships.*

I would follow this speech with others until I had made the people of America so "Golden Rule conscious" that they would begin to live by this great rule of human conduct. I would particularly address myself to the working men of America, directing their attention to the personal benefits to be gained by adopting and using this rule.

Ideas rule the world! This is an idea, but it is not new. In fact, it has been preached for so long that most people have made the mistake of assuming it should be classified along with the many other subjects about which men have been *preaching* but *not practicing.*

The world needs to revive this principle.

If this idea were given one-tenth the front page newspaper space that has been devoted to the discussion of the New Deal, pros and cons, and one-tenth the radio time the president has devoted to political discussions, it would solve all the major difficulties of this country within a few years.

In my appeal to the people of America, I would go over the heads of the labor racketeers, over the heads of the professional politicians, over the heads of the Soviet propagandists working in the guise of labor agitators, and take the laboring men into my confidence. I would tell them the truth about the economic and political setup of this nation through which we have earned the right to speak of ourselves as the *richest* and *freest* country on earth. I would plainly describe to the working men the truth that this country has always been, and of necessity must remain, a capitalistic country. I would frankly admit that the nation has two capitals, one of them purely economic in nature, with headquarters in Wall Street, and the other purely political, with headquarters in Washington.

I would call attention to the fact that men who manage capital and the men who do the labor of industry and business are, and must remain, friendly partners, and I would emphasize the fact that labor represents the physical body of the nation while capital is the lifeblood that keeps that body healthy and alive.

I would plainly tell the working men of America that without the capitalistic system, this nation's political system would have to be changed. I would show them that any organized movement to take away from capital more than is put into it will result in capital's destruction. I would call their attention to the fact that individual happiness comes through individual effort and self-determination, not by mass effort. I would say to the working men that they have every right to organize and negotiate as a group, but I would caution them to use the same philosophy, in their dealings with capital, that an individual must use if he rises to power and accumulates riches without violating the rights of others.

I would go back into the history of the men who have made America, and I would point out to the working men the significant fact that most of these men came up from the ranks of labor, from beginnings as humble as that of any man now living, and I would call attention to the advantages of this privilege and ask if there are any who would wish to have it taken away from them. I would compare the privileges now enjoyed by the working men of America with those of the people of Soviet Russia, Italy, and Germany, and find out how many would exchange what they have for what they might have as citizens of any of those countries. I would bring out the files of the Department of Justice and the State Department, and I would disclose to the people of America the exact conditions existing in countries in which business and industry have been taken over by self-appointed dictators, as they affect laboring men. I would take the working men of America on an imaginary trip through Russia and let them see, for themselves, how many "chickens in every pot and automobiles in every garage" the people of that country possess. I would name the Russian agents now working secretly in this country for the overthrow of our industrial system. I would set the Secret Service men on their trail and expose every move they make. I would put government speakers and propagandists in the field; and for every speech made for the destruction of our industrial system, I would have a better and more logical one made on behalf of this system.

I would organize the churches of this nation and ask them to go to work in earnest and help our people get themselves out of spiritual bankruptcy. I would ask that at least one day each week be devoted to some form of church service with the object of *selling America to its people.* I would ask the newspapers to give over column one on their front pages for the purpose of carrying a daily message to the people on the merits of "the richest and freest country on earth." I would draft the ablest writers to use this prominent space for the purpose of acquainting our people with the multiple blessings we now enjoy; and the reasons for protecting our right to these blessings. I would draft the ablest novelists in the country and ask them to start writing books glorifying the spirit of freedom we enjoy in this country. I would pick out at least one outstanding business in each state, and induce the management of that business and the laboring men who serve it, to adopt and *use* the Golden Rule in all their relationships with one another and with the public they serve. Then, I would ask the public to go out of its way to patronize those businesses and to prove that virtue is not without its direct, immediate, and enduring financial reward.

I would explode, once and forever, that old bromide about the Golden Rule not being practical "with men and conditions the way they are in the world today." I would ask the schools and colleges of the country to begin teaching the principles of success, the principles that enabled Carnegie, Rockefeller, Edison, and others of their type, to rise from lowly beginnings to positions of fame and fortune, and I would call attention to the fact that where there was one opportunity during the early days of these men, there now exists a hundred. I would call attention to the great opportunities, not merely for an occasional individual, but for millions of men and women of all ages, which have grown out of the industrial development and advancement we enjoy in this country through the help of our economic capital on Wall Street.

I would apologize for having made the mistake of referring to the industrial leaders of America as the "Economic Royalists," and I would encourage every working man to aim for leadership in the business or industrial field. I would tell the people of America that from the beginning of civilization on up to this very moment, the great leaders, the successful men in every calling, have always *rendered more service and better service than they were paid to render.* I would tell them that no one has ever been known to enjoy permanent success without giving the best he had to offer, not only in quantity and quality of service, but particularly in *friendly spirit* mixed generously with the service.

What we all need in this country today is information, enlightenment, truth!

We need to know *what we have,* as citizens of this country, and *how we got it!* We need to know more about Andrew Carnegie, Henry Ford, J. P. Morgan, the Du Ponts, and others of their type who have been responsible for industrial America, who have made possible every job in the land paying wages or a salary. The farmers of the country need to know that the surplus food they raise and market is purchased by the industrial system created by the men whom paid agitators are trying to undermine. In brief, we all need to know that this is an industrial, capitalistic nation, and the moment that system is destroyed our freedom goes with it.

We boast of our privilege of a free press and the right of free speech, but we overlook the danger of these privileges. Right now, free speech is being used to undermine the very foundation of individual freedom, as anomalous as that may seem. Let us keep our free press and our free speech, by all means, but let us use them to advertise the virtues and the benefits and the riches and the blessings and the privileges we enjoy. Nature has a queer way of taking away from us the things we do not use. Tie an arm to one's side, remove it from use, and it soon atrophies and withers. Place an arm in back of a heavy tool, give it systematic use, and nature rewards it with strength and power. Neglect the gardens and fields and nature takes them back to the jungle.

Sleep upon our rights to free speech and a free press, and the agents of foreign countries step in and use these weapons to confuse and mislead us.

There are sins of *omission* and sins of *commission*. In this country, we are grossly guilty of both types, but particularly of sins of omission. Our major sin of omission is this: We have no plan for maintaining our freedom by mass thought and action. Fewer than five million men organized in the form of labor unions are in position to establish the price of food and of every other commodity, and the other 125 million of us can do nothing but pay through the nose.

What this country needs, right now, is not a good five-cent cigar but sufficient interest in our own affairs to make the fullest use of our boasted privilege of freedom of speech and press.

35

The Golden Rule in Use

I wear a fine, highly adjusted watch that keeps perfect time. If I took the watch apart, placed all the parts in a hat, and shook the hat the remainder of my life, the parts would not assemble themselves into the splendid time-measuring machine that now serves me. The reason is that at the back of the watch is a carefully organized and thoroughly tested plan that must be followed before the parts can be correlated, organized, and made into a working unit. My watch keeps time because the many parts were assembled in the mind of a man who understood watches and followed a definite plan for putting the pieces together.

I have had the privilege of analyzing thousands of people, some of them among the wealthiest and most successful men known to the American people, some of them complete failures. In every instance, the man who succeeded had followed a definite plan, and the man who failed had neglected to follow a plan. From this observation I deduced that there is always a cause for success, also a cause for failure. As a matter of fact, I learned from my research that there are 17 fundamental principles of success, some combination of which is always used by the person who succeeds in any undertaking.

One of the most important of these principles happens to be the one that most people are neglecting today. It is the principle known as the

Golden Rule, in connection with which thousands of sermons have been preached, without its practicability having been impressed upon the minds of men.

This simple rule of human conduct means that whatever we do *to* or *for* another, we do *to* or *for* ourselves. Understand this distinction and the Golden Rule will take on an entirely different meaning.

I am not going to preach a sermon on the Golden Rule, but I am going to give you firsthand, reliable information about the way it works. To give you this firsthand information, I must use personal illustrations for I can be absolutely sure only of my own motives and emotions—the real motives and feelings of others are necessarily based upon observation.

The view that I here present has nothing to do with morals. It has nothing to do with the hereafter. It deals with the *here* and *now.* It offers a solution of the pressing problems of life, which every man faces from day to day. Moreover, it offers the individual the best possible of all roads to happiness for the very good reason that for one person to succeed under this rule he does not have to cause others to fail.

I was prompted to write this confession because of the futile war now going on between capital and labor. It is futile because both sides are sure to lose when the final count has been taken, for it is a law, as immutable as the law of gravitation, that the man who destroys his neighbor destroys also himself. Have you ever thought of that?

Come with me for a look backward over the years that have flown all too rapidly, and let us analyze some of the results of the Golden Rule applied.

At the close of the World War, Arthur Nash, a Cincinnati merchant tailor, found his business practically on the rocks. He lacked operating capital. His business had fallen off to where the overhead was eating up the profits. He could find no more capital, so, in sheer desperation, everything else having failed (observe well the statement "everything else having failed"), as a last resort he put the Golden Rule to the test.

Calling in all of his employees, he told them the fix the business was in. He said there was but 1 chance in 10,000 to save the business, and with their cooperation, he would take that chance. He offered to take every employee into partnership with him, giving everyone a share in the profits, on the condition that they all would forget hours, forget personal conveniences and comforts, and put everything they had into their jobs. "If that will not save the business," he said, "then nothing can save it, but I *believe if we put our hearts and heads and souls together, we are bound to win.*"

The employees believed so, too. They joined heads, hearts, and hands. And that was not all. They went into old socks, saving accounts, and other secret hiding places and brought out their meager savings and dumped the entire amount into the business. That helped, but the thing that did the most good was the *spirit* they put into the business, the sincere spirit of desire to make the business go. The business did go. In fact, it prospered as it never had before.

I had the privilege of writing the first magazine story about the experiment, and believe it or not, this man, Arthur Nash, and his employees, who did nothing more than *practice* the Golden Rule, made the front pages of the leading newspapers of the country, and they were given generous space in the leading magazines. The unusual experiment had received a million dollars worth of free front page publicity that could not have been bought with mere money, at any price.

When Arthur Nash died some years later, he was a wealthy man and his tailoring business was flourishing as but few such businesses have ever profited. That which he did *for* his employees, he did *for* himself. *They saw to that.*

There are no hidden secrets to this unusual achievement. The episode is now a matter of record, a well-advertised and well-known record at that, yet, almost 20 years have passed since Arthur Nash appropriated the Golden Rule and put it to work in his business. There is no patent right on the Golden Rule. Anyone who chooses may adopt the rule and put it to work. It is one of the few rules any employer, any employee, or any neighbor may put into operation without someone complaining. Perhaps that is one thing wrong with the great rule: it is too *free.* Perhaps if a law were passed making it an offense to apply this rule, more people would begin bootlegging it into operation.

Some years ago, Henry Ford startled the entire industrial world by announcing that from that day on he would pay his men a minimum wage of $5.00 per day, regardless of their positions. Everyone had an opinion about Mr. Ford's new policy, but hardly anyone foresaw the effect it would have on his men and his business. His competitors in industry yelled "treason." His wild scheme, they reckoned, would wreck him and other businesses, too, if others tried to follow his example. They were wrong! Far from wrecking Ford, the move was one of the wisest he ever made. Let us briefly summarize the benefits it brought to Ford. First, it gave him the pick of labor, for everyone wanted to work for a man voluntarily paying such wages. It also cut down the operating expense of the business by automatically making every employee more or less his own supervisor. No employee getting such wages dared take the risk of losing his job by "soldiering" or by turning out work of poor quality or too little in quantity. The benefits did not end here. The plan practically insured the Ford business against labor troubles for over 20 years; because it was so much more liberal than any labor leader could possibly promise, labor union protection in the Ford plants became unnecessary. And, even today, when union labor leaders seem to have lost all sense of self-control, John L. Lewis took good care to pick General Motors for his first battle in the automotive field instead of tackling Ford.

Ford may not have intended to run his business by the Golden Rule when he voluntarily raised wages, but the effect was exactly the same. The *deed* was what counted. Somewhere in my travels, I saw a motto consisting of three short, simple words, which impressed me more than all other mottoes I have ever seen. It said, "Deeds, not words."

The more I see of men, those who succeed in a big way (financially), and those who go down in utter failure, the more I am convinced that too many reverse this motto, reading it backward, "Words, not deeds." As a group of words, the Golden Rule is nothing but so many sounds, of themselves without practical benefit. When translated into deeds, these words tell another and a vastly different story.

The Golden Rule, when translated into deeds, is the equivalent of rendering more service and better service than that for which one is paid. Moreover, to benefit to the fullest by this great rule of human conduct one must render that sort of service, a truth that all leaders would do well to learn and to impress upon their followers.

I have made a very startling discovery about the power of the Golden Rule, something I never knew before, and of which I have heard nothing, viz, when a man is in difficulty the very best thing he can do to overcome it is to find some other person or persons who, likewise, are in difficulty and help them out. In doing so he will find, with but few exceptions, that in having helped his neighbor he has also helped himself. "Help thy brother's boat across and lo! thine own hath reached the shore."

Varied and far-reaching are the effects of rendering service based upon the Golden Rule, service that gives the best one has to offer. All the labor unions on earth could never provide any individual with the advantages he may gain for himself by adopting and living the Golden Rule, putting into his efforts the best he has, not once in a while, but always, as a matter of principle. Those who render that sort of service never need the help of a labor union, or of any other power, to gain for themselves the best that life has to offer.

People who literally live by the Golden Rule possess an almost uncanny power to attract and please others and have no difficulty in gaining willing cooperation. Not long ago, I was invited to spend a day with Herman Schatzman, of the Western Union Telegraph Company, who volunteered to take me on a long automobile trip that brought us into contact with many people under many different circumstances. I was astonished to observe the manner in which people everywhere went out of their way to be courteous to Mr. Schatzman, a fact that was so obvious that I began to analyze him to determine the cause. On one occasion, he drove up to a private estate that was guarded by a policeman at the entrance gate. Before waiting for the policeman to speak, Mr. Schatzman said, "We are interested in seeing the estate; will you be good enough to open the gate for us?"

The policeman turned and started to open the gate, then hesitated, looked around and asked, "Whom do you wish to see? The public is not admitted here, you know." Instantly, Mr. Schatzman replied, "I want to show my friends this beautiful place." Without another word, the policeman opened the gate and we passed through. On our way out I saw him looking us over very quizzically, obviously wondering why he violated his instructions by admitting us. I, too, wondered why he allowed us to enter. Before the day was over, I learned the secret.

Shortly afterward, Mr. Schatzman had the misfortune to have one of his tires go flat in a crowded section of Newark, New Jersey. To make matters worse, the tire went flat right in front of a private business entrance, where we were compelled to block the passageway. A policeman was directing traffic not more than a hundred feet away. When he saw the predicament we were in, he walked over to the car, looked at the flat tire, and was about ready I am sure, to order us to get out of there, when Mr. Schatzman spoke up with a broad smile on his face and said, "Now isn't this just a man's luck, to have a tire go flat in a busy place like this?" The policeman changed the scowl on his face to a broad grin and answered back, "You said it, brother!" Then, to my amazement, he volunteered to direct traffic around us, and gave Mr. Schatzman directions to the nearest garage. The job required nearly an hour, but that policeman did not utter a single word of reprimand, and when the tire had been changed and we were ready to leave, he walked over to us, smiled generously, and wished us better luck the next time a tire went bad.

Later in the day, Mr. Schatzman got to a red light a few seconds too late, but decided to go on through. When he was about halfway across the intersection, a police whistle blew loudly, and a big strapping policeman walked over with that "I've got you this time" manner about him. Again, Mr. Schatzman beat him to the draw and began by saying, "How stupid of me not to look up at that light. When I looked at it about a block back, it was green." The policeman just looked at him for a few seconds, then smiled and waved us back into position, without opening his mouth.

After I had traveled with Mr. Schatzman the better part of an entire day, and had seen him treated with the utmost courtesy by taxicab drivers, policemen, and diverse other persons who usually do not take the trouble to be courteous, I discovered the secret. It was simply this—Schatzman truly likes people—all of them. He reflects this liking not only in all his deeds but in all his thoughts as well. On occasions, when I ventured to analyze some person in the public eye whose personal conduct I did not approve, Schatzman always came back with an expression of some virtue or good quality that person possessed that I had deliberately ignored.

Here, then, is a man whose very personality is so thoroughly charged with positive, constructive thoughts of others that they quickly pick up this attitude and reflect it back to him as their own. This is one of the queer, imponderable traits of human nature, but it is decidedly a trait; *people act toward us, in thought as well as deed, in a manner corresponding to our thoughts.* Not only do people do this but animals as well. A dog knows instantly when he meets a stranger who dislikes dogs, and generally he shows his dislike in return. Thoughts do have a way of telegraphing themselves from one brain to another. As I rode through the country with Herman Schatzman that day, I wondered what it would be worth to every concern employing men and women if his spirit of love for his fellow man and his refusal to speak ill of others could be injected into the minds of both the employer and the employees.

That simple spirit, alone, would end all labor disputes such as those that threaten the very foundation of this country. It would do more than that: It would bring to men and women poise and peace of mind, such as never can be known by those who load their minds with greed, malice, hatred, and envy.

Before my day with Herman Schatzman was ended, I did some philosophizing by asking myself why, with all of our marvelous systems of education, no one has ever thought of teaching boys and girls, as they go through the schools, the advantages of thinking in terms of human kindness! Also, I could not help wondering why the leaders of both capital and labor have never discovered the manifold blessings they might enjoy for themselves and their followers by the simple procedure of thinking of one another in terms of human kindness.

I fear that one of the greatest weaknesses of most of us is our tendency to look everywhere except to *our own state of mind,* for the causes of our difficulties throughout life, and I know, beyond any room for doubt, that we are where we are and what we are, financially and spiritually, *because of the dominating thoughts that occupy our minds.*

36

Mental Attitude Must Be Right

NOT long ago, I had the privilege of spending an evening with Madam Esperanza Garrigue, an internationally known teacher of singing who gave me an interesting account of the early experiences of Graham McNamee. Mr. McNamee wanted to be a singer, but he lacked the money to pay for his education. Madam Garrigue looked him over, studied him carefully, and reached the conclusion he was worth her effort after she learned that he wanted to become a singer so badly that he was willing to starve, if necessary; so she took him on and gave him the best she had.

After he made a reputation as a radio announcer, and money began to come freely, Mr. McNamee went to Madam Garrigue and offered to pay up his debt to her. She refused to accept money, so he asked her to let him pay in another way, by giving to some other young man the same opportunity she had given to him when he was without money; the bill to be paid by him. They spent more than $150 advertising for a suitable young man, and finally found him (strangely enough working as a page boy in the broadcasting studio). After six year of training, the lad was launched on a very promising career as a singer. McNamee's debt had been discharged. It is little wonder that he is making a fortune as a radio announcer. It is little wonder that the public likes him. Perhaps most people do not know why the voice of Graham McNamee is so pleasing—I am sure I did not until I learned about his philosophy of dealing with others—but the truth is, he colors his voice with a mental attitude that reflects the Golden Rule. He thinks kind thoughts of his fellow men, he lives the Golden Rule in his thoughts and in his deeds, therefore he is prospering. When I say he is prospering, I have reference not only to material opulence but also to spiritual riches, for Graham McNamee must need to be at peace with himself because he is at peace with his fellow men.

"Whatsoever a man soweth that shall he also reap." Thousands of sermons have been preached from this text, but few of them conveyed the real meaning of the philosophy back of the short sentence. Probably the greatest fortune in America, if not in the entire world, is the Rockefeller fortune. For more than a quarter of a century, the Rockefellers, father and son, devoted most of their time to giving away money. So that it might be given away wisely, a large staff of scientists and business experts are employed through the Rockefeller Foundation. Their business is to see that the money is used for the greatest good to the greatest number. Despite these huge gifts, amounting to nearly a billion dollars, the Rockefeller estate continues to grow and to prosper. Everything the Rockefellers touch turns into riches. And one of the strange facts concerning the Rockefeller gifts is that they *are not made for the purpose of getting.* The last sentence contains a thought well worth analysis by those who wish to make practical use of the Golden Rule. The elder Rockefeller may or may not have used cruel methods in dealing with his competitors during his younger days when the Rockefeller fortune was not so great. The fact remains that the Rockefellers have been generous to the public in the use of their money and something, some power not easily isolated, has been generous to the Rockefellers by bringing back more money than they ever gave away.

Charles M. Schwab was fortunate enough to become associated with Andrew Carnegie when he was a very young man. I have Mr. Carnegie's word for it that Schwab needed no one to supervise him, no time clock to record his coming and going. Schwab was his own supervisor, and as for hours, well, he was on hand when needed, no matter how many hours he had to put in. Did Mr. Carnegie demand this sort of service? He did not! It was young Schwab's own idea. Did it pay him to render more service and better service than Mr. Carnegie asked of him? Wouldn't he have been better off if he had been flanked by a labor union whose leaders would have seen to it that he did not put in more than eight hours a day? The answer to that is interesting. By setting his own hours, by giving in both quality and quantity of service far more than any employer could possibly have asked of him, Mr. Schwab set his own wage scale, more than any labor union could have demanded, and Mr. Carnegie was happy to pay it. Sometimes the pay amounted to as much as a million dollars in one year.

When Schwab went to work for Carnegie, he was inexperienced and poor. His schooling was slight indeed. However, he had a certain state of mind, a mental attitude one might say, that gained for him advantages and privileges often withheld from men who insist on measuring their services out by the time clock and union wage scales. This state of mind, which proved to be so very profitable to Mr. Schwab, was, as Mr. Carnegie expressed it, "very contagious." Those who worked with Schwab quickly picked up his mental attitude, and they, in turn, passed it on to others, and this led to harmony throughout the works. Harmony is an intangible thing, but it is worth a lot of money to those who can inspire it.

You can't overestimate the value of this principle. Use it wherever you can.

Schwab inspired harmony and good feeling *because* he had the right mental attitude toward other people. It was this same mental attitude that gave him the reputation of being one of America's greatest salesmen. Of course, he is a great salesman. He is great because his mental attitude is constructive and contagious. Other people who contact him pick up his state of mind and reflect it back to those around them. A young stenographer who once worked for Schwab said, "To be privileged to contact his mind daily is worth more than all the college degrees in the world. It has the effect of causing one to want to be decent to other people."

What a tribute! Yet, Schwab's mental attitude cost him nothing but self-control plus a genuine desire to be pleasant to people. Such an attitude has many advantages. It not only attracts and pleases people and causes them to willingly cooperate, but it also gives one peace of mind and personal satisfaction such as may be had in no other way. Schwab converted his mental attitude into millions of dollars. He made it supply employment to hundreds of thousands of men, to whom he has paid out and continues to pay out hundreds of millions of dollars in salaries and wages. Verily, the Golden Rule attitude is an Aladdin's lamp that never fails.

How long will it be until men learn the importance of mental attitude? How long will it be until men learn that their own state of mind, and nothing else, fixes their incomes and measures their worth to the world? How long will it be until men begin to control their state of mind? Answer these questions and you will become as rich and famous as Schwab, Rockefeller, or any of the others who, very evidently, knew the answer. If there is one thing more than all else that makes a person indispensable to his employer, or to the public, it is right mental attitude.

While I am on the subject of Carnegie and Schwab, I may as well here call attention to the fact that Carnegie's mental attitude was right. He knew the value of mental attitude, of pleasing personality, and did not hesitate to pay a high price for these qualities. But few employers would have permitted Schwab to receive a million dollars a year, no matter how much he may have been worth. The common tendency during Mr. Carnegie's day was to chisel men down to the lowest wage possible. He knew better! He knew that the best of all possible ways to gain and keep the sort of service rendered by Schwab was to permit such men to receive reward in proportion to their actual value. The fact that Carnegie made more millionaires than any man engaged in the steel business speaks loudly in support of his superior wisdom.

Almost constantly I hear men say, "Oh, yes, I believe in the Golden Rule, and I would like to apply it in my business, but to do so would be financial suicide, *because others would not live by the same rule!*" I must confess that I, too, was at one time guilty of taking the same erroneous attitude toward this great rule of human conduct.

The truth of the matter is that those who live by this rule cannot be cheated of their compensation, no matter how many others may refuse to live by it, for the very simple reason that those who practice this rule build in themselves that imponderable spiritual something known as the right mental attitude, which attracts friends, favorable opportunities, ideas, and circumstances they could neither recognize nor embrace without this attitude. *Like attracts like!* Suppose those with whom you do business refuse to live by the Golden Rule, while you observe it. The loss will be theirs, not yours. True, they may cheat you at trade when they have the opportunity because of your scrupulous observance of this rule, but for every person who does so you will attract a dozen who will go out of their way to favor you, and you will be more than repaid for any losses you may have sustained. The law of compensation works in this way.

I have often heard it said that when one is ready for anything it always puts in its appearance. The first time I heard that I doubted the truth of it. That was because I lacked understanding of the Golden Rule; also because I did not know the real meaning of being ready. Had I not been ready all my life for plenty of money, and had I not been ready for complete happiness, and had I not been ready for plenty of friends, without any of these desirable things having shown up? No, the truth is I had not been ready for these things. Readiness to receive means clearing the mind and developing the right mental attitude. Many people make the error, too, of confusing their need for things with their readiness to receive. There is but little, if any, connection between one's *needs* and *what one actually gets.* We all need money, we need friends, we need opportunities, but we may receive none of these things until we create the right mental attitude.

Through some strange form of mind chemistry with which science is not familiar, those who literally live by the Golden Rule, and know why they live by it, thereby create the mental attitude so essential to attract the desirable things of life. Remember, I do not expect you to be impressed by these statements unless and until you get firsthand knowledge of the truth I am trying to convey. The magic power of the Golden Rule is something that cannot be described, or imparted to another, by *words* alone. Knowledge of this great law comes only through *deeds.* Start to live the Golden Rule and soon you will know more of its nature than I could convey in a hundred years of continuous effort. Perhaps this clue to the nature of this rule will be helpful. You will *never receive the benefits of the rule by merely believing in it or talking about it.*

More than 25 years ago, I began to study the causes of success and failure. For almost a quarter of a century, I stuck to my chosen purpose, although my labor brought no monetary income. Many of my friends believed that I was wasting my time because I had to earn my living in other ways as I went along. The trouble with their reasoning was that they misjudged what constitutes pay. It is true that I helped thousands of people to find a solution to their own problems without, in any way, gaining monetary advantages for myself, but consider for a moment what these thousands of people gave to me. By studying their problems and helping to solve them, I gained the knowledge necessary to write a practical philosophy of individual achievement. That philosophy now serves men and women throughout the world, and provides me with all the income I need. My income is not derived from the people to whom I have rendered service directly, but it comes from others who willingly pay me for the knowledge I gained while rendering that service. In this way, the law of compensation does work.

37

Some Personal Experiences

GOING back again to the question of right mental attitude as being the first step toward making one's self *ready* to receive the blessings of life, I want to describe the most dramatic and the most important experience of my life.

While waiting for the business depression to pass, I was approached by two men who induced me to go on a nationwide lecture tour with them. As I learned later, their motive was thoroughly dishonest and entirely selfish. They wanted to use my name as a means of gaining the confidence of people whom they could not approach without this entre. Their purpose was to sell stock in a moving picture project. These men not only cheated many of my friends whom they met through me and caused me great embarrassment, but they also cheated my relatives and myself out of rather large sums of money. Some of my friends wished to have them arrested, but I protested, saving them from jail. Moreover, I assumed full obligation for every cent they took away from my friends, and this is why I did so. While I was on the lecture tour, I met a lady who later became my wife. She brought into my life such priceless spiritual and mental assets that I felt it my duty to give full credit to these misguided gentlemen who had cheated my friends, because it was they who were responsible for my meeting her. They cheated me of money but, whether they intended to do so or not, they paid me in something much more precious than all the money in the world. Doubtless, these gentlemen will be surprised to learn that by cheating me, they removed themselves from the possibility of sharing an opportunity that would have yielded them, in cash, more than 10 times the amount they actually procured through their dishonesty.

Every adversity brings with it the seed of an equivalent advantage.

There never is an exception to this rule. That is why many so-called failures prove to be blessings instead. The late Thomas A. Edison emphasized the truth of this when asked if his deafness had not been a great handicap to him. "No," he replied, "it has been a blessing because it forced me to listen from within. This led to the development of my sixth sense through which most of my inventions were perfected."

Emerson was right when he said, "No one can damage you except yourself." Not long ago, my wife originated and perfected a game designed to make the player conscious of the hazards of automobiles. After it had been perfected, she turned it over to one of our acquaintances to market, with the understanding the money received would be divided equally between them. The next she heard of her game, it had been patented in his name, and he had sold it to a large manufacturer of games on the representation that it was his own property.

Did we take him into court and ask that he be jailed for fraud? We did nothing of the sort. No court in the land could have settled the transaction as satisfactorily as we settled it for ourselves. Here is exactly what we did. First, we went to the lawyer who filed the patent in this man's name and pointed out to him that the application for the patent was based on fraud, that the patent really belonged, in its entirety, to the creator of the game. We submitted evidence to support our claim, after which the lawyer acknowledged that the game belonged to my wife. Then, we agreed to accept an assignment of a percentage of the royalty returns in lieu of our rights, a smaller percentage than we originally agreed to accept. Our offer was accepted and the matter closed.

Now, let us take inventory and see who was the loser in the transaction. There was a hidden asset in the transaction of priceless value to both my wife and myself, an asset that no court could possibly have evaluated, an asset that even the man who tried to cheat could not have recognized had it been called to his attention, an asset that gives a clue as to why it is true that "Every adversity brings with it the seed of an equivalent advantage."

That asset consisted of the discovery that my wife possessed a genuine creative talent. It took the foul intentions of a dishonest man to uncover this talent and center our attention upon it. Starting from that point, with that discovery as a guide, we made another discovery of still greater importance—we discovered that this same creative ability could be transmuted into other channels. This newly discovered ability of my wife's is destined to be of great service to me in a thousand ways.

Do we hold a grudge against the dishonest acquaintance who, as far as his own intentions were concerned, would have cheated my wife out of her rights to her own creative ability? We do nothing of the sort! Instead, we include him, almost at the top of the list, in a group of people whom we bless daily—people who have contributed in one way or another to our personal development and advancement. Right underneath his name are the names of the two men who swindled me out of a large sum of money and led me on a wild goose chase through the South, where I met the one person who has brought to me the richness that can come only from spiritual growth.

Earlier in life, I looked upon philosophers such as Emerson as long-haired gentlemen who had a lot of theories but little or no practical ability to cope with the pressing problems of life. Now, I have reversed myself. My reversal was forced by life itself. I now know that every person should be skilled in at least the elementary fundamentals of philosophy. Every person should at least know every effect has a cause and should know how to judge causes by their effects.

38

The War between Employers and Employees

IN this battle which is now raging between capital and labor, we may see, if we look, the benefits of philosophy. Take John L. Lewis, for example, and study the man and his *deeds!* Obviously, his purpose is to gain control of both industry and the government. For the time being, it looks as if he were winning. It would seem that everything of advantage is on his side. Even the government, through its leaders, has been temporarily thrown into the balance on the side of Lewis. But these facts are apt to mislead those who do not go deeper and study cause and effect.

"Whatsoever a man soweth that shall he also reap."

In that brief sentence, you may find the answer as to what will happen to Lewis and all who are encouraging and supporting him. You need not be a skilled philosopher or a prophet to foretell what will happen to Lewis. It is certain he will pass out of the picture by the operation of a law just as inexorable as the law of death. And the reason for this is the fact that many leaders *destroy instead of build.* Time is the mortal enemy of the person who destroys. Time is the friend of the person who builds. Not all the men in the world could change this law. No president or politician can give Lewis surcease from this immutable law. When his political end comes—mark this statement and remember it—it will come as the result of his own handiwork, and the power that will bring about his end will be supplied by those whom he now calls his followers.

American workmen may not be schooled in letters, but they do have a lot of sound horse sense. When they come to themselves, as they always have in the face of a national crisis, they seem to know what to do and they have the courage to do it.

While we are making references to Lewis, let us also turn our attention to those who are opposing him. Lewis has cast his own doom, so there is nothing anyone can do about it. With the employers of labor whom he is so viciously fighting, the situation is different. Although many of them have made grave mistakes in their dealings with labor, there is still time for them to save themselves. Any employer who chooses to do so can immediately and permanently set up a barrier against Lewis and the Lewis philosophy, a barrier that neither those in control of the United States government nor Lewis can possibly remove.

Henry Ford almost discovered this barrier when he put into operation his famous $5.00 a day minimum wage scale, over 20 years ago. Walter Chrysler faintly flirted with it when he voluntarily raised the wages of his workmen by a total of more than $50 million. But neither of these gentlemen went quite far enough.

There is available to the employers—and to Lewis, too, for that matter—a law that no Supreme Court can reverse or declare unconstitutional. It is none other than the Golden Rule, the varied combination and applications of which I have tried to describe.

If Walter Chrysler had gone over John L. Lewis's head and dealt directly with his men when he announced that $50 million wage increase and had frankly told them from then on they were *partners in the business* and as such would be permitted to *share in the profits* the same as the stockholders who bought a share of those profits with monetary investment, he would have had Lewis stopped forever. Of course, there should have been strings attached to the privilege extended to the men sharing in the profits, one of which should have been the condition that they change their mental attitude and put into their work not only a certain number of hours of time, but a definite *spirit of willingness* to do their very best. The offer should have carried with it a complete list of the conditions under which the men would be permitted to share in the profits. The conditions should have called for "Golden Rule services in return for Golden Rule pay."

There is nothing to stop any employer from going over the heads of self-appointed labor leaders and dealing directly with his own people on the Golden Rule basis. All the Wagner Acts in the world cannot stop an employer from dealing with his men on the Golden Rule basis, and all the labor demagogues on earth—and there are many of them—could never gain control of the employees who were in partnership with their employer on the Golden Rule basis.

Some will say, "Oh that will never work. No employer is going to pay wages to his men and then give them a part of the profits, too." With that viewpoint, I cannot agree. The truth is this, nothing less: *The employers, all of them, are going to be compelled to deal with their men on the Golden Rule basis or lose their right to remain employers.* Everything, by which civilization may be judged, points in this direction. These are changed times in which we are living. It clearly indicates a sharp turn in the path of civilization, a turn that is destined to *force men to deal with one another on the Golden Rule basis!*

But waiving this viewpoint on the ground that it is merely a theory, or that it is too idealistic, let us take another view of the situation. The employer, who voluntarily takes his employees into his business on a profit-sharing basis, will earn greater profits than he earned on the old basis of paying only wages. In the first place, the superior *quality* and *quantity* of service the employees will render, under the Golden Rule treatment, will supply the extra money the employer will pay them, not to mention the savings in strikes and damages to property. Arthur Nash proved that point beyond any room for doubt. Moreover, the money now being spent by many employers to fight Lewis and other labor leaders would, if given directly to the employees, under some practical working plan based on the Golden Rule, be sufficient to pay this employee dividend fee.

Henry Ford came very near to the adoption of the Golden Rule policy when he launched his $5.00 minimum wage scale. *He fell short because it was then and it still is obvious that his move was cleverly designed for the exact result it produced, namely, to outwit the labor unions and insure greater efficiency from his workers.* It produced those effects, but the thing that was lacking in the deal, the *power that would have made it stand out like the Rock of Gibraltar against all foes who might have tried to control the Ford business, was the Golden Rule spirit.* The policy was inaugurated in too cold-blooded a manner. It reflected the cold, unyielding determination of Henry Ford, but not the warmth of brotherly love so plainly laid down in that brief sentence by the Master in the Sermon on the Mount.

The Chrysler $50 million wage increase might just as well have been dumped into the ocean for all the good it did his company. Everyone knows that it was a last-minute sop thrown to his men as a bribe to keep out of the hands of Lewis. The *deed* itself, was commendable, but the *spirit* in which it was done was without that vital force that moves mountains.

In these two cases, both well known to everyone, may be found a hint to employers of America as to the way out for them. *There is no other way out* except surrender of their property and perhaps their privilege of free citizenship. Perhaps the line, "It Can't Happen Here" was sound enough for the title of a bestseller, but few real thinkers doubt that *it can happen here,* because it has already happened in spots throughout the country.

In all this conflict between capital and labor, the contending parties and most of the public seem not to have thoroughly understood the meaning of the word capital. Capital and labor consist of three factors, namely: 1) men who labor with their hands, 2) money or its equivalent in the form of credit, and 3) *the brains that manage and direct the use of both labor and money.* The last item is by far the most important of the three, for brains capable of managing and directing the efforts of men and of conserving and using money intelligently, are rare. In the ranks of labor, very little of such brains can be found, and none whatsoever among the so-called leaders of labor. Not 1 laboring man in 10,000 could or would care to assume the responsibility of managing the business in which he works, if that opportunity were given to him on a silver platter. This fact is so well known that it needs no evidence to support it.

The brains that manage capital must not only guide and efficiently direct the efforts of men, but they must also find a market for the products created. That, too, calls for highly skilled and specialized talent not to be found in the ranks of labor, except in rare instances. The products of labor must be transported from where they are manufactured to where they are consumed. That calls for highly specialized management in the field of transportation.

It seems strange, indeed, that laboring men could be misled into believing that their troubles are over as soon as they appoint Lewis to speak for them. The most that a labor leader can do is to collect union membership fees and embarrass employers by tying up their business. This, however, does not solve the working man's problem; it only complicates his troubles.

As a matter of fact, no single mind is, of itself, complete. Men who succeed in life in any undertaking of any proportion worthy of mention do so through alliance with other minds. Carnegie surrounded himself with many highly paid, highly skilled scientists, chemists, technicians, and business advisers. Without their friendly cooperation, he could not have accumulated his millions. It is worthy of note, however, that he paid them well.

Suppose that some labor leader, with the aid of the United States government, drowned out the steel plants and starved them to death, then took them over. What then? Who would run them? Who would supply the necessary money to keep them operating? Who would sell the output of the mills? Who would transport the materials to where they were needed? Could Lewis run the steel mills as efficiently as Charles M. Schwab or Tom Girdler or Myron Taylor? Is there a single man in all the ranks of labor who could do so? Personally I doubt it!

These are some of the questions that both capital and labor should ask and answer before they are too ready to destroy one another.

Everybody's business is nobody's business! Therefore, the proper side to take the initiative in settling this conflict is, without question, the *men who control capital.* As a matter of fact, they are the only ones who are capable of ending the conflict because they are the only ones really capable of managing the great industrial, financial, and economic structure on which this nation stands. Organized labor is manifestly a cause worthy of every consideration. In fact, it is so great a cause that it is entitled to, and should have leadership of the type of Lincoln, men with a sense of justice, level heads and, above all, honest hearts. No one known to the public in the ranks of labor leadership today comes within miles of meeting these requirements. Moreover, most of the labor leaders are looked upon by both their own followers and the public as being unfit to negotiate in a businesslike way with men of the type that manages capital. This does not make a pretty statement, but it has one redeeming feature: *It is true.*

All of which is but another reason why the responsibility for taking the initiative in settling this labor dispute lies squarely on the shoulders of the capitalists. Power and superior intelligence, no matter where these virtues are found, carry with them the responsibility of duty and wisdom in their use.

For every problem, there is a solution. It often happens that the person best fitted to solve a problem is someone not directly connected with or influenced by it.

Oh yes, there is a solution for this labor racket! And let's call it by its right name, because that is just what it is, a plain, cruel, debasing racket. Two groups of people suffer most from this racket. One is the unfortunate victim who is coerced or misled into paying membership fees to support the racket, and the other is the public *who pays the bill when the smoke of battle finally clears away.*

It is about time these two groups put their heads together and ended this fat racket, therefore, we propose that every employer immediately announce that henceforth his business will be run by the management representing the men who supply the money, and properly chosen representatives of the men who furnish the brawn, under a Golden Rule policy of fair distribution of profits. We propose, also, that each employer appoint an advisory board made up of well known, disinterested persons of the community who will sit in with the two groups representing capital and labor for the purpose of representing the third party, the public.

If any industrialist made such an announcement, and backed it with *deeds,* all the labor leaders would be about as welcome in the ranks of their workers as Leon Trotsky would be if he should set foot in Russia.

Capital has brains, lots of them! Why, in the name of high heaven, then, doesn't someone in this group awake to this opportunity, become real smart, and forever put an end to racketeers who collect huge tolls from both capital and labor every year?

Here is a chance for some business leader to make himself and his business immortal by selling this idea to the industrialists and the public. This can best be done by deeds, not words.

39

The New World

WHEN the sea of life shall once more have attained to calm and when the world shall once more have settled down to its business of ordered living, peace, and prosperity, new leaders and a new brand of leadership will have made their appearance. In the fields of business, industry, religion, politics, and in fact, all fields of human endeavor, leaders will find more compensation in helping their followers than in accumulating millions of dollars for themselves.

A New Religion Is in the Process of Being Made

When this calm shall have come, and come it will, a new religion shall come with it, a religion of life, not a religion of death; a religion that will help people to live as well as to die; a religion whose followers will worship through the spirit and deed of useful service to one another instead of worshipping a dead ancestry; a religion whose leaders will teach the love and beauty of cooperative effort among men instead of fear and superstition; a religion whose followers will be made up of those who found dogma and creed inadequate for their needs and believe instead in the effectiveness of deeds.

When this calm shall have come, politics and statesmanship shall have been removed from the category of racketeering and graft, and the people will find leaders in men and women who have caught the spirit of the new age, men who will understand and live by the Golden Rule.

When this calm shall have come, nations will be led by men and women, who will settle all differences by arbitration and not by war. Warfare will be branded and regarded as what it really is—murder! Then Woodrow Wilson's name will take its rightful place along with those of Washington and Lincoln, and the world will pay more willing homage to the man who advocated a settlement of differences among nations by arbitration rather than warfare, and who finally fought a "war to end wars" and then sought to establish an international accord to insure permanent peace.

When this calm shall have come, men who cheat and steal and besmirch the reputations of their fellow men, in order to accumulate millions of dollars which they do not need and cannot use, shall be treated with the contempt and scorn that they deserve.

Visionary and Utopian!

Perhaps, if viewed from the level of intelligence on which the world now stands, but levels of intelligence change. Come back to these statements a dozen years hence. They will not then seem quite so visionary.

If you had been told 20 years ago, that a score of passengers could be transported through the air at the rate of 150 miles an hour, you would have called that "visionary." Or if you had been told 30 years ago, that the ether all about you was filled with all manner of beautiful music, you would have cried out in amazement, "Crazy idea!"

We are living in a world of rapid change. Ignorance and superstition are on the run. Men no longer fear the punishment of fire and brimstone after death as they once feared it. Men no longer look upon God as cruel, capricious, or arbitrary. The truth about life is beginning to be known, and with it is coming considerable truth about God, and that which may happen after death.

Truth makes men free. This is an age of experimentation and discovery. The world is learning to cut the fetters of ignorance and superstition and fear that have bound struggling mankind all down the ages. Today, man is beginning to stand erect and free above his self-sprung chains.

It is no wonder that dogma and creeds are becoming less popular, and life and its needs more interesting. "Whatsoever a man soweth that shall he also reap." Many religious leaders of the past have been among the most prolific sowers of the seed of fear. The world is now reaping the crop.

Bigots and zealots of the past perpetuated their creeds largely through the weapon of fear, and up to the eighteenth century they effectively retarded civilization by discouraging men of science who sought to acquire and to spread truth and knowledge. Moreover, they discredited the philosophers and thinkers who endeavored to enlighten humanity. The immortal Emerson, at the time of his death, was *persona non grata* in the eyes of many leaders of orthodoxy. Thomas Paine was crucified on a cross of poisoned public opinion, and the same fate would have been Robert Ingersoll's, except for the fact that public opinion had become more generous and a bit more courageous during his time.

The religion of the future will be a religion of faith, not a religion of fear. It will be a religion of life, not a religion of death. Its clergymen will do more teaching and less preaching. The fight between religion and science will cease, and the clergyman will prove that which they teach by scientific principles and by the laws of nature. The clergyman of the future will take his text from the known realities of life. He will prove by these facts that there is but one God; that this God permeates every atom of matter and every unit of energy throughout the universe; that He may be reached by every person who desires to approach Him, not for a price, but through harmony and understanding, aspiration, and prayer.

This is an age of unfoldment of the human mind, and with greater understanding of life will come leaders who will be capable of lifting us into still greater heights of wisdom and understanding. We are in the embryonic stage of that new age now. The colleges and universities of the world have hastened its dawn. The scientists have done their share and the clergymen, be it said to their everlasting credit, are falling in line and adapting themselves to the trend of this new age. Dawn is on the eastern hills—a new light is aglow in the sky. A new day is breaking, a day in which man will control his institutions and not be driven as a bond slave before them—a day in which the humanities shall prosper!

Already, there is a widespread interest being taken by the clergy in the changes of civilization that have made the modernization of religion a necessity. Not long ago, the author had the privilege of attending a series of Sunday evening lectures delivered in the Mt. Vernon Place Methodist Church of Washington, D.C., by a group of statesmen and businessmen who spoke frankly of the new relationship developing between the church and industry. Significant was the fact that practically every pew was occupied! So, too, would the pews of every church be occupied if a part of its services were devoted to the solution of the pressing economic and personal problems that have enshrouded the world.

Religion, like business, is undergoing and must continue to undergo radical changes and reformations. The religion of the future must be a religion of practical service to humanity; it must help men to satisfy their temporal as well as their spiritual needs. The religion of the future must be based upon practice as well as faith.

Business has found it expedient to eliminate fear and oppression. Religion has done likewise. Business and religion are going to be more interdependent in the future.

The author has wanted for more than 20 years to express these truths, but fear has stilled his pen. Age and experience, plus the rapid change that has taken place in the world since the beginning of the World War, have supplanted that fear with courage. Moreover, the changes that have taken place during the past 20 years have brought with them evidence of the soundness of these statements.

Fear is man's worst enemy. Like a demon of hell, it sits upon one's shoulder and whispers, "You can't write that. It will hurt your business; it will deprive you of an income. You can't write this or you can't do that because of public opinion. You must not express new ideas nor advocate new ways of doing business because people will laugh at you."

Fear of poverty and fear of criticism are two of man's worst enemies. They deprive men of their initiative; they stay the hand and the mind of the genius who might advance civilization a thousand years in one generation; they deaden the faculty of creative imagination and cause it to atrophy and die because of lack of use and expression.

This is an age when the world needs men of courage who will search for the truth and express it, no matter whom it may affect, for weal or for woe.

When the suffering of the recent business depression shall have passed, it will make way for a new and better freedom than any the world has ever known because it will be a freedom based upon faith and not upon fear, truth and not ignorance, training and not guesswork. The new freedom will give men the necessities of life and as many luxuries as may be actually needed to bring contentment, and in return for fewer hours of labor. It is a disgrace that men must labor 8 and 10 hours out of every 24 in order to gain just enough clothes to wear, sufficient food to eat, and a roof over one's head. Four hours a day should be ample time in which to earn the three bare necessities of life.

The new age of freedom will give the laborer a more equitable share of that which his labor produces. Employers will think in terms of human happiness and less in terms of dividends. If not out of choice, they will be forced to do so by necessity.

The man who labors with his hands will enjoy freedom, not only from those who have exploited him in the past, but he will enjoy also freedom from that type of so-called labor leader who has in the past been more of an exploiter than a leader. Moreover, labor organizations in the future will operate under a system that recognizes the triumvirate of interests of: 1) labor, 2) capital, and 3) the public, which both capital and labor serve. They will also, of necessity, operate under a system that will recognize and adequately reward individual superiority, instead of the present system that claims for the inefficient worker (as long as he pays his union dues) the same rewards and the same privileges as those enjoyed by the more efficient.

Slaves and slave drivers, no matter in what walk of life, are becoming more and more a relic of a barbaric past.

The Crime We Commit against Children

The new freedom in its fullest form will protect little children from ignorant parents who plant the seed of fear in the minds of their offspring through corrective measures of brute force. Children will be managed by suggestion and by constructive example rather than by the rod. Moreover, the new freedom will permit children freedom of thought as well as freedom of action. Their minds will not be warped and limited through teachings that fill them with fear of God and of man. This new freedom must begin with absolute freedom of thought for children; the customs of the new age will not tolerate the practice of filling the minds of children with so much of the food of fear that they never actually come into possession of their own minds.

Any emotions, and especially emotions of fear, planted in the minds of children through highly colored stories that appeal to the imagination, imbed themselves in the subconscious minds of those children and may remain with them all through life!

It is a crime to plant in the mind of a child any negative thought no matter what may be its nature or purpose. No human being has the right to hamper a child's chances of success in life merely because that person may have been responsible for the child's birth. Children do not belong to their parents. The parents are merely the custodians by whom a most precious temporary responsibility for their children has been assumed.

A human being's earthly destiny may be, and usually is, fixed for him through the influences of his childhood.

Children are often taught to steal and to tell lies as the result of mismanagement by parents. Ignorance of proper management on the part of mothers often brings about the degradation of thousands of young girls every year. There are no secrets of life that should be kept from children who reach the age of comprehensive understanding. The "mystery" of where children come from and why they come into the world should be explained to them as soon as they are old enough to understand it. Lies that parents tell their children about storks plant in the subconscious minds of those children the impulse to lie about other things. Children grow up, learn to think for themselves, and finally learn the truth. Often, their resentment against those who deceived them becomes marked and permanent.

The Inferiority Complex Must Go

The age of freedom will not tolerate the practice of teaching children that men are worms of the dust, conceived and born in sin and should, therefore, fear God. On the contrary, it will teach children that man is conceived and born in the image of God; that man is limited in his achievements only by his own power to appropriate and use Infinite Intelligence. It is one of the glorious signs of the new age of freedom which has already dawned that the youths of this generation are not accepting in blind faith all the orthodox teachings of their elders.

Let it be understood that the author's only charge against orthodoxy is that it has been the chief purveyor of fear all down the ages. The indictment is not against individuals; it is against a system that has enslaved alike the minds of its leaders and followers.

The new age of freedom will teach the young the beauty and possibilities of the emotion of sex instead of treating the subject as if it were a thing of ugliness and sin. The subject of sex will be shorn of its mystery and it will be taught in the public schools by clean minds in a clean manner. Youths will be taught the true function of sex, including the values that may be had through transmutation of this beautiful emotion. They will be taught the truth about sex energy; that it is the most powerful of all the human emotions; that it has a therapeutic value unknown in the connection with other emotions; that it is capable, when controlled, transmuted, and intelligently directed, not only of perpetuating life, but of developing business or professional genius as well.

The object of this book is to provoke thought! It was not written with the purpose of reformation nor with the purpose of destroying faith in any religion, nor with the purpose of influencing others to think as the author thinks. The author does not claim to be infallible, and he is more than willing to have his opinions and beliefs passed upon by a jury made up of people who have been disciplined in the art of accurate thought.

The writing of this book has been truly a labor of love, and the author has been paid for his labor a hundred times by the thoughts that have kept him company as he worked; thoughts that inspired him with courage and left no place in his mind for despondency or fear; thoughts that attuned his heart to these words of Max Ehrmann:

"Let me do my work each day; and if the darkened hours of despair overcome me, may I not forget the strength that comforted me in the desolation of other times. May I still remember the bright hours that found me walking over the silent hills of my childhood, or dreaming on the margin of the quiet river, amid the tempests of the changing years. Spare me from bitterness and from the sharp passions of unguarded moments. May I not forget that poverty and riches are of the spirit. Though the world know me not, may my thoughts and actions be such as shall keep me friendly with myself. Lift my eyes from the earth, and let me not forget the uses of the stars. Forbid that I should judge others, lest I condemn myself. Let me not follow the clamor of the world, but walk calmly in my path. Give me a few friends who will love me for what I am; and keep ever burning before my vagrant steps the kindly light of hope. And though age and infirmity overtake me, and I come not within sight of the castle of my dreams, teach me still to be thankful for life, and for time's olden memories that are good and sweet; and may the evening's twilight find me gentle still."

The Future Demands Dreamers with Courage

The whole world now needs, and is demanding, a new group of pioneers who have the capacity to conceive new plans, new ideas, new inventions; men and women who have, also, the courage and the initiative to blaze new trails in every walk of life.

These new leaders and discoverers will be required in politics, in religion, in banking, in transportation, in industry and business, in education, in the professions, on the farms, in city planning, in art, music and literature, in journalism, and on the screen and stage.

The business depression marked the death of one age and the birth of another.

This new changed world will require dreamers who can put their dreams into action!

The dreamers have always been the patternmakers of civilization.

Through faith, courage, and imagination, they harness the intangible and unseen forces of unborn opportunity and build great skyscrapers, convert forests and deserts into cities, and turn frontiers into marts of trade.

Any person who, in the future, cherishes a lofty dream and holds fast to it will be more than apt to see that dream become a reality, for this is an age that is favorable to the practical dreamers.

Columbus dreamed of an unknown world and discovered it!

Copernicus dreamed of a multiplicity of worlds and revealed them.

Henry Ford, poor and uneducated, dreamed of a horseless carriage, steadfastly held to that dream, and now the evidence that he dreamed soundly belts the entire earth.

Edison dreamed of a machine that would record and reproduce the sound of the human voice and stood by his dream, through countless failures, until his dream became a splendid reality.

Whelan dreamed of a chain of cigar stores, transformed his dream into action, and now the United Cigar Stores occupy the best corners in every city in America.

Lincoln dreamed of freedom for the black slaves, and a united North and South have translated his dream into a reality. Other dreamers, of the Lincoln type, are going to dream of freedom for the "white slaves" of America and live to see their dreams come true.

The Wright Brothers dreamed of a machine that would conquer the air and now one may see evidence that dreams can be made to become true, because this evidence fills the air in flocks all over the world.

Marconi dreamed of a system for harnessing the intangible forces of the ether. Evidence that he did not dream in vain may be seen in every radio set in the world.

"The greatest achievement was at first, and for a time, a dream!"

"The oak sleeps in the acorn; the bird waits in the egg; and in the highest vision of the soul a waking angel stirs. Dreams are the seedlings of reality."

Awake; arise, dreamers of America. The world is filled with an abundance of opportunity, such as the dreamers of the past never knew.

A burning desire to be and to do is the starting point from which the dreamer must take off.

Dreams are not born of indifference, laziness, or lack of ambition!

The business depression was one of the greatest blessings the world has ever known. It paved the way for the dreamer-doers and provided them with opportunities they never would have known without it.

Don't say "there isn't a chance today."

The world no longer scoffs at the dreamer nor calls him impractical. Instead, it beckons to him to bring forth his ideas and plans and sets up before him prizes of both money and glory equivalent to a king's ransom.

You have been disappointed, have undergone temporary defeat, have felt the great heart within your breast crushed. Take courage from the knowledge that these experiences have tempered the spiritual metal of which you were made; that they are assets of incomparable values.

Remember, too, that most men and women who succeed in life get off to a bad start and pass through much struggle before they arrive. The turning point in the lives of those who succeed usually comes at the moment of some crisis through which they are introduced to their other selves.

Lincoln became great only after disappointment over his love for Anne Rutledge had penetrated and illuminated his soul.

John Bunyan wrote *The Pilgrim's Progress,* which is among the finest of English literature, after he had been confined in prison and sorely punished because of his religious belief.

O. Henry discovered the genius that slept within his brain while confined in a prison cell, in Columbus, Ohio. Being forced, through his misfortune, to become acquainted with his other self, he discovered himself to be a great author instead of a miserable criminal and outcast.

Thomas A. Edison was a "tramp" telegraph operator, and failed innumerable times before he was driven, by his temporary defeats, to the discovery of the genius that slept within his brain.

Milo C. Jones accumulated a fortune of more than $1 million from the exploitation and sale of "Little Pig Sausage," after he had been stricken with total paralysis. Prior to that emergency, he had been trying to earn his living with his hands. His physical handicap introduced him to his own brain and to that other self that dwelt within the brain.

Charles Darwin was considered a dull boy, but his imagination became fired with a burning desire for knowledge and lo! The world had discovered a genius through whom civilization has been stepped up no less than a thousand years.

Demosthenes stammered, but his desire to become a great orator was stronger than his physical handicap. He wrote his name deep in the records of men who achieve success because they made stepping-stones of their handicaps.

Charles Dickens began his career by pasting labels on blacking pots.

Helen Keller became deaf, dumb, and blind shortly after birth. Despite her misfortune, she has written her name indelibly in the pages of history, and her entire life has served as evidence that men and women are never defeated until they accept defeat in their own minds!

Robert Burns was an illiterate country lad, was cursed by poverty, and grew up to be a drunkard in the bargain. The world was made better because of the beautiful thoughts that he clothed in poetry.

Booker T. Washington was born in slavery and cursed by his race and color. He left his impress, for good, upon an entire race of people.

Napoleon began as a private in the French armies. Adversity, disappointment, and temporary defeat drove him to contemplate suicide before his star began its ascendancy.

Beethoven was deaf and Milton was blind.

Neysa McMien slept in an attic, in New York City, before her front-page magazine cover drawings began to bring $3,000 each.

"The road to success lies through many a thorny course, over many an obstacle, from which the fainting heart is often tempted to turn back. But hope and a sense of power within inspire the struggling person still to continue the conflict, till at last courage and perseverance meet with their just reward, and success comes."

—HENRY IRVING

We come now to the end of our journey. Before our paths separate and we go our respective ways in life, the author wishes to leave with you these thoughts, the accumulation of which has required much experience and struggle and hardship.

Nothing which you have or ever may have in the way of worldly possessions is worth the price of fear and worry.

Nothing brings enduring happiness except achievement in that sort of service that brings happiness to others. Human longings cannot be satisfied by things of monetary value alone.

Happiness is not possible without freedom of both body and mind. Freedom is an aim for which every human being is striving, whether that fact is recognized or not. Great riches do not always bring freedom; usually wealth brings only more responsibilities and fears and worries. No man is free as long as any evidence of fear finds housing in his mind.

These are hazardous times through which all mankind is passing; hazardous because of the spirit of discontent and indecision and fear that are everywhere in evidence. Be careful not to be caught in the maelstrom of this chaos. If you should become engulfed in it, remember that no one can extricate you from its overpowering current of despair except yourself. You are truly the master of your own fate, the captain of your own soul, because you are what you are as the result of your own habits of thought. Habits may be changed. In this book, you have been informed of the principles through which thought habits may be changed. Here, your guide must leave you. The remainder of the journey must be completed by you alone. Whether the trip is beautiful or ugly, pleasant or unpleasant, will depend upon what use you make of your own power of thought.

If it were required of me that I condense the substance of this book, and state it in one sentence, these are the words in which I would do it: You have a mind which you may control, and inasmuch as this mind can penetrate Infinite Intelligence, at your will you possess, therefore, the answer to all your problems, and the medium by which you can acquire all material things you need.

Before departing, the author wishes you an abundance of courage and peace and faith. If you have these states of mind, all other things that you need will come to you when you need them. Pray let Emerson express my thought for me, in these words:

"Every proverb, every book, every byword that belongs to thee for aid or comfort shall surely come home through open or winding passages. Every friend whom not thy fantastic will, but the great and tender soul in thee craveth, shall lock thee in his embrace."

40

Rounding Out Your Success Qualities for Leadership

RARE it is to find a man with an *all-around* equipment for success. As a general rule, people are *strong* on some success qualities and *weak* on others. Broadly speaking, anyone's success is determined by two things: 1) His ability to *get;* 2) His ability *to hold.*

All around you, you can see brilliant men who are past masters in the art of *getting* what they want—money, position, friends, influence, customers—*anything they want.* But when they get these things they are unable to *hold* them.

Obviously, in a book of this size devoted mainly to teaching the basic principles of *How to Sell Your Way Through Life,* it is impossible to include the wide range of facts necessary to make the fully rounded out Success Mind.

Other books have been prepared that do this in a practical, fascinating, sure way. Because of the sincere hope that every reader of Napoleon Hill's book will come to possess a high degree of both 1) ability to *get,* and 2) ability to *hold,* we ask your indulgence in the following.

A Few Words from the Publishers

Frankly, this is the Business Department of the Ralston Society. We want to have a little chat with you as you come to the end of this book. For over 50 years, Ralston has supplied hundreds of thousands—yes, probably millions—of ambitious men and women with home study books that bring health, wealth, power, and happiness.

We have many unusual, private, exciting instruction books embracing all human powers. From time to time, we will extend an invitation to you to read these courses. But for the time being, let us concentrate upon the inspiring message that Napoleon Hill, author of *How to Sell Your Way through Life,* has for you.

So great a businessman and master of success as John Wanamaker, merchant prince of New York and Philadelphia, speaking of earlier books written of Mr. Hill, said:

"If I had a young son I would insist that he read every word of the books by Napoleon Hill, and the books by Dr. . . . These two men are, perhaps, the most inspirational writers in the world. I know the 17 fundamentals of success are sound because I have been applying them in my business for more than 30 years."

Napoleon Hill Has Written a Postgraduate Course for You

It is because we sincerely feel that every reader of this book should go on into this postgraduate course, known as the Law of Success, that we take the liberty here of giving a few brief highlights upon this brilliant work.

The Law of Success presents, for the first time in the history of the world, the true philosophy upon which all lasting success is built. Ideas, when translated into intelligent plans of action, are the beginning of all successful achievement. So the Law of Success proceeds to show you how to create practical ideas for every human need.

It does it in easy-to-understand lessons.

Napoleon Hill spent the better part of 25 years in perfecting this philosophy of success. During the long years he has worked on it, some parts or the whole of it, have been reviewed and praised by many of the greatest Americans of our times.

Among them are included four presidents of the United States: Theodore Roosevelt, Woodrow Wilson, Warren G. Harding, William H. Taft; Thomas Edison, Luther Burbank, William J. Wrigley, Alexander Graham Bell, Judge E. H. Gary, Cyrus H. K. Curtis, Edward Bok, E. M. Statler—dozens of glowing names in politics, finance, education, and invention.

Andrew Carnegie Started It

Over 25 years ago, Napoleon Hill, then a young special investigator for a nationally known business magazine, was sent to interview Andrew Carnegie. During that interview, Carnegie slyly dropped a hint of a certain master power he used: a magic law of the human mind—a little known psychological principle—which was amazing in its power.

Carnegie suggested to Hill that upon that principle he could build the philosophy of all personal success—whether it be measured in terms of money, power, position, prestige, influence, accumulation of wealth.

That part of the interview never went into Hill's magazine. But it did launch the young author upon over 20 years of research. And today, we open to *you* the discovery and methods of using the revolutionary force that Carnegie quietly hinted at. The thrilling methods of using it are now taught in eight textbooks known as the Law of Success.

In the trail of the Law of Success lessons, become accomplishments, not mere entertainment and time-killing diversion. There come larger businesses, bigger bank accounts, fatter pay envelopes; small, struggling enterprises given new life and power to grow; low-paid employees shown how to gain advancement by leaps and bounds.

It is impossible in this small space to give any real idea of the inspiring, revealing lessons in the eight textbooks of the Law of Success. But, you will realize that a wonderful treat is in store for you when you read what some American leaders, who saw parts of the philosophy while in process of creation, have said.

"Allow me to express my appreciation of the compliment you have paid me in sending the original manuscript of the Law of Success. I can see you have spent a great deal of time and thought in its preparation. Your philosophy is sound and you are to be congratulated for sticking to your work over so long a period of years. Your students will be amply rewarded for their labor."

—Thomas A. Edison (world's greatest inventor)

"Your work and mine are peculiarly akin. I am helping the laws of nature to create more perfect specimens of vegetation while you are using those same laws through the Law of Success to build more perfect specimens of thinkers."

—Luther Burbank (world famous scientist)

"Certainly I will supply you with the information you request. This I consider to be not only a duty, but it is a pleasure as well. You are laboring on behalf of the people who have neither the time nor the inclination to ferret out the causes of failure and success."

—Theodore Roosevelt (former president of the United States)

"Our entire business policy, in the management of our hotels, is based upon the 17 fundamentals of the Law of Success, of which I am a student."

—E. M. Statler (founder of great hotel system)

"I feel greatly indebted for the privilege of reading your Law of Success philosophy. If I had had this 50 years ago, I suppose I could have accomplished all that I have done in less than half the time. I sincerely hope the world will discover and reward you."

—Robert Dollar (steamship magnate, The Dollar Lines)

"Napoleon Hill has produced what I believe to be the first practical philosophy of achievement. Its major distinguishing feature is the simplicity in which it has been presented."

—David Starr Jordan (Leland Stanford University)

"The best evidence of the soundness of the Law of Success, with which I am personally acquainted, is the noteworthy achievement of Mr. Curtis, who has built one of the greatest publishing businesses in the world by applying the principles of this philosophy."

—Edward Bok (former editor, Ladies Home Journal*)*

"You may say for Mr. Rockefeller that he endorses Mr. Hill's 17 fundamental principles of success, and that he recommends them to those who are seeking the highway to achievement."

—*Secretary to John D. Rockefeller*

Evidence that Money Could Not Buy

The foregoing is evidence and praise seldom accorded *any* course of education. Money could not buy such letters of endorsement from men who are, or have been, leaders of our times.

Millions of books have been written to amuse, to entertain, to help you while away your idle hours. But here in the Law of Success are eight vibrating, power-radiating books that shape your destiny, enrich your future, and turn your hopes and dreams into solid success realities.

Don't waste your own precious years blindly searching for the hidden road to the heights. Profit by the dearly bought experience of America's leaders. Over 500 great and prominent men of America were minutely analyzed—their methods, motives, strategy—to find out the secrets that put them on top.

No matter whether you are rich or poor, you have one asset as great as the richest man living, and that is time. But with each setting sun, you become one day older and have *one day less* in which to attain the success and wealth you desire. Thousands of progressive people throughout the North American continent have realized this mighty truth and have sought the help so clearly and inspiringly taught in Napoleon Hill's Law of Success.

You cannot afford to let day after day slip into eternity without getting possession of this course. You will profit greatly from the lessons in *How to Sell Your Way Through Life.* You will take even more brilliant and gratifying rewards from the Law of Success. The cost is trifling; the benefits are tremendous.

May we tell you in detail about the Law of Success? If you say "yes," then write us that you are a reader of this book and would like detailed information about the Law of Success.

—The Ralston Society
Dept. 2 Meriden, Conn.

You need have no fear of competition from the person who says, "I'm not paid to do this and I'll not do it." He will never be a dangerous competitor for your job. But watch out for the fellow who remains at his work until it is finished and performs a little more than is expected of him, for he may challenge you at the post and pass you at the grandstand.